THE SURVIVAL
of
JUAN ORO

Also by Max Brand
in Large Print:

In the Hills of Monterey
The Lost Valley: A Western Trio
The Secret of Dr. Kildare
Seven Faces
Vengeance Trail
The Sheriff Rides
The Stone that Shines
The Fugitive's Mission
Men Beyond the Law

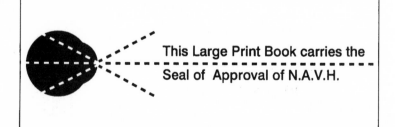

This Large Print Book carries the
Seal of Approval of N.A.V.H.

THE SURVIVAL
of
JUAN ORO

MAX BRAND

Thorndike Press • Thorndike, Maine

Published in 2000 by arrangement with
Golden West Literary Agency.

Thorndike Large Print ® Western Series.

The tree indicium is a trademark of Thorndike Press.

The text of this Large Print edition is unabridged.
Other aspects of the book may vary from the original edition.

Set in 16 pt. Plantin by Minnie B. Raven.

Printed in the United States on permanent paper.

Library of Congress Cataloging-in-Publication Data

Brand, Max, 1892–1944.
    The survival of Juan Oro / Max Brand.
       p. cm.
     ISBN 0-7862-1336-1 (lg. print : hc : alk. paper)
    1. Outlaws — Mexico — Fiction.   2. Apprenticeship
programs — Mexico — Fiction.   3. Large type books.
I. Title.
PS3511.A87 S88   2000
813'.52—dc21   99-046980

THE SURVIVAL
of
JUAN ORO

Chapter One

Indians

When the wind turned to the south, it came over the shoulders of the hills like a breath from a furnace, and madame complained of the heat. Young José Fontana meditated over this complaint for some time. He prided himself upon his inventiveness, but it was difficult to control the weather to any effective degree.

However, since he had brought his Lady Anna to his own estate in Mexico for the sole purpose that their first child might be born on lands over which he was king — for what could be more absurd than to call Fontana a mere *citizen* of Mexico? — he felt that everything must be done to make her comfort perfect. He had done everything as a Fontana should do it. He had brought down three nurses from New Orleans because rumor had it that American nurses were incomparable. He had brought a fine doctor from Vienna, at a staggering cost. And when one has worked on such a scale, it is a little irritating to have the weather inter-fere. Don José determined that weather should *not*.

This was his invention. He had a lattice-work screen erected on the balcony opposite the windows of madame, and this lattice was interwound with the tendrils of green, climbing vines. A dozen peons were em-ployed to carry water in buckets to the bal-cony and pour a continual stream of water over the lattice. At the same time another dozen peons worked great fans with all their might and so forced a powerful current of air through the lattice, through the intertwisted vines drenched with the water, and so created a steady current of cooled air into the open windows of the chamber. Two overseers managed the affair, seeing that all was done in silence. If a man slipped and brought down his pail with a jangle — if there was a single grunt of effort — the whips whirled in the hands of the overseers and gave the unlucky laborer a reminder that he would not soon forget.

It was killing labor. Every four hours a new shift was put to work. In the course of the day, nearly a hundred and fifty men had used their hands and the sweat of their brows, standing in the torrid sun under the whip, in order that the temperature of madame's room might be reduced some vital degrees.

However, the word came forth that madame was resting easily, and that she was content. Therefore, Fontana also was content. When this word was received the hour of his daily visit to the child had arrived. His secretary, a discreet, learned, thin-faced old man, came to announce that time had come.

Straightway Fontana arose, and from two corners of the room there stepped forward two members of his bodyguard. Soft-footed, keen-eyed as imprisoned leopards, they stole behind their master. Two *mozos* opened the door before him. Two more house servants opened the door at the farther end of the hall. He moved in the state of a prince — indeed, he moved in the state of two princes!

So he came to see his infant daughter. The doctor leaned against the wall at the farther side of the room. He was the only person in the "presence" who seemed to care very little what was being expressed in the face of Don José. But the three nurses were all there, their heads canted a bit to one side or the other, their faces full of foolish fondness as they looked down on the youngster.

Don José leaned above the pink-faced baby. He considered it gravely. He knew

9

that he was expected to say something, but what the thing should be he could not imagine. He wanted to compliment the tiny creature, but to save his soul he could think of nothing except to remark that its face was very red and its eyes very foolish. Neither of these remarks, of course, would have been fitting from Don José, and he knew it. He was perfectly aware, also, that he was wrong, and that he was himself a perfect idiot for not seeing something in the child that was worthy of compliment. There was no doubt that it was an exceptional little girl because, forsooth, it was a Fontana, and when in history have the Fontanas failed to be remarkable?

So Don José was at a loss. He had been at a loss upon all the other days when he went in state to see the child, but on each occasion he had found something to praise. First there had been a hand to remark, and then a foot, and then the smile. But even human anatomy begins to be exhausted after a time.

He said to the doctor: "May the child be turned so that I may see the back of her head? May this be done without harm?"

At this, the irreverent doctor stared very hard at Don José and grew red in the face.

"My dear sir!" exclaimed Don José, lifting

10

one slender, aristocratic hand. "I ask your pardon, if I have begged an impossible thing."

The answer of the doctor was rude. But, after all, he was a barbarian, and wild things were to be expected of him. He strode across the room and shoved his hand under the tiny back of this newly baptized Alicia Calderón Fontana. With that, he flipped the little lady over on her face. There was a gasp from the *mozos* who made up the background of the picture. The bodyguards of Don José settled their hands upon the hilts of their knives, more ready than tigers to strike. But although Don José recoiled in horror at this barbaric freedom with his offspring, he could not help seeing that the little lady, Alicia, was crowing with great content and punching her fat and dimpled fists into the pillow.

"Sir," said Fontana. "I cannot help observing that such roughness with a newborn infant may be dangerous . . . with all deference to your superior knowledge, Doctor."

"Stuff!" said the doctor, and turned his back.

Once more the hands of the bodyguards leaped to their knives, but, observing that they received no direction from their master, not so much as the lifting of a finger, they swallowed their rage and removed their hands once more.

The master had turned his attention to the back of the child's head.

He could not help saying: "It seems remarkably bald!"

Then he could have bitten out the tongue that pronounced the stupid words. Of course, there could be nothing at fault with the daughter of Fontana. He himself knew it. But the outcry of the ladies convinced him. They pointed out a dark fuzz upon the head of the little girl. They declared that these tresses were unusually thick and long for that age.

He said: "At least the head seems well-shaped . . . she will surely have intelligence."

"She will be brilliant! She will be a genius!" they cried to him.

Don José smiled in deprecation. "We shall see," he said, and, turning slowly, so that the procession might have time to form behind him, he moved from the room as slowly and as grandly as he had entered it.

Going down the wide stairs, he heard a clamor from the patio, a jangling of many voices. Don José stopped short with a scowl. He turned to the two tall guards behind him.

"The fools!" he said. "Stop them! And

bring the chief noise-maker before me!"

The guard, with a flash of savage satisfaction in his eyes, leaped down the stairs like a soft-treading panther to carry the message and to execute the command. Don José, with pleasure, watched him go. He felt that he had made rather a fool of himself in the chamber of his new-born daughter, and now he was glad to show himself the master again.

But, before he reached the bottom of the stairs, his messenger came hurrying back with a changed face, and what he cried was: "The fires are on the mountain, *señor!* The fires are on the mountain!"

At this, *Señor* Fontana forgot his dignity enough to break out in an exclamation and to hurry — almost run, it might be said — into the patio, where two score dependents were already in confusion, pointing and clamoring.

Yonder, from the high head of the mountain to the north, three columns of dense smoke rose steadily into the air and then leaned over in the wind and streamed to the north like three great, white flags.

"The Yaquis!" cried the two score in the patio.

"The Yaquis!" breathed Don José, and turned pale. He added: "Fernando Guadal!

Where is he? Where is Guadal?"

"Our Lady bring him soon! Our Lady bring him quickly to our rescue!" moaned a dozen voices around him.

They poured in from the patio beyond the walls of the great house and into the open in time to see the famous Fernando Guadal himself approaching, and coming as lightning streaks through the gray heavens of a storm. He, too, had seen the signal. For behind him, armed to the teeth, rode thirty of his men — those thirty who were kept constantly under arms, constantly drilled, mounted on fast horses, and ready at all times either to pursue and crush small parties of marauders on the domains of Fontana, or else to form the nucleus of a larger body in case of a greater crisis.

He swept to a halt, leaped from the saddle, and strode through the cloud of dust that his horse had raised. So he stood before his master, a squat half-breed with a flat, expressionless face and a pair of dull eyes, but with something about him, even more than his reputation, suggesting strength, patience, courage, wisdom so often proved.

He said: "I have examined the messengers. The Yaquis have swung down from the north. It is the same story. Murder, fire, torture."

14

"How far have they come?" gasped Don José.

"To the town of San Juan de Cordoba."

"Ah," sighed Don José with relief. "And how many in their army?"

"A thousand, the messengers say."

"God be with us! As many as that?"

"If there were, I should not care. But the messengers lie. They always lie. If there are more than four hundred in that war party, I am a fool! And they shall be four hundred dead men! I shall be ready to strike them in a day. I have sent out for men in every direction."

"Take armed men from the house! I, too, shall ride with you, Fernando."

"*Señor,*" said Fernando, "forgive me . . . but that is not wise. Keep all your men here. Let them be armed. If the Yaqui devils escape from me and come on against the *hacienda,* you will be here to command, and you will stop them. I shall take the others . . . there will be plenty. We will find them, if we can."

Once more Don José sighed with relief. "You are wise, Fernando," he said, "and, if you blot the Indians from the face of the earth, you will be not only wise, but rich. Remember, for I have spoken."

A little glimmer came in the eyes of the leader, a little yellow glimmer, as though

15

gold were reflected there. And, in another moment, he was gone, and all his men behind him.

It was the beginning of a time of great bustle around the *hacienda*. From the house and from the neighboring fields all the men were gathered in. They were armed with their heavy, sharp machetes at the belt and with fine, new rifles. Ample stores of ammunition were distributed to them. No fewer than seven hundred men were gathered together to drink pulque and boast of what they would do in case the Yaquis dared to advance against the great house of the master.

As for the master, he reviewed their ranks with some satisfaction, for they had numbers enough to stand a battle or a siege, at the worst. But he also knew that the Yaquis were devils and that numbers mean nothing to them when they have determined to make a rush. And he knew that his peons knew it, also. Stories of Indian ferocity, Indian daring, had been instilled in their minds since childhood.

With all his heart, Don José prayed that Fernando Guadal might find the enemy and crush him far off.

Chapter Two

Juan Oro

Guadal ended his hurry as soon as he was well beyond the eye of his master. He kept with him a dozen of his best men. The others he furnished with messages to as many places as there were men. Each was instructed to pick out only good riders, good shots, men familiar with their arms and with the courage to use them. For numbers were not what Fernando Guadal wanted. The estates of the master, stretching some seventeen leagues in breadth and thirty in length, had many villages, yes, many towns in its extent, and could furnish forth thousands, if he wished them. He had no wish for thousands, however. He wanted only a handful of chosen men to do his work.

When the messengers had departed, he went on slowly with his remaining handful. For two days he worked gradually to the north, never traveling more than three or four leagues in a day. But at every stopping place along the way, he found the recruits that had poured in, responding to his call. They were truly picked men. They rode on little horses with lumpish heads and roached backs, but with the speed and the endurance of antelope. Each had his rifle; each had his revolver and his knife. They knew no discipline, and they would have scorned to know it, but one and all they looked up to Fernando Guadal as a wise and lucky man.

So, by the end of the two days, he found that he had gathered around him fully eight hundred warriors. With these he was content. For, in the meantime, a hundred stories were pouring in upon him every day. He knew that the Yaquis had finished the looting and the burning of a town. Glutted with all their booty, they were proceeding more slowly in their march. And they were ready to turn and whirl back to the north and to their own wild mountains and deserts where they would escape all pursuit in case an overwhelming force blocked their path.

That was not the intention of Guadal. When his forces were gathered in sufficient numbers, he sent messengers before him up to the very van of the advancing Yaquis that he was coming straight at them with five thousand men. They would get the tidings by torture from some prisoner, and the news should turn them back. It was upon the recoil that he planned to ensnare them.

In the next twenty-four hours, he pushed fifty miles in a shallow semi-circle to the north, putting out scouts toward the Yaquis all the way. At the end of that march he was at the head of a narrow valley, walled with steep hills upon either side. Here, his scouts brought him word that the Indians were coming, making a leisurely retreat, like lions gorged with food which they had stolen, and ready to turn and strike down any too rash pursuer.

All was as the excellent Guadal desired. He rested his men after he had disposed them behind the shelter of cactus, brush, and rocks. He saw that they were fed and their canteens filled with water. He distributed to them each a small ration of fiery tequila. And then he waited for the Yaquis.

They came in the blazing heat of the next noon, a wild rout rolling up the valley without order, without suspicion, for all their scouts had been put out to their rear, and so the head of the column came within the curve of Fernando's half circle.

He waited until they were well within the horns of his army. Then he gave the signal, and the response was a roar of rifles. There

19

had been time to draw careful aim for that first volley, and it decimated the five hundred Yaquis. They rolled back upon one another in yelling confusion and in a denser mass. And out of their repeaters the men of Guadal poured in a rapid fire that blasted the Indians down in heaps. The remainder started to flee for the hills, and then Fernando played his main card.

He sounded a whistle as shrill as the scream of an eagle, a prolonged note that rang, at last, through the gaps in the noise of rifles. It brought every man into the saddle, and, streaming down from their heights, they swarmed over the Indians.

Let it be said of Fernando that his net had been so skillfully drawn that not one escaped. A scattering reached the hills, only to be overtaken there and riddled with bullets. When all was ended, Fernando counted his cost and found that fifty-three of his men were dead and wounded. For every Mexican, ten Yaquis! Whereas the usual rate of payment was vice versa. There was no wonder that Guadal, as he gave the order that the wounded Indians should be killed, was delighted.

The work of slaughter began at once and quickly ended. There were a few groans — no screams — and in a trice all was quiet except for the shouts of the victors. It had been marvelously simple, marvelously complete. But here, as he pressed through the battlefield, he broke through an excited circle of his men and saw the same strange picture that they were watching.

Standing upon a heap of Yaqui dead was a boy of fifteen years or so, naked except for a twist of cloth about his loins, his bronze body flashing in the sun, and long, bronze-colored hair falling about his shoulders. He wielded in his hand a machete that might have wearied the arm of a grown man. But machete play is a science as accurate and mysterious as rapier play, and skill counts more than strength. So well had this child mastered the art that, with his supple, sinewy muscles, he swung the heavy steel weapon as though it were a thing of gilded steel. The wind caught his hair until it flashed like gold, also. And as he stood, he shouted to them in good Spanish.

"Mexican buzzards . . . I, Juan Oro, defy you!"

There was a cry of hate from some of Fernando's men. The sun winked on a dozen rifles as they were raised. Guadal's voice cut them short. "We will take the young cat home to show the master what the big ones were like. Take him alive, friends! Take him alive!"

And he, loosening his lariat of suppled rawhide, made his horse dart forward. He made his cast as his horse flew past the young brave. A rawhide lariat drives as a bullet drives, swift and straight and inescapable, but faster than the leap of the rope was the flash of Juan Oro's machete. It severed the loop of the rawhide and the leather struck him harmlessly. But, the next instant, another loop dropped over his head and pinned his arms to his sides, and a second later he was swathed from head to foot. Now that resistance was in vain, he ceased all of his struggles. They tied his hands; they threw him on a horse and bound his feet together beneath its belly.

"Kill me now!" said Juan Oro, "for, if you take me back with you, I shall surely be to you like poison to a sick man!"

But Fernando Guadal was himself more than half Indian and, for that matter, so were all of his followers. They saw in the youngster something to admire, so he was brought along in the return. And there was conversation about him as they rode.

"For," said Fernando's most trusted lieutenant, "he is not a Yaqui at all, but a *gringo!*"

"Because his hair is copper?" asked

Fernando. "But I have heard of such things even in an Indian."

"Look!" said the other.

He rode to the side of the boy and lifted his arm. Even in the pit it had been reached by the sun and tanned a little, but, nevertheless, that skin was pale — paler than the skin of any Yaqui — paler, indeed, than the skin of Fernando himself or of any man who rode in his train.

"This is very strange," said Guadal. "I have never heard of a white Yaqui!"

"He is some child stolen from the *gringos*," said the other. "Let me pass a knife between his ribs. Good may come out of even a Yaqui. Even a wildcat may be tamed a little. But the *gringo* is always wild and can never be tamed."

"He has the ways of a Yaqui," said Guadal thoughtfully. "He is full of a devil, that is, a Yaqui devil. No, friend, we will take him to the master. The white skin may please him. Who can tell? His own skin is weak and white."

This was the salvation of Juan Oro, who, hearing the conversation concerning him, stirred not a muscle in his face. But he said at the end: "You, Fernando Guadal, are a fool . . . and the other man is wiser."

"Am I a fool?" said Fernando. "This will teach you better!"

And he gave the boy the lash of his quirt across the face. It raised a great weal across the eye and the nose and mouth of Juan Oro.

"If you are *not* a fool," said the boy, "you will stab me now, for I shall never forget you!"

Chapter Three

Before the Great Don

To the very excellent *Señor* Don José Fontana, word came soon by the first messenger of winged rumor that a victory of the first dimensions had been won by his general, Fernando Guadal. *Señor* Fontana considered the matter for some time, but, as he said to himself, this was a real triumph, and there was no good reason why Guadal should enjoy all the glory undisturbed. So he galloped away in person with some twenty or thirty people behind him and joined the ranks of Fernando Guadal as that brave came in to report his success.

"I have come out to thank you, at once, and before any other could reach you," said Don José, smiling upon his lieutenant.

"God give the don long life," said Fernando in a voice of the humblest joy. But, nevertheless, he knew very well that this visit was aimed purposely at reducing the size of his laurel wreath. However, there was nothing he could do, and all his men were so stupid that they failed to see the point at all.

Instead, they were so immensely flattered by the visit of the maestro that they pulled their hats off their heads and yelled and brandished their rifles on high, and without hands on the reins, guiding the mustangs by pressure of knee and sway of body, they swung their fiery little mounts in front of *Señor* Fontana, making the air shudder with their battle screams. As though they were saying: "Thus and thus, did we rush upon the Yaquis . . . and thus were the Indians slain."

They were more delighted, one would have thought, by the visit of Don José than they had been pleased by the outcome of the very battle itself. At least, they made far more joyous noise at the sight of him. Only their leader himself — only Fernando Guadal said to himself: "He is stealing my poor happiness from me. He is making me one of the followers. I can no longer return at the head of the column, which is my proper place."

Accordingly, since there was death in his heart, Fernando made his face into a very sun from which shone nothing but the happiest of smiles. This was because he was half Mexican and half Indian. The only greater dissembler than the Mexican is the Indian, whose blood, after all, flows thickest in his veins. And Fernando Guadal possessed the qualities of both races.

Fernando had to tell his tale of the battle, and he and the maestro were at the halt while the long column rode by them. How they sat their horses when they saw they were about to pass immediately under the eye of the Fontana himself. For the falling of that glance might translate them to heaven — who could tell? A glance was enough to make the maestro elevate or lower. Men had been made for life and their children after them because of what? Because the maestro had happened to enjoy a certain sort of soup — or he had been pleased with a horse — or the manner of a rider — or the face of a flower garden.

Such was the way of the maestro. Not like God's way, to be sure, all-wise, all-seeing, all-knowing — but a far more delightful way, for it rewarded more often the unworthy than the worthy. And who, after all, is really worthy of great happiness? No one, no one surely! How far more exciting, then, to live on earth under the rule of one who picked at random here and there — bestowing that happiness where he happened to choose, and blindly?

At least, so thought the men who were under Fontana. They were not free men. They had fewer rights than the peons on most estates. And yet they were content. Worse than slaves, in fact, they preferred their situation to that of the free man. Because they loved excitement. And, indeed, fresh hundreds, every year, begged of the overseers of Fontana that they be allowed to come into his country and work for him — let him set his foot upon their heads. And, every year, he was forced to turn the hundreds back.

Now, as the procession of the gallant riders wove past him, the will of the Fontana began to work. Here went by a withered man, a little old, but very straight.

"He was a hero," murmured Fernando to his master. "I saw him attacked by two Yaquis. One he brained with the butt of his empty rifle. With the other he grappled, took the knife from the savage, and buried it in his heart."

"So?" said Fontana. "Ah . . . who is that?" And he pointed out a carefree youth, set off with much red silk, a very dashing cavalier, very conscious of his own brilliance.

"He?" scoffed the leader. "Oh, he was too busy during the fight, seeing that all his ribbons were in place."

"Did he?" chuckled Fontana. "Well, a man who thinks about ribbons under rifle fire is more of a hero than he who rushes into the fire. Call him out."

So the youth was called and, at a gesture from Fernando, took his place in the little cavalcade behind *Señor* Fontana. He took that place, trembling with joy. And he was greeted with keen, eager glances from the rest of the cavalcade. As for the men who had ridden before and behind him in the procession, they followed him with bright glances — not of envy, but of a sort of joy. For though they knew that the honor had fallen where it was least deserved, so much more the heart of every common man was lifted with hope — so much more the real heroes and worthies of the fight said to themselves: "If his eye *should* chance to light on me, how would he reward me, if he will do so much as this for a common dog?"

In this way, everyone was happy. He picked some sixteen or twenty men from the procession. And of the sixteen, perhaps six or seven were men who had really distinguished themselves in the battle. They gave a tone to the entire choice.

"There is a wisdom in the maestro. He can never be altogether wrong." — was the most frequent saying on the estates of *Señor*

Fontana, and it was heard now.

Only Fernando was more and more dissatisfied. For he saw that this personal review at the hands of their maestro had made the army quite forget him. When the journey began again, all glances were for Fontana; all the pride of the army was their pride in their master and not in their general.

"Truly," said Fernando to himself in bitterness, "there is a wisdom in the maestro."

"But where," exclaimed Don José presently, "did that naked boy join the troop?"

"He is a Yaqui, *señor*," said Fernando. "We caught him, and we kept him alive to show you and your house, *señor*."

"He has strange hair for a Yaqui. However, I am glad to have him. I have always wanted to have a tiger cub for a plaything . . . something to tame and watch and discover the growth of the wildness and the madness in it. For I am one, Fernando, who despises tame obedience. I love strength. I rejoice in courage. I have a heart as wild as those mountain peaks. And most of all . . . I love to see rebellion . . . and to crush it . . . so!"

Thus spake exquisite Fontana, and to illustrate his words he closed his delicate right hand slowly, destroying invisible life in the midst of the air. Fernando Guadal observed and made his eyes great with wonder. If Fernando was disappointed and sore-hearted on this day, he was so pleased by the skill of his own acting that he well-nigh forgot all else.

"So," said Fontana, "let this wild young thing be brought before me."

They conducted the boy before him, and Fontana looked him over slowly, and had him turned around and around.

"He is only the merest child," he said. "However, his eyes are not black, but brown, I think. Who has told you that he is a Yaqui?"

Fernando murmured: "*Señor*, if it may please you, the skin beneath the pit of his arm is also white. He is a *gringo*, but knows it not. He thinks of himself as a Yaqui. Is that not well?"

At this, the grin of Fernando became less broad than the grin of the Fontana.

"You were beginning to bore me, Fernando," said the maestro, "but I am glad to see, again, that you are not completely a fool. Very well, this is truly an idea. We keep the young tiger cat and see it grow. In time, the spots will begin to appear. It will turn *gringo*, will it not?"

"So it is said," answered Fernando seriously. "I have heard it said that a *gringo* must have a free life, or else he will prefer to die."

"They are swine!" declared Fontana. "What of their laws? Are they not worse than slaves, living by such laws as those which they have?"

"Yes, it is true," said the lieutenant, "but those laws have strength only because they all agree to bow down to them."

"Bah, bah, bah!" sneered the Fontana. "They are swine. I say it, who know them well, I, José Fontana!"

He raised his head. It was as if he directed his words above the earth to the divine ear.

"That is very true," said Fernando.

"I am rejoiced that you agree with me, Fernando," said the maestro dryly.

"Ah, *señor,* they are poison in the air that I breathe. I live only to hate them!"

"I believe you, Fernando. I begin to see more and more in you that is amusing. Very well, I shall not forget you."

"Ah, *señor,* this is kindness . . . *señor,* you are my father! But as for the boy, even now that he thinks himself a Yaqui, he is still a *gringo* in spots."

"Is he so? Madame Fontana will be pleased to see the young beast. I may keep him in a cage until we have made sure he will not use his claws." He added: "Bring the boy closer. I wish to speak to him. Does he know Spanish?"

"A better Spanish than I use."

"I shall see. What is his name?"

"Juan Oro."

"John Gold? That is an odd name. But I see the sun on his hair . . . that, perhaps, is the reason. Boy," he said as the captive was brought forward, "why did you go with the Yaqui to battle? You are a child. Was your father a great man among them?"

"I went with them to kill Mexican dogs like you," said the boy, looking him fiercely in the face.

There was a gasp from those who had heard. Only Fernando smiled inwardly. But one could never tell how Fontana would act. Sometimes a kind word made him rage; sometimes impertinence pleased him. Now he merely smiled at the youngster. He said to his man of war: "Fernando, is not that a whip weal across his face?"

"It is, *señor*, and for the same reason."

"And still he talks! Well, he amuses me. But I think that I shall teach the young dog tricks! Tell me, Juan Oro, have you ever killed a man?"

The eye of the boy glistened. "Yes," he said.

"This is prodigious. With what weapon?"

"The machete."

33

"Tush! Your arm is not large enough to swing it."

The eye of Juan Oro glinted to the side. He nodded toward a skulking cur, half mongrel, half coyote, that had come near.

"Give me leave to show you," he said readily.

"Unbind his hands," said the maestro. "I shall see."

"*Señor*," protested Fernando, "this is not safe. The young tiger may put his teeth in a man's throat."

"There are guns ready and aimed at him even now," said the maestro. "His hand will not move faster than a bullet. Unbind him and let him have a machete."

It was done. Juan Oro, receiving the weapon, sent the machete straight to its mark.

"Excellent, is it not?" cried the maestro to Fernando. "This boy has the hand and the arm of a man now. To what will he grow?"

There had been a little stir in the circle; for a moment all eyes were diverted from the boy himself to the work which he had just accomplished, and in that instant of relaxed vigilance he acted. Near him was one in whose belt the handle of a heavy hunting knife thrust out. The fingers of Juan Oro snatched that weapon with a gesture faster than a glint of light, drew it back, and with a scream of joy and rage hurled it straight at the breast of the maestro.

Nothing could have saved him, had not one wary hunter in the train kept his eye constantly upon the youngster. His rifle tilted barely in time, and, as the hand of Juan Oro flicked forward, the gun barked. Too late to recall the flung knife. The bullet knocked the boy flat along the back of his horse. As for the knife, the maestro at the sound of the gun turned with an exclamation — and so the bright death flew by him, and the blade of the knife was buried in the shoulder of him with the scarlet silken sash. His yell of pain and fear arose above the universal shout.

"Kill the Indian devil!" cried fifty voices.

"He is dead already," said the maestro, "and I would to heaven that I had him alive again. This breed of hunting dog is to my liking."

Chapter Four

The Doctor's Miracle

Although a bullet had smashed through his back, Juan Oro was not dead. He lived to be taken to the great house, where the Austrian doctor looked at him and wondered.

"He is made of leather from head to heel," said the doctor. "He is dead, however. He cannot live through the night. There is little more pulse than in a stone, you might say."

But when the next morning dawned, it shone into the living eyes of Juan Oro.

"If that is the case," said the doctor, "he *is* worth saving. And I shall save him."

So he neglected his principal charge. The wife of *Señor* Fontana could be cared for well enough by her nurses, according to him. He spent day and night laboring over Juan Oro. And it was the struggle of a fortnight. At length, he pronounced the boy out of danger. He went to Fontana with his report.

"As for the boy," said the don, "I care nothing! But Madame Fontana might have died of neglect, sir."

At this, the doctor smiled broadly. "I will tell you about these women," he said. "The more care you give them, the more care they will need. And they will make child-bearing a mystery so long as you are willing to foot the bill."

Don José blinked at him a little.

"As for the boy," went on the doctor, "he is gold. He was named correctly. I have given him enough torment, in dressing that frightful wound, to break down the nerve of an army of giants. But he has never murmured."

"It is the Indian way," said Don José, shrugging his shoulders.

"Indian?" chuckled the doctor. "He has bleached out. He is as white as bone."

"What is the color of the skin?" asked Fontana. "The mind is the thing, and his mind is Yaqui."

It was the doctor's turn to show surprise, and he stared rather wildly at Don José.

"This is true, beyond a doubt," he said. "However, he is more than half tamed, and with the proper care. . . ."

"Why," said Fontana, "should I give him care?"

This the doctor pondered for a moment. He said at length: "There are a great many knives and a great many guns in this

37

country, are there not?"

Señor Fontana enlarged his narrow chest. "Each country has its peculiarities," he said with much pride. "The English are traders, the French are lovers of romance, the Americans hunt dollars, and Mexico is a nation of warriors!"

The doctor bit his lip. "A nation of warriors," he repeated. "And they love war so well, sir, that they are apt to take up their tools at any moment and fly to their trade . . . which is killing."

"Yes," said Don José, "it is true."

"Suppose, then, that a man could be sure of a guard who cared more for his master's life than for his own?"

"Ah?" murmured Fontana. "I, *señor*, have guards who follow me night and day. They are trained fighters."

"They are paid men," said the doctor, "are they not?"

"Certainly. They receive four or five times in cash what a laborer gets. Besides, there is the honor of guarding Don Fontana, which is really the main thing."

"Honor is a peculiar thing," said the doctor, "and pay usually corrupts it, I believe. But devotion can never be bought."

"I do not understand," said Don José with a blank face.

"Have you been paid," asked the blunt doctor, "to love your daughter?"

"¡Señor!" cried Fontana.

"Very well. Was your wife paid to bring that life into the world and endanger her own? That is devotion, señor. Now I speak of devotion in another way . . . devotion of a man to a man. Who can buy that? Napoleon had many marshals. He had only one Lannes. You, Don Fontana, have many guards, but which one of them would willingly lay down his life for you?"

"It is much to ask," muttered Don José.

"It is much to ask. It is about all that *can* be asked. Now I say, my friend, that this little Juan Oro has bulldog in him."

"Yes, his teeth were once almost in my throat."

"Perhaps. But I have seen a bull terrier with the man who trims his ears. First he hates the man for the pain he has suffered. But afterward, because that man bathes the wounds and relieves the pain, the dog comes to love him more than he loves any other man. Do you understand?"

"I understand. That is nature, I presume."

"Bull terrier nature. Go a step further with me. This Juan Oro lay day after day, making no sound, asking no questions. And expecting nothing, he was ready to die. But he was treated kindly. He began to wonder at me. He said to me, at last . . . 'Why do you do this?'

" 'Because *Señor* Fontana will have it so,' I said. 'Otherwise, why should I waste my time over you?' At this, he frowned and closed his eyes to think.

"I came the next day, and he said at once . . . 'Why does *Señor* Fontana do this thing for me?'

" 'Because he is a kind man,' I replied.

" 'I would have killed him,' he said.

" 'He loves courage and even fierce courage,' I said."

"That is true," broke in Don José. "In that, you represented me accurately."

The doctor rubbed his chin and looked askance at his employer. "Very well," he said. "Every day I have had a few questions from the boy about you. It seems exceedingly strange to him. He said to me a little time ago . . . 'If I, *señor*, had found *Señor* Fontana alone on the desert, do you know what I should have done?'

" 'Killed him?' I responded.

" 'Yes,' he said. 'But now he gives me this care. He takes my lost life in his hand. He gives it back to me.' The tears came into his eyes.

" 'Are you sad, Juan?' I asked him.

" 'Is this not a sad thing?' he said. 'Have I not been worse than a wolf?'

" 'Yes,' I said, 'you have.'

"He said . . . 'The don shall see that I can be better than a wolf, also.'

" 'What will you do?' I asked, very curious.

"He thought of this for a long time and could not find any good answer. But the next day he had it ready, when I came in to him.

" 'I have thought of it,' he said.

" 'Of what?' I said, having forgotten what was on his mind.

" 'Of what I shall do for the don.'

" 'Well, what is it?'

" 'I shall find a way to die for him!' was his reply."

"Did he say that?" broke in Fontana.

"That was his saying. Now, *señor*, ask me again if he is worth saving?"

"I spoke like a child," admitted Don José. "Yes, *señor*, I live in the most constant danger of my life. Ten thousand people hate me because I am rich. If I died tomorrow, a hundred men and women would benefit by my death. The food I eat is tasted before I touch it. The water I drink is sampled before me . . . a little from every glass."

He leaned forward to the doctor: "Twice the tasters of my food have died, *señor* . . . died strangely and suddenly, filled with agony. Such is the life that I lead."

"The devil!" said the doctor. "Is it as bad as that? In this century?"

"All centuries are the same in Mexico," said Don José moodily. "But if this is true about the boy, I shall cherish him."

"No, no!" broke in the doctor. "If you do that, you ruin him. He was in the beginning like an Indian. Continue him in the same way. Treat him like a brute. Let him have one human emotion only . . . the love of you. For the rest, let him be a wolf. In that way, you can be surer of his devotion."

"Doctor," said Fontana, "I think that this may mean as much to me as your work with my wife."

"It is far more," said the other. "For your wife and new daughter are only women, but in Juan Oro, I am giving you a man!"

Chapter Five

<u>Garcilasso's Slave</u>

The more that *Señor* Fontana thought over
the doctor's advice, the better it appeared to
him to be. At length, he went in person to
visit his captive. He was shown to a pleasant
little garden attached to a tiny cottage that
belonged to his chief groom.

"How," said Don José to the doctor, "is it
possible to keep him at liberty and yet be
sure that he will not run away?"

"I shall tell you," said the doctor. "In the
first place, I have promised him a very fine
hunting knife, if he stays here until he has
my permission to leave. In the second place,
he hopes against hope that he may be able to
see your face before he goes. You are not a
man, *Señor* Fontana. You are a god to that
boy."

"Very absurd! Very absurd!" said Don
Juan, but he could not help smiling, for it
was not unpleasant to play the part of a god,
even to a renegade Yaqui boy.

There was no doubt as to the youngster,

however, the moment that Don José laid eyes upon him. He was still tanned. The sunburn of many years could not be shed too quickly. But a thousand outer coats of brown had been thrown off. He was pale, indeed, to an extent which none of *Señor* Fontana's household could claim. He himself was not so fair, only his wife could claim a complexion like the boy's.

Upon this point Fontana pondered a little. His skin, indeed, might be called perfectly white except for certain shadows in the corners, so to speak — and a certain trace of smokiness in the whites of his eyes. Nothing to speak of — nothing to notice. Men from the south of the United States, to be sure, had a way of looking very straight at him. But he could go through the length and the breadth of Europe not as a Mexican, but as a Spaniard. And it was of the old Castilian blood in his veins that Don José loved to speak.

But, now and again, something brought him up with a start. Sometimes it was a whisper among his servants, swearing that somewhere in the past of his ancestors there had been a cross into red blood or black. It was the secret cross that the noble Fontana was forced to bear. And sometimes, when he thought of his own greatness and nobility, he wondered if heaven had not arranged this bar sinister, or the whisper of it, so that he might seem more like his fellow creatures.

For, after all, what the don most keenly felt was the immense distance which existed between himself and the rest of the world. In Europe he found those with whom he could talk freely — the dukes, the counts, the blue blood. But here in the New World, he was almost alone. Those who were of ancient lineage were mostly poor. It was distressing.

Some of all of these thoughts passed through the mind of *Señor* Fontana, as he stood looking from a window of the house into the garden of his head groom. Juan Oro lay with body stretched in the sun, but his head was in the shadow of a tree, and pillowed on the side of a big sheep dog.

Then Don José went forth to speak with the boy. He went forth alone and stood above him. Juan Oro was asleep, but in the twinkling of an eye, as though the shadow that fell over him was enough to waken him, he had bounded to his feet. The sudden effort made him stagger a little, but presently he steadied himself and stood blinking at the don.

"Now, Juan," said the don, "have my servants healed you?"

"They have healed me," said the boy.

"And are you happy here?"

Tears rushed to the eyes of Juan. "Ah, *señor*," he said in a trembling voice, "you are so kind that it makes me sad. I would have killed you, and you have made me like your son. But I shall grow strong again, *señor*, and I shall find a way to die for you."

"Live for me, Juan," said Fontana, "and do not die."

He went back to the doctor. "You are right," he said. "This boy may be worth as much as his name . . . he may be worth his weight in gold."

"He may," said the doctor. "These Anglo-Saxons are a queer people. They talk a great deal of freedom, but they love to be slaves. Even in the old days, when they were freest, what was the highest honor to which they could aspire? To be the hearth companions of some chief . . . that is, to sleep around his fire at night, and fight for him in the day. They were pledged to die for their master. You can make such a man of this boy . . . stronger than steel and ready to die for his master."

Upon this problem, as upon a new toy, the don pondered for a long time. At last he said to Fernando Guadal: "Fernando, what man in my country is the greatest warrior? What man is the surest shot, the deadliest hand with a knife, the greatest lover of battle?"

The answer of Fernando came instantly: "There is only one. That is Matiás Bordi!"

"That is the half-breed?" said the don.

"That is he."

"We have given him a house and lands to keep him from plundering and murdering our people."

"That is true. It was easier to do that than to catch him. Five times we rode out to catch him. Five times we left our dead men behind us and rode back without Matiás."

"But this Bordi, is he a quiet man now?"

"No, but more secret. He does no harm on the lands of the don. But he rides out with his men to other places. He goes out like a hungry wolf, and he comes back with his belly filled. He has killed a hundred men, *señor*. He will kill another hundred before he dies."

"Take this Juan Oro to him," said the don. "Tell him that he is to teach Juan Oro all that he knows."

"He will kill the boy," said Fernando.

"It will be one *gringo* the less," said Fontana. "Before you take Juan, bring the boy to me."

All of this was done. When Juan Oro could walk straight and there was only the weakness of his wound in his body, he was carried to Don José.

The great man said: "Juan Oro, you are now to be taken to a strong and fierce man who will teach you things that you wish to know. But what things, Juan, do you most wish to know?"

"To ride a horse, *señor,* to shoot straight, to use a knife."

"That is very well. But what of the lariat, Juan?"

"That is to catch cattle. I, *señor,* wish to catch men."

"You will be taught these things and more by Matías Bordi," said Fontana. "Stay with him."

"For how long, *señor?*"

"When Matías Bordi is dead," said Don José, "then you will be worthy to come back to me and serve me."

And the eyes of the boy flamed. "I shall be back!" he breathed. "He will be dead, and I shall come back."

Don Fontana smiled. He knew a good deal less of fighting and fighting men than he thought he did, but at least he was quite sure in his estimate of Matías Bordi.

So Juan Oro was sent away. He was well-dressed, like a little man rather than a boy; he was placed on a silver-mounted saddle on the back of a prancing mustang. Although he was still very weak, he endured the ride with perfect ease and grace and kept the wild little horse well in hand.

In this fashion he swung his hat at Fontana and darted away with his escort, consisting of Fernando Guadal and another. They rode forty miles, out of the plains, into the hills, and into the sweetness of the pines. Then they found a ranch house as naked and sun-scorched as a thing out of a furnace. There were no trees near it. The careless improvidence of those who lived there had simply cut down the nearest trees for firewood and had kept on cutting in a growing circle. Now the ground was made hideous, for a thousand stumps of varying sizes were all about, and the house itself was without shadow in the noonday.

A score of fierce mongrels rushed out at them. When Fernando Guadal quirted one across the nose, instead of running away with its tail between its legs, it leaped at his throat. Fernando shot it without hesitation.

"And these," said Fernando to the boy, "are only the dogs!"

Juan Oro listened and understood.

Presently, in the entrance to the patio, he saw a tall, bearded man leaning on a rifle. The stranger said: "The price of that dog is ten *pesos*, Guadal."

"Listen to me, Bordi," said Fernando Guadal. "The brute flew at my throat."

At this, the bearded man tossed his rifle into the crook of his elbow. "The price is ten *pesos,*" he repeated without changing his voice.

Juan Oro, who understood, reined his horse to the side to get out of the possible path of the bullet.

"Very well," said Guadal. "I have not come to quarrel. Understand, Bordi, that this is the money of *Señor* Fontana, and not mine."

He counted out ten *pesos,* and, as he dismounted, he put it in the hand of the tall man.

"Good!" said Bordi. "I would rather have his money than yours. Come in, friends."

He clapped his hands and two or three ragged *mozos* appeared. They were directed to take the horses.

"Let them hold them and not tether them," said Guadal. "I talk with you for five minutes, Bordi, and then I return. The day is half done."

"We cannot talk with dry tongues," said Bordi. "Come in, then."

He led them through the patio. It had been a garden spot at one time. Now there remained only a few stumps of bushes that had been eaten down by horses; dust rose under their feet. They sat on the porch that circled the patio, and Guadal sent Juan Oro to look about the place. Then he said to Bordi: "I have brought you a pupil."

"The boy?" said Bordi.

"That is it."

"Am I a schoolmaster when I cannot write my name?"

"You can write it with bullets," said Guadal.

"Well?"

"*Señor* Fontana has sent up this boy. He sends you, also, five hundred *pesos*."

"He is kind. But I do not need money."

"You are to take the boy and teach him," said Guadal.

"For what? That he may learn how to put a bullet through me when he is grown up?"

"Perhaps that is the reason," grinned Guadal.

At this, Bordi smiled in turn, although he was one who seldom relaxed his expression.

"Whose son is this?" he said.

"He belongs to no one. He is a Yaqui taken in a fight."

"He has a white skin."

Tequila was brought, like water with a blue shadow in it. They drank that liquid fire.

"Well," said Bordi, "I may take him. I shall make him a man or . . . a dog. I think I shall send back a dog to *Señor* Fontana. You may tell him that."

"I do what I am told to do," said Guadal. "I bring the boy to you . . . I give you the money . . . here it is. For the rest, you are your own master."

"That is true."

"Farewell, then, Matiás Bordi."

"Farewell, Fernando Guadal."

Guadal mounted his horse and rode off with his companion, rode on the spur without so much as looking back, as though he feared lest Juan Oro might be fleeing after him.

When he was gone, Bordi called, and his son came softly out to him. He was a beautiful boy of the height of Juan Oro, but a year older. He fastened his great black eyes upon the face of his father.

"There is a new *mozo* come for you, Garcilasso," he said. "Have you seen the boy?"

"I have seen him," said Garcilasso.

"He is a present to you from *Señor* Fontana. He is your slave, Garcilasso. He will run, when you tell him to run, and walk, when you tell him to walk. Go take him!"

Chapter Six

Bordi Loses a Son

Juan Oro looked up from his examination of the burro which he had found, and saw the enemy standing over him.

"Are you my *mozo?*" said Garcilasso.

"Am I what?" Juan asked softly.

"Are you the present which *Señor* Fontana sent to work for me?"

"You are a fool and the son of a fool," said Juan pleasantly.

Garcilasso leaped at him like a tiger, and, too late, Juan remembered that he was not strong enough to resist. The wound was healed, indeed, but he was filled with weakness — water instead of blood. At his first effort to resist, his arms gave way like the arms of a girl. He was crushed to the ground with the fingers of Garcilasso fixed around his throat. So he lay passively, and presently the fingers were taken from his throat. Still he was motionless and unresisting while Garcilasso bound his hands.

"Now stand up!" said Garcilasso.

Juan arose.

"Today," said Garcilasso, "you are my horse, and first I teach you the whip. Run!"

He whirled the quirt and lashed Juan Oro with it. It seared his back with a great welt.

"I shall not run," Juan Oro said patiently. "I have been sick, and I am too weak to run away."

"Are you not my *mozo?*" screamed Garcilasso. "Will you not run when I command? Dog!"

He fell into a wild fury and lashed at Juan with all his might, and Juan set his teeth and endured.

"Now," gasped Garcilasso, "you have had a lesson. You are like a child to me. I break you in my hand like dead leaves. If you try to run away, I shall catch you. So!" He cut the rope with which he had tied the wrists of Juan Oro. "Walk before me!" he commanded, and directed Juan into the house and up to his own room. There he found some outworn clothes, a shirt, and a pair of trousers.

He tossed them to Juan, saying: "Take these and put them on. Give me those clothes you have on. They are too good for a *mozo*. They are a present to me from *Señor* Fontana."

Juan Oro obeyed in silence. Garcilasso

Bordi sat on his bed and spoke in the meantime: "You will clean my guns and sharpen my knives," he said. "You will bait my fishhooks, and carry the fish that I have caught. You will catch my horse and saddle it for me. At night, you will sleep there." He pointed to a corner of the room. "Bring some straw in. That is good enough for you!"

Presently Juan had taken off the clothes and donned the new suit of rags. Garcilasso instantly slipped into the discarded finery.

"First," he said, "we will find my father. I wish to show him how well I have trained my slave."

So they went down and found Bordi, sitting on the porch behind the patio still sipping tequila. He observed the pair with quiet eyes that were as black as charcoal and as lifeless.

"Watch him," he said to Garcilasso. "He is a Yaqui, and they are as patient as time."

"If he lifts his hand," said Garcilasso, "I shall kill him! Do you hear, Juan? If you ever lift your hand against me, I shall kill you!"

But Juan looked steadily at him with neither anger nor fear in his eyes. He was waiting. It might be a month or a day, but it was folly to resist until his strength had come back to him.

However, now began a wretched servitude. Juan was never allowed to be free from the eye of his young master. And there was not a moment in the day when he did not find something for Juan to do. But this was not what hurt Juan the most. He could bear with the insolence and the blows of Garcilasso, but the mockery and the laughter of the men cut him more than whips.

There were never less than a dozen men at the house of Matiás Bordi. They seemed to have nothing to do. They lounged in the shadow and slept during the day. At night they made the place ring with their songs and their shouts. And gúns and knives were ever at hand. Three men were wounded during that first month, while Juan fought to regain his strength.

He never had leisure for thought, except at night a moment before he closed his eyes, exhausted. Then he wondered how it could have been that *Señor* Fontana had sent him among these brutes. He could only explain it by saying to himself that these must be the bad servants of the great man. When he told *Señor* Fontana how they had ill-treated him, the great man would put out his hand and punish them. For there was nothing but goodness and justice in the mind of the great don.

There was a large stone behind the house. When Juan had first come to the house of Matiás Bordi, he could barely stir that stone from side to side. He said to himself: *When I can raise that stone, then I shall fight with Garcilasso until he begs me to stop.*

So, every day, he found a chance to tug at the stone. And every day it seemed to him that he came nearer to lifting it. That life in the open air and constant drudgery in the service of Garcilasso were clothing him constantly with new power. The body of a child is an elastic thing. And so is his mind. The tyranny of Garcilasso passed out of his thoughts every night, and he slept sweetly and soundly. And the labors for Garcilasso toughened him by day, and a whole month ended with the day when he laid hold upon the stone and heaved with straining back and closed eyes. At length it came up by the roots, and he went at once to find his young master.

He found Garcilasso stretched in the shade, his eyes closed. He did not open them, but he knew his *mozo* by the sound of his step.

"Go to the cook," said Garcilasso. "Get me two tortillas wrapped around slices of fried pork. Hurry! I am hungry."

Juan Oro leaned and gathered a handful of sand. He tossed it in the face of Garcilasso. "Eat dirt," he said. "It is good enough for the belly of a pig."

As one touches a match to a dead pine tree and the flames leap up, so Garcilasso leaped to his feet. "Now I shall beat you until you are all running blood!" he screamed at Juan Oro. "Son of a dog! Yaqui cur!" And he smote Juan Oro upon the root of the nose.

But to Juan it was not more than the touch of a gentle hand. There were thirty days of shame and thirty days of hatred locked up in his breast. He laughed as he pushed aside the next blow of Garcilasso and gathered him in his arms.

"Squeal, pig!" said Juan, and hurled the other to the ground.

He fell with his enemy. They were locked in a mutual embrace like two fighting wild-cats. Then they rolled away from one another and came to their feet. As for Juan, he was in no hurry to end the thing, because he had been tasting victory from the first instant of the battle, and the taste was wonderfully sweet. But Garcilasso was in great trouble. He was bewildered by this sudden rising of a slave. He was maddened with the pain. He was thoroughly frightened, too, and, as he rose to his feet, he scooped up a broken branch which made a cudgel that comfortably filled his hand.

With that he drove at Juan Oro's head, but it was like striking at a dead leaf. Juan Oro floated out of the path of the blow and leaped in with hungry hands. When one has wrestled and fought with Yaqui boys twice one's weight, one has learned how to take punishment and how to deal it out. Now his hard fist flailed against the face of Garcilasso and knocked him flat on his back.

"You have killed me," moaned Garcilasso.

"I have only begun," Juan said, and leaped on his fallen foe. He took him by the hair and banged his head on a rock. "Are you beaten?" he said through his teeth.

"I am beaten," moaned Garcilasso.

"Will you call me *mozo* again?"

"Never," gasped Garcilasso. "Let me go. You are tearing out my hair by the roots."

"Am I your master?"

"Yes, yes! Do not kill me, Juan," he pleaded.

"Coward and pig," Juan pronounced. "I will not dirty my hands in your grease." He arose from his victim. "Stand up!" he ordered.

And Garcilasso stood up.

"Walk before me into the patio where your father is with the other men."

"No, no, Juan! He will kill me, if he knows that you have beaten me."

"If you do not go, I, Juan Oro, will kill you now . . . with my hands. Now, go!"

Garcilasso, trembling and groaning, walked before the victor through the dust of the patio and stood before his father. There were a dozen others there, rough men with brown, shining faces and glittering eyes, drinking tequila and gambling. They stopped their talk and turned to stare. Straight up to his father walked Garcilasso and then threw out his arms and raised his bleeding face.

"The *mozo* you gave me," he cried, "jumped on me from behind and made me like this."

At this, Matiás Bordi half rose from his chair, his fingers kneading the handle of his knife. He glared at his son. He looked past him at the unmarked face of Juan Oro.

"Lying dog!" cried Matiás, and smote his son to the ground. He said to the horrified *mozos* who were near: "Pick up the coward and take him away. Never let me see his face again!"

Then he caught Juan by the arm and

dragged him carelessly into a chair beside him.

"Look, *amigos*," he called to the men around him. "I have lost a son, and I have found a son!"

Chapter Seven

<u>Juan Stands the Test</u>

To Juan Oro it seemed like the beginning of some frightful jest, but by the serious faces which the other ruffians turned upon him he began to guess that Bordi was in earnest. Presently the chief said to a trembling *mozo:* "Call Isabella!"

The servant disappeared. A moment later a pretty half-breed woman came from the house onto the porch. Matiás Bordi turned upon her an absolutely expressionless face — for, when he was most moved, his features became most mask-like.

"Isabella," he said sternly, "come near me."

At this, her smile went out. It was as though a coating of ashes had fallen, yellow, upon her face. She came to him with a faltering step. The sharp eye of Juan Oro could see the difference now. Bordi was quiet, but it was the quiet of a tiger before it leaps.

"Woman," he said, "our son has proved himself a coward. Take him away. He is no longer mine. Here," he added, "is money." He reached into his pocket, drew out a handful of gold and silver, and gave it to her. In another moment she had scurried away.

Bordi then turned and seized upon the arm of Juan, and his steel fingers ground the flesh against the bone. But Juan Oro looked calmly into his eyes and changed not a muscle of his face. Bordi dropped the arm with a smile of contentment.

"To whom," he said, "do you belong?"

And Juan answered: "To the *Señor* Don José Fontana."

"Now, little fool, you have left him. You are free. Living with me, you will have horses to ride . . . not lump-headed mustangs, but blood horses! You will have guns, knives. You will have no work. Tell me, Juan Oro, do you become mine?"

"No, *señor.* I belong to *Señor* Fontana."

"Ah, and why?"

"Because, *señor,* I tried to take his life. I came within the snap of my fingers of taking his life. Only a bullet stopped me. Then, *señor,* he did not leave me to die. He took me to a great doctor, a very wise man. My life was given to me after it was going away. For that I belong to *Señor* Fontana. He had my life . . . he gave it back to me."

Bordi turned his black eyes upon his companions. There was a little murmur of approval from them.

"We shall see," said Bordi, "if you will stick to it. Take him," he said to two *mozos*, "and tie him against that post so that he cannot so much as stir a finger."

They seized upon Juan Oro and bound him with the entire length of a lariat against the stone pillar on the farther side of the patio. He could not, indeed, so much as stir a hand. And Matiás Bordi stepped out into the flare of the sun with a revolver in his hand.

"Do you hear me, Juan Oro?"

"I hear you, *señor.*"

"You will belong to me or to no one."

"No, *señor,* for I belong to *Señor* Fontana."

"Then you die, Juan. When I touch the trigger of this gun, you die!"

Juan Oro cast one glance into the sun-paled blue of the sky. There was no cloud, but a tiny speck of black — a buzzard — was tracing a great circle in the heavens. And Juan Oro thought of the only heaven of which he had ever heard among the Yaquis — a strange and misty place where men hunted again as they had hunted on earth. He looked back at Bordi and set his teeth.

"Do you hear?"

Juan did not answer. He could remember

one lesson, more clearly than all others, and that lesson was that it is folly to speak when words serve no purpose. Therefore, he stirred not a muscle. And his mind was busy saying to himself: *I must die like a man. I must watch death come and smile. Otherwise, after death, my soul will never grow to be a man. I shall be a boy always.* Thus said Juan Oro to himself. And he watched the line of light steadying to a point on the top of the barrel of the Colt.

"It is your last chance!" cried Matiás Bordi in a terrible voice. "Do you hear me, Juan Oro?"

But there was no answer. Then the gun clanged — and the eyes of Juan Oro did not so much as blink. Was this death? No, here he hung against the pillar still, and there was the wisp of smoke that the wind was jerking away from the muzzle of the gun. Matiás Bordi could not miss. Then what had happened?

"Did you see?" cried Bordi to the others.

A tall man with a pale, villainous face stood up and strode across the patio. He set his bony fingertips in the throat of the boy and forced up the head of Juan Oro. The pungent scent of tequila breathed strongly in the nostrils of Juan.

"Well," said the tall man, turning suddenly away, "his heart is going no faster than mine. That is enough, Matiás."

"It is enough," agreed Bordi. "Set him loose."

The two *mozos* fairly ran to him and set him free. The biting coils of the rawhide had stopped the flow of his blood. For a moment he staggered, but after that he walked slowly toward them.

"Now, Juan," said Matiás Bordi, "you are free to go, if you wish to go."

"Ah, *señor*," said the boy, "I could ride back to Fontana and tell him what you have done."

Bordi glanced at his friends, and they in turn fastened their eyes upon the youngster.

"What would the *Señor* Fontana do?" he asked.

"He would send his men. He would not need to come himself. He would kill you all. He would burn your house. That is what he would do."

Matiás Bordi leaned back in his chair and laughed long and softly. "Do you hear?" he said to his men.

They grinned wickedly.

"Then go tell him," said Bordi.

"No, *señor*, I shall remain and learn from you. I was commanded to do that."

"Juan Oro," said Bordi, "let me speak the

truth to you. I, Matiás Bordi, have been to this weak fool, this *Señor* Fontana, what a wolf is to a blind shepherd. I have seized what I would. I have torn and rent the flock. What did he do? Did he chase me to a corner and pull me down with the dogs he calls men that follow him? No, Juan, but like a coward and a sneak he sent to me saying . . . 'Rob wherever else you please, but let my lands go safe. I will forgive all your crimes against me. I will give you a great house for you and your men. I will give you cattle to eat. I will send you corn and peppers. You shall have no cost while you live on my land.' I listened to what the coward said. And that is why I am here. Do you understand me?"

"*Sí, señor.*"

"Do you believe me?"

"No, *señor!*"

The hand of Bordi darted out, but he checked it in mid-air. "So!" he said. Then he stood up and began to pace back and forth. The eyes of his men flicked back and forth, following every turn, but Juan Oro merely stared straight before him. At length the lean hand of Bordi darted forth and fastened upon the wrist of the boy. Juan was dragged into the house and with a great key Bordi unlocked a room and thrust Juan Oro into it.

He, expecting to be hurled into a prison cell, recoiled with a cry of wonder. For he saw before his eyes all the heaped-up treasures that the world could offer. He saw saddles covered with shining gold worked into fanciful patterns. He saw saddles glittering with spangles and with silver. He saw golden spurs and golden bridles. He saw revolvers jeweled and chased with precious designs. He put out his hand and picked up a knife whose hilt was roughed with emeralds and sapphires.

"Take what you want . . . as much as your arms can drag," said Bordi. "It is yours."

Then the small body of Juan trembled with desire. But he whipped up the knife and flung it from him with all his might. The keen blade sank into the wooden frame of the window and stuck there, raising a sharp and wicked song of humming like a hornet enraged.

"I want nothing," he said.

Matiás Bordi stared at him as though a miracle were being performed before his eyes. And, from that moment, he never looked at Juan Oro without a touch of reverence.

Chapter Eight

Juan Attempts Bordi's Life

By wolf-like sense of hearing, Juan Oro watched the road. For the rest, he gave himself up to the trees around him. Now and again, in the near distance, he heard the munching of his horse, as it found the tufts of grass that grew here and there. Another sound of horses was what he waited to hear. He lay flat on his back with his arms stretched out over his head and his hunting knife lying flat along the palm of his hand. Three times a squirrel had darted around the trunk of the tree and looked at him. Three times he had moved his hand to throw the knife, and three times the squirrel had flicked out of view before he could make his cast. Now he was ready for the try the instant the nose of the agile little creature should come in view.

He was no longer the Juan Oro of old. He had gained his full height, which was an even six feet. He was still slender. Now, as he lay on his back, his ribs arched high above a flat belly. But although he was spare, he was sinewy. There was hardly a wasted ounce of flesh on his body. A few years and he would grow heavier, stockier. But just now he was supple as a whiplash and well-nigh as swift and elusive in his movements.

This was Juan Oro at twenty. Five years among the men of Matías Bordi had given him a skin as deeply brown as theirs. For five years he had lived with gun, horse, and knife. He had learned to gamble with cards and with dice. He had learned to drink the fiery poison, tequila, and keep a level brain. He had learned to shoot by instinct, as other men speak. He had learned to make a bucking horse squeal with agony as he raked it with his spurs. He had learned to swim like a gleaming, twisting fish in the icy mountain streams and their colder pools.

He had learned how to drop a mask over his face also, and ride suddenly out before a traveler, turning his voice to coldest iron as he bade the stranger halt. For after five years with Bordi, the education that had begun under the Yaquis had been completed. There was neither kindness nor tenderness or honesty in his soul. His body was supple steel. His mind was steel also.

But robberies did not lie upon his conscience, because he had no conscience. Neither did he have a religion. He knew that some men went to churches, but, when church bells rang, they were no more to Juan Oro than the bell under the goat's neck that the poor sheep follow.

When he was a boy, his voice was as shrill and as biting as any other youngster, but now it had changed; it had altered completely. It was pitched in a middle register, and was wonderfully soft. It fell upon the ear like velvet on the touch. It was gentler than dew forming upon grass, this voice of the young robber. Only when he chose to put steel in the ring of it was it like the voice of a stern man. For the rest, it was such a sound as made women pause and turn with a smile even before they saw him. And when they saw him, they saw a brown young god. Most men are like cheap watches — they keep time a little awry. But the masterpiece of many jewels runs with frictionless ease, perfect truth. So it was with Juan Oro. He had no nerves to interfere. If he bade his hand to be steady, his hand was steady. In every finger there was a separate intelligence, so it seemed. And the card tricks that the gamblers had taught him, from time to time, he had picked up as though he were born to the knowledge of them. And so, adroitly fashioned, he had that strength of nerve and will and perfect harmony that surpass the strength of bulky muscle. When he tussled with the stalwart youths in the band of Bordi, he put them on the ground with snaky speed and a grip of iron.

Such was the body of Juan Oro, but his face, as has been said, was the face of a god. There was no flaw in it. It was a creation of perfect beauty. Too femininely perfect, some might have thought — a beauty, too, like the beauty of his voice. But that was before they looked into his brown eyes, as cold as the still mountain pools that hold the shadows of the trees. His hair was worthy of his name. In shadow it was deepest bronze. But in the sun it was dark, rich gold.

Such was Juan Oro in his twentieth year. And if one were to search all through his strange nature, it would have been hard to find in him a single virtue, except that virtue which goes with strength — he was brave. But, a black shadow to match this light, he was as cruel as he was brave.

Now he lay flat on his back, unstirring, only in his eyes was there a centering of brilliant light as he watched the place where the squirrel might next appear. And here it came — a tentative tip of the nose — then a glitter of tiny eyes — and the hand of Juan Oro flashed up over his head. A long streak of light left his palm, and, flying up, was extinguished in the soft bark of the tree. He had missed, and the shrill chattering of the little squirrel struck on his ears as it raced higher through the branches.

Juan Oro leaped to his feet with a snarl of rage. He leaped for the first low branch, caught it, and swung himself into the higher limbs like a climbing monkey, then up he went. No sailor ever sped for the loftiest yard with half such speed. He reached the knife, tore it out, and poised it again — and just in time to see a fluff of fur dart around the trunk higher up. He hurled again, and this time the knife struck with a soft, heavy sound. The weight of the heavy weapon lifted the little creature with it for an instant. Then knife and victim dropped back through the branches — struck a little bough, and began to whirl, over and over — until the knife and the body landed with a light thud among the pine needles far beneath.

Juan Oro, like a beast of prey, licked his lips and sighed with satisfaction. He was content. But sooner than have that squirrel elude him, he would have hunted it through half a day. He peered through the branches of the tree and looked down the road. Through the golden light of the afternoon he could see the thing he wanted — a single horseman mounted on a gray that was running freely down the trail. He saw that wished-for vision and smiled evilly to himself. Beyond, he let his glance rest upon the mountains, and saw where the dark belts of evergreens ended and the naked summits began above the timberline.

After that, he went down the tree, dropping cat-like from branch to branch, catching by his hands, and dropping again. A circus performer would have been proud of such a trick. He landed unfatigued on the ground beneath, drew his knife from the soft skin, and kicked the poor little dead body with its fixed and lifeless eyes under a heap of dried leaves. Then he went to his horse.

By the time he was in the saddle, the hoofbeats were ringing nearer and nearer, and, as he pushed his horse into the open where the trail wound, the traveler was almost upon him. It was Matiás Bordi who now drew rein with a shout of welcome and a wave of his hand.

"Hey, Juan!" he cried. "You have come to meet me, my boy?"

Juan Oro pushed his hat back from his smooth forehead. "Stay where you are, Matiás," he said. "I have come to meet you, yes." He put his hand on the butt of his revolver as he spoke, and, although he smiled, Matiás Bordi changed color, for he had seen that smile before and knew that there was danger before him.

"You have been drinking that ten times damned brandy," he said to the boy. "It always makes you a devil! What is wrong now?"

"Nothing is wrong. All is right. We have our meeting at last, Matiás."

"What meeting do you mean?"

"I have been your pupil for five years, have I not?"

"You have. You have learned what I could teach, Juan. And what of that?"

"Only a fool would learn lessons without using them."

"That is true, Juan. You are not a fool. Why do you look at me in that manner?"

"When I told you that *Señor* Fontana sent me to you, I forgot to tell you the last thing he said."

"What is it, then? What did that woman in man's clothes have to say to you?"

"That I was not to come back to him until you were dead, Matiás. That would be my proof that I am a man."

"Sacred devil," breathed Bordi. "Is that true?"

"It is true."

"I shall start today. I shall burn the house over his head and shoot them as they run out like singed rats!"

"You will never see him unless he meets you in hell, Matías. This is your last day on earth."

"Juan, Juan, do you mean that you will try to do the thing he wants?"

"I shall, *señor!*"

"Ah, Juan, you kill me without bullets. I have loved you as a son is loved."

"If you, *señor,* are a fool, is there a good reason why I should be a fool, also?"

"But this would be the work of the devil. You have eaten bread and meat with me for five long years."

"They have been very long. I have been waiting, always, for the coming of this day. Now it has arrived."

"Why this day?"

"I am twenty. I am a man."

"You are a poor child. You wish to have me murder you, Juan? No, I shall not raise a hand against you."

"Do you hear me, Bordi? If you will not raise a hand, then I will kill you in cold blood. Afterward, I shall discharge one bullet from your revolver. Then I shall go to other men and tell them how the great Bordi fought me . . . and how I, a boy as you call me, killed Bordi in fair fight."

"You are a devil!"

"Perhaps I am. That is what I would do."

"Will you force me, Juan? It would be drawing a gun on the only thing under the blue sky that I love."

"You will fight, Bordi, or else die without fighting. That is all I have to say."

"In the name of mercy, Juan. . . ."

"Bah! Do you talk to me of mercy? I have no mercy! I have learned in these five years with you, Matiás Bordi. Take your gun!"

"I shall be murdered, if I do not. Ah, Juan, God forgive you, if you kill me . . . for He will never forgive me, if I kill you. But you force me. Go for your gun!"

"Shall I take advantage of you? No, I do not need it. You are as slow with your hands as a bull is slow with his feet. Take your gun, fool!"

"On *your* head," groaned Bordi, and snatched out his weapon.

What shall we say of Juan? That there was some small shrinking of his heart as he seized his own weapon? That some mist of kindness rose before his eyes? No, he had only one hunger, and that was to drive his bullet into the brain of Bordi. He had no doubt as to the outcome. He had measured with his eyes a hundred times the speed with which Bordi drew and fired. In his soul there was the cruel superiority of the cat that plays with the mouse. So he whipped his hand at his own revolver butt.

Once in ten thousand times a revolver binds against the barrel. There was a slight tug of steel against leather as Juan drew his weapon. That instant of delay was enough. As the muzzle of his gun came clear, Bordi's gun exploded. There was a clanging of metal. Juan was knocked cleanly out of his saddle, as though an invisible lance had lifted him forth.

Chapter Nine

Matías Bordi's Gang Attacked

For the bullet from the gun of Bordi had knocked the gun from the hand of Juan Oro and flicked it up against his head. When he recovered his senses a little, he found that his head was supported in the lap of Matías Bordi, who was pouring water from a canteen over his face and groaning: "Holy Mother, restore him. I vow at the shrine of San Mateo...."

Here Juan Oro decided that it would be less embarrassing if he gave warning that he was about to waken. He groaned loudly and then opened his eyes and sat up, holding his hand to a lump that had formed on his head. Bordi had already recovered his feet and stood before him, looking down with an anxious eye.

"How is it with you, Juan?" he asked.

"My head spins," said Juan. "You are a lucky man, Matías. My gun stuck in the leather. Otherwise, you would be here ... and I there. Now finish me."

"God forbid," said Matías with much solemnity. "You have been saved from me, and I have been saved from you. Let us vow, Juan, never to raise a hand against one another again."

"I shall make this vow," said Juan Oro, "never to raise a hand against you, until I have repaid you, life for life, according to what you have done on this day."

"Look, young fool, you are in my power. I have only to raise my gun and shoot!"

"And you are a greater fool, if you do not. *I* have not begged. I have told you what to do. On your own head, if you refuse."

A vein of anger swelled in the temple of the outlaw. But he bit his lip and controlled himself. "Have I not made you as a son to me, Juan?"

"I have given an oath," said Juan Oro, "that I shall never go down the mountains until you are dead."

"What are oaths to you?" sneered Matías Bordi. "I have seen you break a hundred of them."

"To fools and enemies, yes. But this was to the man who had my life in his hand and who gave it back to me."

"As I do on this day."

Juan Oro studied that thought with a sigh of effort. At last he shook his head. "I shall repay you," he said. "Until I do, I am your man, to work for you as before, Matiás. But after you are repaid . . . then beware of me!"

"You are not a man," declared Bordi in anger. "You are ten devils gathered into one flesh."

Juan Oro stood up. "Here is my hand," he said, "that I shall never forget . . . until I have repaid you, Matiás."

The outlaw took the hand reluctantly. "Ah, Juan, God give you a soul at last. For you have none now."

But Juan Oro merely laughed. One would have thought, to see him swing into his saddle again, that nothing had happened — that he had not been striving to take this man's life the moment before. He rode cheerfully at the side of Bordi on the way back to the old *hacienda*. Neither did he ever mention what had happened to any other in the band, nor did Bordi himself speak of it. But Bordi, for a month, was an incarnate devil of cruelty.

Matters went worse and worse with the great Bordi. The law, baffled for some time by the protecting arm that Fontana stretched around the outlaw, had finally traced him to his new domicile. On a day when Juan Oro was in his twenty-second year, he rode back with Bordi and a dozen followers, and, as they topped the last hill before the *hacienda*, they gave the spurs to their horses and rushed down to see who would be first. Juan Oro himself was near the lead, and gaining constantly as he jockeyed his racing horse along. Before them, the *hacienda* was a blaze of light — illumined by the *mozos* to cheer their homecoming?

Then a long line of fire ran along the black ground in front of them. Out of that ground, shadowy forms of men rose with rifle at the shoulder. Another volley crashed among the outlaws.

To turn back was madness. A broad-faced moon hung in the east, climbing swiftly, and making every shadowy horseman a perfect target against that mild light. But most of the gang turned and strove to flee back in the direction out of which they had come. They died, every one.

Only two had sense to see that salvation lay only in breaking through the cordon and galloping beyond. One of the pair was Juan Oro. As he came at the line, he dug the spurs deep. And while the squealing, terrified horse leaped forward, he fired his revolver into the face of the soldier straight before him. He saw the fellow spin around with a scream and clap his hands to his face. Then Juan Oro was through the line.

He rode straight for the house. Half a dozen pursued him, running, screaming, shadowy figures. He shot one down and stopped that rush. They preferred to go to the front again and join their comrades in looting the fallen bandits and examining their faces by the growing moonlight.

Upon this, Juan had counted. In the meantime, he said to himself, the great Bordi was doubtless among the dead, which left him free to return to *Señor* Fontana and tell him the work was done, although by other hands than his. But why should he go back with empty hands? There was treasure in that house, and he knew where it was.

He slipped from his horse, dove through a window, and ran to the upper story. He had kicked his boots off, so he moved with no more noise than a cat, and, when he gained the upper gallery off which the treasure room opened, he heard the sounds of a subdued struggle.

There he saw a soldier struggling on the floor, and a familiar form above him, with hands fixed around the warrior's throat. The conqueror turned his head — it was Bordi!

When the soldier struggled no more, but lay still with swollen face and fixed eyes, Bordi and Juan Oro ran together into the prize room. Silver they could not regard. But they gathered fifty pounds of gold and gold coins — a comfortable little fortune. They went through a casement and so, climbing like cats, to the ground. A moment later they were in the saddle and swinging away through the darkness, leaving the soldiers behind them, shouting and dancing drunkenly to celebrate their victory. A great victory for the soldiers. A headless triumph, for, while Bordi lived, the destruction of a dozen of his gangs meant nothing.

At the edge of the trees Bordi halted his horse and extended his left arm to Juan Oro. It had been slashed from wrist to elbow by a grazing bullet, and, while Oro bandaged the wound, the chief rolled a cigarette with matchless dexterity with one hand, lighted it, and watched the revels of the conquerors. And while he watched, he laughed. They had taken his men, but his own life was spared, and he had come away with the cream of his treasure.

"I shall make them groan for it," he said to Juan. "But before we go, we still have work to do."

"Well?" said Juan, wondering what deviltry was still in the mind of the leader.

"We can catch half a dozen of the best of the horses," said Bordi, "and take them with us. The rest, they're welcome to. I'm glad they came, curse them! For it was beginning to be too hard to get firewood."

It was not difficult to get the horses, for the best of them were the tamest, and in half an hour they were off again with their prizes tethered one to another.

However, that midnight coup of the soldiers was a blow to the prestige of Bordi. Thereafter, men were more cautious about joining him. His charm, it was held, was broken, and, since misfortune had begun to come to him, some prophesied that it would continue to rain thick and fast.

He and Juan Oro were all that composed the gang at the first. They drifted here and there through the mountains, descending now and again for plunder or for food merely, then retreating again into the hills. Bordi constantly begged the boy to stay away from the robberies; Juan as constantly refused.

"For," said Bordi many a time, "before long you will be known. And then there will be a price upon your head. Believe me, Juan, between outlawry and law there is all the difference that lies between heaven and hell."

"But you," said Juan Oro, "choose outlawry."

"Shall I tell you why?"

"Tell me, then."

"I was a farmer, Juan. If I had one great wish, it was to have more cattle and fatter ones. I was an innocent."

Juan Oro laughed.

"You, Juan, cannot understand. You have never been young. You have never been foolish, except to give a madman's vow to *Señor* Fontana. You have always been filled with ten devils. But I was once a gentle child with a man's body. I believed that all men were good. Of course, it was only a matter of time. At length a cruel and clever scoundrel by the name of Díaz found me. He showed me a great scheme for reclaiming an old mine that had been abandoned. If I were to sell my farm and give him the money, he would buy great machines and open that mine again, and we both would have a million *pesos* in a year. Then I could buy a great farm, build me a huge *hacienda . . . ah, well, how my heart jumped, when I heard him talk.*"

"And then?" Juan asked, rather curious.

"I did everything as he wished, and, of course, he disappeared. I followed him and found him at last. He was a rich man much respected in his town. I went to the judge and told him my story."

" 'You are a madman,' he said, and sent for Díaz. Díaz looked me up and down and shook his head.

" 'I have never seen this poor fellow before.'

" 'Rascal,' said the judge to me, 'begone!'

"I went away and sat by myself. 'I have been wronged,' I said to myself. 'And why have I been wronged? What have I done? I have been kind to the world, and the world has been unkind to me.'

"I went to Díaz and managed to find him alone.

" '*Señor,*' I said, 'tell me in what way I have ever wronged you, and why you have stolen my property from me?'

"He only laughed at me.

" 'A fool,' he stated, 'and his money are soon parted. And you, Bordi, are the greatest fool I have ever known.'

"Then it came upon me, like a flash of yellow lightning, that he had taken my money out of mere cruelty and avarice. I drew my gun and shot him through the heart . . . and in five minutes the posse was after me. They rode hard. I wore out three horses, stole new ones, rode them to death one by one, and on my fourth horse rode away to liberty.

"A fortnight later they cornered me. I

87

killed two men and wounded three more, and then I escaped. Since then I have been wounded many times, but never more seriously than this last cut across the arm."

"Tell me, Matías, how old are you?"

"How old are you, Juan?"

"I am twenty-three."

"I am twenty years older than you."

"Ah, but you look not more than thirty."

"I shall never grow old," Bordi declared calmly.

"And why?"

"Because Providence wishes to keep me young for this work."

"So you really work for Providence, then?"

"Foolish boy," said Bordi, "do you think it is chance that has saved my life these many years?"

Chapter Ten

The Life Story of Bordi

To Juan it was most curious — like reading a mysterious book. For it was the first time that Bordi had ever talked of himself. Perhaps it would be the last time. They sat under giant pines that towered up toward the steel-black sky, set coldly with white stars. The fire at their feet was a feeble thing of fluttering yellow wings that struck at the darkness and then cowered away to nothing again. They had finished their night meal, a simple matter of cold tortillas and beans, washed down with icy water from a stream whose voice still murmured in the background.

"So," said Juan coldly, "Providence has much to do with you?"

"It has," answered Bordi with perfect surety.

"How can you tell? Your life has been saved because you shoot straighter and faster than other men."

"That is not so. You, Juan, are a quicker and surer shot than I. I have seen you practice. Also, I have seen you shoot. The play of your hand is like the play of a cat's foot . . . a wonderful thing to watch. And there are other men I have seen . . . none, perhaps so deadly with weapons as you are, but terrible men, nevertheless. And yet I have stood up to them and beaten them with no trouble. It is Providence, Juan."

"Do you think," asked the boy, smiling to himself, "that Providence is pleased with your way of life?"

"Yes," said Bordi with the same astonishing nonchalance. "Providence is unquestionably pleased with me. Otherwise, I would not be preserved."

"That is strange talk. How do you serve Providence?"

"A divine spirit is in me."

"What?"

"I tell you, a divine spirit is in me."

"And does it guide you?"

"It does. I turn to it always. I say to it . . . 'What shall I do?' And the spirit answers . . . 'Follow your own will, Matías Bordi. Follow your own will, for that is the will of Providence.'"

At this expression of egotism so gigantic that it ceased to be vanity and became something profound, impersonal, Juan Oro stared and said nothing for some time. But he kicked some of the embers of the fire together, and as the trembling flame pushed a tentative hand up into the darkness by that light, he watched the face of the chief. And the face of Bordi was lifted to the stars, and there was a perfect peace upon it.

"You have murdered, robbed, taken by stealth," said Juan Oro. "What are your good acts?"

"My killings and my robberies are my good acts," said Bordi.

"Ha?"

"That is true. The Lord puts His hand forth, and it is fire. He punishes the sins of the evil-doers. I am His hand. I strike down His enemies!"

"*¡Diablo!*" hissed Juan. "This is very strange talk."

"You, for the first time, hear my mind. No other man has ever heard it. For this work I was taken from my little farm. Weapons were put in my hands. I, who had hardly shot so much as a squirrel, suddenly faced fighting men and killed them without trouble. Yes, it is the will of Providence."

"Well," said Juan, "I shall not say no to you."

"Besides," said Bordi with the same assured calm, "I do other things that are of a

91

divine will. The money which I take is not mine. Do you wonder why I have so much gold constantly passing through my hands and yet I am always poor?"

"I have wondered at that."

"I give it away, Juan. My charity is as great as my robbery. Here, there, and again, I see a poor man's face, or a woman in agony. Then the voice within me says . . . 'Give, Matiás Bordi,' and I give."

"That is why they have not caught you, then. You have too many friends here and there. But twice they caught you, Matiás, and twice you escaped."

"And if I am caught again, I shall escape again."

"How is that?"

"There is a certain great man whom I pay. Five thousand *pesos* every year goes from me to him. Now he is dead. I must go to see his son, and he will do for me what his father did. When I am closed behind steel bars, he finds a way to open them for me. It is very simple. And that is why, when I am cornered, I do not fight to the last. No, I surrender. They take me down to the towns so that the people may stare at me, and they may be applauded. But after I am safely locked in the jail, then the door is opened for me. Do you see?"

Juan Oro sighed. "Is this the will of Providence also?"

"It is the will of Providence, also."

"All your work is good, then?"

"All is good. Consider yourself, Juan. You are a tiger. When you beat that dog, Garcilasso, a voice within me said . . . 'Save this child. He is yours.' I have made you mine."

"But I am not yours, Matías."

"Do you think not? You will find, when the right time comes, that I have secured you to myself."

"But I have warned you again and again, Matías, that when I have repaid you, life for life, my hand shall be against you."

"That is nothing. If you do not force me to kill you, I shall save you in the end and make you gentle."

"And yet you yourself, Matías, have said that I shoot straighter and more quickly than you do."

"What are bullets to a man who is protected by Providence? You have stood before me once."

"That was when my gun stuck in the holster."

"What held it there?"

"Matías, you are mad!"

"Well, you will see. No man can kill me. I am safe. I am free."

"And what will your end be?"

"When Providence has ended his purposes that I may accomplish, then will it send a destroyer!"

"Perhaps I, Matiás, am that man."

"Ah, yes, Juan. Perhaps."

"But you have no fear?"

"Am I a fool to be afraid of fate? No! I wait."

So their talk ended on that evening, but Juan Oro lay awake for a long time, wrapped in his blanket, listening to the wind singing in the trees, and wondering at what he had heard.

And, three days later, they committed the robbery on the gold train from Chihuapa that made the fame of Matiás Bordi greater than ever before. Fifty armed men guarded the burros which brought down the gold from the great mine, and, where the trail wound around the edge of a cliff, Bordi and Juan Oro crouched on the farther side of the ravine and watched the burros, looking like goats walking on the sheer face of the cliff, so narrow was the footing on which they went. There was a guard before and a guard behind, but Matiás Bordi said to Juan: "Shoot for the heads of the burros."

So he put his rifle on a rest, and, as the burros came around the curve, one by one, he shot them. Three times he fired, and the little animals rolled dead over the edge of the trail.

There were the horses of Bordi and Oro. They transferred the packs and rode through the heaped fragments of rocks until they gained the trees, with a pattering hail of rifle bullets falling around them from the height above.

When they were alone in the shelter of the trees, Bordi looked at his young companion with a complacent smile. "Now, Juan," he said, "what made their bullets go astray?"

"Shooting down from a great distance," said Juan. "It is hard to shoot straight, when one is shooting down and at such a distance."

"Is that your reason?" smiled Bordi. "Well, perhaps you are right." But he laughed to himself, and Juan Oro knew what was in his mind.

What he felt toward Bordi was that the man was mad — plainly insane. And yet, since that evening in the woods, his heart changed toward his chief.

They lay up in a cave well above timberline after that robbery.

"Because," said Bordi, "we need time while the excitement dies away. But, in a month, men will forget everything . . . even the danger of death, to say nothing of lost money."

"Why do you take precautions," asked Juan mischievously, "if Providence is with you always?"

At this, Bordi groaned. "Young man," he said to his friend, "remember this always. The hand of Providence must not be borrowed for little things that are within the power of man. Providence strikes when there is no other help to look to. For the rest, it is left to our own hands, our own wits." He added: "But ask me no more about it. I am only a poor servant, not one who can pretend to know this divine mind, saving when its spirit speaks within me."

When that month of lazy loitering in the bare regions above timberline had ended, they started down from the heights and went leisurely toward the richer lowlands, which at last they could see checked and patterned with little farms and, in the distance, a white city, streaked across with mist.

"To what are we riding?" asked Juan.

"We are riding," said the chief, "to find the new Pedro Maldonado."

"And what is he?"

"He is the son of my old friend, whose name was Pedro, also. We are to make a new accounting with him in place of the old one."

So they dropped down from the hills and crossed the rolling lands in the night. And though they could see the city first from the mountains, they spent two nights of riding before they reached its walls. For it was an old town that dated back almost to the Conquest. Through the streets they rode by night, until they came to the house of Pedro Maldonado.

Chapter Eleven

Pedro Maldonado

When they reached the Plaza Municipal, Bordi began to ride more slowly. All the central part of the park was a growth of grand old trees through which the street lamps on the farther side twinkled only now and again, like watchful eyes.

"When I was a young man . . . when I was of your years, Juan," he explained, "my greatest happiness was walking in these boulevards at night. When the evening crowds began to circle the plaza, I would come out dressed in my best. I would ride in from my little farm for the sake of that walk. There was a pretty girl who was always with a big, man-faced woman. I used to search for her. I loved her. She loved me. As we strolled around the plaza and passed once in each round, my eyes found her, her eyes found me. That was enough. One glance . . . it was a book. Three or four times in an evening we had glimpses of one another. Then there would come days and days when I did not see her. But at last she would appear again."

"Who was she?" asked Juan.

"I never knew. I had few friends. I was a dull fellow, and there were few men who cared to stroll with me. And I knew that I could not point her out and ask who she was without letting my face show why I asked. As for following her to her house, I was too proud for that. And, before I found out her name, I killed Díaz and had to ride for my life. Since that time . . . since they have put up my picture in ten thousand places, I have wondered what she thought, when she saw my face and beneath it . . . twenty thousand *pesos* reward."

"Is it so much?" asked Juan.

The bandit chuckled softly. "You, who wish to take my life one fine day . . . do you not know how much money it would bring you?"

"Ah!" cried Juan in disgust. "Do you think that I would take blood money?"

"Would you not? *¡Diablo!* You love nothing but fighting . . . nothing but blood."

"Perhaps. But to kill for money? That is to be worse than a dog. *Whist,* Matiás! There is someone coming toward us . . . I think I saw a glint of gold on his shoulders. It is a gendarme, I think. Shall we turn and ride the other way?"

"Certainly not. Then he would be suspicious. If we ride past him, he will think nothing."

They drew nearer, and now, passing a street lamp like a small, dull, orange moon, by that light they saw that it was a gendarme, indeed. They saw his white cotton trousers, his gold-braided, epauletted coat, his brilliant cap. He was swinging his stick, and his saber clanked as he strode. When he was closer, he took up a position immediately before them and raised his club.

"Stop!" he commanded.

Juan Oro began to draw rein, but, seeing that his companion kept on, he pushed his horse straight ahead. Not until his mount was almost trampling upon the startled gendarme did Bordi stop.

The *policía*, in alarm, had drawn his revolver.

"Keep back," he commanded, "and give your names! It is past midnight!"

"Fellow," said Bordi harshly, "do you dare to stop me?"

The gendarme, starting, peered earnestly toward the face of the stranger, but the night shadows were sufficiently thick to veil him.

"*Señor,*"he said in doubt, "I cannot recognize you."

"You cannot!" roared Bordi in an apparent passion. "It is very well for you that I am a good-natured man, or I should report you to your captain. Stand out of my way!"

The gendarme moved as precisely as a soldier to the side, and saluted. Bordi and Juan Oro rode on past.

"That is very well," chuckled Juan. "But what if he follows us?"

"He will be afraid to do that. For a month he will be expecting to lose his place. What is that?"

"Some old woman. She is going to sleep there in her blanket, I suppose."

It was a huddled form, squatted in the brush at the side of the boulevard. Bordi rode straight toward her.

"A good evening, *señora*," he said.

"There are no good nights for the old and the weak and the poor," answered a cracked and dismal voice.

"You have had misfortunes," said Bordi with more gentleness than Juan had ever heard in his voice before.

"I have had them, God knows."

"Are there no people in this town to help you?"

"They have helped me too long. They are weary of helping, *señor*. They are tired of my face. And I do not accuse them."

"But I," said Bordi, "am not weary of you. Here is something that will keep you comfortably for half a year. May it bring you happiness, *señora*." He handed her a weight of money that made her gasp.

She breathed: "You are an angel God has sent to me. Ah, *señor*, let me see your face . . . and tell me what name I shall pray for."

"I shall show you," said Bordi. "Perhaps you will recognize me?"

With that, to the utter astonishment of Juan, he lit a match. That spurt of flame showed Juan Oro the withered, seamed face of an ancient Indian woman, with a ragged black mantilla slipped back from hair shining as though with oil. She, on her part, opened the thin slits of her eyes and moaned with terror and surprise.

"Matiás Bordi!" she whispered. Bordi let the match drop into the darkness.

"*Adiós,*" he said.

"God save you! God give you fortune!" said her trembling voice. "*Adiós*, kind *señor!*"

"She will be at the ear of the *policia* in five minutes," Juan commented as soon as they were at a little distance.

"She?" chuckled Bordi. "No, no, Juan. She would lay down her life for me."

"But what good would her life do you,

Matiás? It is nearly ended. It is nearly gone. Why did you waste so much money on her?"

"When I heard her speak, the voice rose in me and told me to give. I could not help it," said Bordi. "Now, slowly, for we are almost there."

They had turned from the plaza down a side lane, very narrow, very black, untouched with the light of a single street lamp. Presently they paused in front of a great house, all of whose lower windows were strongly secured with new steel bars, glimmering faintly through the starlight.

"How will you find him?" asked Juan.

"That is easily done," answered Bordi, and, raising his voice, he broke into a weird old Indian song, more wail than music.

When he ended, Juan asked: "Is that the signal?"

"It was the signal for his father," said Bordi.

"Ah, but what will that mean to the son?"

"His father was not a fool. He would not die and disinherit his son from five thousand a year. No, you may trust that the new Pedro Maldonado knows all about this little song. Look!"

As he spoke, the light went past one of the windows of the big house. It appeared again at another casement immediately above them.

"Who is there?" asked a strained, uncertain voice.

"A friend of your father's. Will you see me, Don Pedro?"

"I? My father's friend? *Señor . . . señor . . .* well, ride into the patio."

"The gate is closed."

"I shall open it instantly."

The light disappeared, and there was a faint murmur of hurrying feet. By the time they had reached the great gates that closed the entrance to the patio, someone within was working the lock. Now the gates swung wide, softly, telling of good balance and much grease. They walked their horses into the courtyard.

Their guide, with a muffled lantern, led the way across the court and passed through a low, narrow doorway. There was a flood of light that announced that the lantern had been unveiled.

"Matías," murmured Juan. "Do not go in. If those gates are closed behind us, we are hopeless prisoners."

"You think, Juan," Bordi said with his usual, unruffled calm, "without remembering the five thousand a year. All will be well. Stand at the door and keep the heads of the horses turned toward the gates of the patio. If you see anyone stealing toward those gates, shoot. I will be with you instantly, and we will be away like two bullets. For this new Maldonado, after all, may prefer twenty thousand *pesos* in reward at once to fifty thousand spread over ten years."

So said Bordi as he dismounted. Juan Oro, keeping his own saddle, backed the horses close to the door. By bending a little, he could look through the door behind him and watch everything that happened.

What he first saw was a young man of twenty-five, perhaps, hastily dressed, his hair a little disordered, and a linen robe thrown on carelessly. But even those clothes would not disguise what he was. His quality spoke in his blood, in his refined and handsome features, in the thin carving and the bold arch of the nose, in the big, bright, steady eye. The hand that held the lantern was almost as delicately made as the hand of a woman. And his other hand gripped the barrel of a rifle. He was manifestly on his guard, and he carried himself with perfect courage and composure.

When Bordi stood before him, he said: "I must ask you first, *señor,* for what reason you have come to me tonight, and who you are."

"I am not a vain man," smiled Bordi, "and yet I am surprised that you do not know a face which is worth twenty thousand *pesos*."

If Maldonado was stirred, it was only so slightly that even the keen eye of Oro could not detect a change. He looked steadily at Bordi and shook his head.

"That," he said, "does not help me to understand."

Bordi shrugged his shoulders. "A man who does not wish to see is worse than blind!"

"*¿Señor?*" said Maldonado coldly.

The tiger was up in Bordi, and Juan Oro expected that anything might happen, but his chief now strode slowly up and down the little room. At length, controlling himself with an effort, he added: "I was useful to your father . . . your father was useful to me, *Señor* Maldonado."

"My father," said the young man pointedly, "is dead."

"True, *señor*. But you, also, my friend, may be able to use five thousand *pesos* each year of your life . . . while I live."

"Five thousand *pesos?*" stated the confused Maldonado. "I do not know what you mean."

"Certainly not, *señor*. Nevertheless, a little thought may make you see the use of it. However, although I need a *patrón*, I do not need to beg for one. There are others, of course, whom I can have. But Maldonado is an old name and a strong name. It has been of such use to me, and I have been of such use to it, that I did not wish to change. If you do not need me now, say so for the last time, *señor,* and I am gone."

But here, just as young Maldonado was shaking his head, a new thought seemed to come to him and made him glance aside at the darkness of a corner.

The devil was the only deity of which Juan Oro felt that he had any intimate understanding; and now it seemed to him that he saw the devil, like a visible shade, pass over the face of Maldonado.

"Wait, *señor,*" said the young don. "There is another thing of which I have just remembered. But first I must close the door. We must speak alone."

Chapter Twelve

Juan's Wild Indian Capers

It seemed madness to Juan Oro that his chief should put himself altogether in the unknown hands of this stranger. But that was what he did. The door was closed which shut him off from his retreat, and Juan Oro was left alone in that well of darkness — the court — with the white stars strewn above his head.

But of what avail was it to shut a door against ears that were trained from infancy to hear every whisper in the forest? He drew back his horse against the door of the house, and, bending his head, he listened. The voices from the room were carefully lowered, and yet he heard every word.

"Money," he heard Maldonado say, "is not the only current coin in the world. There are other services."

"It is true," answered Bordi.

"Very well. Of money I have no need. My father was wealthy. I myself am about to complete an alliance which will put me beyond the consideration of money."

"May I ask with what great fortune?"

"With that of *Señor* Fontana."

"I did not know that his daughter was of marriageable age."

"She is dead. His wife cannot have more children. His heiress has come from Spain. She is his niece. I am about to be married to her, *señor.* You understand?"

"I understand," Bordi said a little dolefully. "Money, then, is nothing to you. What else can I pay you?"

"A great service has just come into my mind, *Señor* Bordi."

"You have remembered it together with my name?"

"Exactly!" And Maldonado laughed. "I know you, frankly, from my father, *Señor* Bordi."

"He has given me a good account, then, for we never failed one another."

"That is exactly as he worded it. He told me that you are a valiant man . . . the whole world knew that before. He told me, also, that you are a faithful man. To be faithful, in my eyes, is a greater worth than courage, *señor.*"

"Well?" Bordi said tersely.

"But this affair that I would open to you is such a thing as cannot be talked of freely with a stranger."

"Consider that you are your father, and not yourself. Speak freely. He had no secrets from me, *Señor* Maldonado."

"Are you a *gringo*-lover, Bordi?"

"They are nothing to me, *señor*. The Americans are neither one thing nor the other. I do not consider them."

"At least, you are not to them as to a brother?"

"Tush! They are nothing to me."

"You would not see them come in to marry the great fortunes out of our Mexico?"

"I would see them dead, first."

"Now, Bordi, you speak in a way that I can understand. You would see them dead!"

"It is my meaning."

"Now, *señor,* there is a certain man at the house of Fontana . . . with the bigness of a bull, and the quickness of a panther. Let me tell you what manner of man he is. He rode off into the hills, hunting. Six Mexican bandits watched him go and trailed him. When he was far away among the hills, alone, they attacked him to make him prisoner and hold him for a ransom from *Señor* Fontana. Ah, *Señor* Bordi, four of them he left dead, and brought back the other two living as his prisoners. First he showed them to the people. Then he made them confess all that they had done and all that they had tried to do. Then he tied their hands to a tethering post. He whipped them until they were screaming and begging for mercy. Then he turned them loose . . . not to the gendarmes . . . but free!"

"Ah?" murmured Bordi. "This is a man!"

"A man? A devil! Has not our brave nation been disgraced by one such thing? And besides, does he not owe us four lives?"

"Well, you wish to have this man killed?"

"*Señor*, I put myself in your hands. You are a man of honor. My father has told me so. Now, *señor*, this marriage which I intended has been contracted for by *Señor* Fontana. That is well. You must understand, however, that his niece, long before, had traveled much and lived in the United States with a dear friend. Why should I make it a long story? There she found this Steven Marshal. There she found this big man. She is young. She is not eighteen, *señor!* Well, Bordi, I tell you all these things so that you may understand why the thing must be done. Who will marry a woman whose heart is over the hills? It is a dangerous thing."

"That is true. But, in case I do this thing . . . ?"

"Name what you wish. It is yours!"

"Our alliance is compact?"

"It is sealed forever in whatever way you wish."

"Your hand, *señor*, is enough."

"Very well. *Señor* Bordi, this is a day that we shall never forget."

"I trust we shall not. Is it *adieu?*"

"*Adieu*, Bordi. Only, before you go, I must caution you again. The man is, truly, a tiger. There is force in his hand to smash bones."

"He is a Texan, then?"

"Yes. He is a Westerner, I believe. A great, blood-loving barbarian! It is right that he should die by the gun. But, *señor*, if I were you . . . to make sure . . . I would use every care to come at him with an advantage. Do you understand me?"

"It shall be done," said Bordi. "The man is already dead. Farewell!"

He came out from the room and leaped into his saddle. There was a wave from the hand of Maldonado, white in the flash of the lantern light, and they were away. But as they rode through the gate, they saw two armed men crouched on either side of it, close to the shadow. That was the reason, then, for the boldness of Maldonado in showing himself to these strangers at midnight.

"Tell me," said Juan Oro, "what will you do?"

"I shall ride south to *Señor* Fontana. I shall see this man, this great *gringo*."

"No," said Juan. "*I* shall do it."

"Young blood-drinker . . . young ferret . . . man-killer," Bordi murmured. "What makes you wish for this work?"

"I wish to see this strong man . . . this bull . . . this great fighter. When I have finished seeing him, I shall kill him, Matiás."

"Without knowing what manner of man he is?"

"Why should I care? When he is dead, what will he be to me?"

Matiás Bordi threw up both hands. He cried: "There is no heart, no soul, in you, Juan!"

"Now you begin to talk of Providence," Juan Oro said sullenly. "I shall not listen. Have you not promised to murder him?"

"I promised to see him. No more than that. Perhaps he is a fool and a villain . . . a treasure-hunter who has made this girl love him. Well, Juan, in that case it would be my pleasure to show him a shorter way out of the world. That only was in my mind."

"You have more angles in your thoughts," muttered Juan, "than a prickly pear has spears. I see nothing more to this . . . the man is worth fighting . . . the man is worth killing. That is the end."

"You are a Yaqui," said Bordi.

"I am a man . . . the Yaquis are men."

"Tush! Wild beasts!"

"Your people have run before us, Matiás Bordi. We have beaten you and robbed you and harried you. We have made you turn white at the name of us."

"Peace . . . peace . . . peace," said Bordi with a shudder. "When I hear you purring out such words, it turns my soul sick. Alas, Juan, in another word you would have your knife out and. . . ."

"Between your ribs . . . yes," said Juan through his teeth.

"No, I have no fear of that. Well, Juan, you will not go to this Steven Marshal."

"No?"

"I shall do the work. You may remain behind me."

"I shall not stay!"

"As you please, then. But my horse is faster than yours."

"Bah!" snarled Juan Oro. "If you go to him, he will tie you up like a pig and beat you. I shall be near to watch the beating, you may be sure. Go, then, I shall laugh, when I hear that you are hanging by the neck . . . and the *gringo* has taken twenty thousand dollars and put it in his purse. I shall be glad . . . I shall laugh!"

"Black devil!" exclaimed Matiás Bordi. "I believe that you will!"

But Juan Oro, his transport of fury growing, because he had been robbed of this gentle mission, spurred his horse suddenly forward. He sent it racing down the alley and swung off through the boulevard around the central plaza.

Was it that same gendarme who stood before him, waving his club and demanding a halt?

Juan Oro rent the air with an Indian yell that stabbed the ears as a knife stabs through flesh. He abandoned his grip upon the reins, and, winding his lithe legs around the body of the horse, clinging with spurs thrust deep into the leather of his saddle, he swayed far to the side and rushed at the unfortunate *policía*.

That frightened man had barely time to whip out his revolver, but his shot went wild. He had no time to shoot again. Juan Oro was upon him. He was gripped by strong arms. The shock knocked the wind from his body and staggered the running horse. Then he was lifted, trussed by mighty hands that made him a child, and suddenly swung across the pommel of the saddle and into a deep ditch of mud. There he sank to his chin. And Juan Oro, still yelling like a demon, raced on through the town. He had a revolver in either hand. And when he saw a light gleam at a window on either side of the street, he fired, heard a crash of glass, and went whirling on.

Chapter Thirteen

Juan to Meet the *Gringo*

It was a sulky tiger that Matiás Bordi overtook outside the town, his horse reined under the shadow of a great cypress that stood by the bank of a little winding stream.

"Now tell me," said Bordi, "what made you do it? You have raised the whole town . . . look, yonder they go now."

Not a furlong away, a party of a score of horsemen, issuing from the town's walls — white as the wings of a moth in the starlight — went lurching off through the night. But by their own bad luck, they had chosen the wrong road, and, although they were close to the fugitives now, they would be farther and farther away as they galloped on. But Bordi, watching them go, muttered angrily to himself.

"Bah!" sneered Juan Oro. "What should a man do? Live like a tamed dog, afraid that his master will beat him?"

"Only fools," declared Matiás Bordi, "go from their way to find danger."

Suddenly Juan began to laugh. "I am a fool, then, but I am a happy fool. Did you not hear the *plop* he made when that *policía* dropped into the mud?"

"I heard it," said the bandit.

"Did you not laugh?"

"I never laugh, when I make an enemy."

"An enemy? Why, that man is only a fool . . . a stupid fool, Matiás."

"Listen to me, Juan. Hatred makes even a fool into a wise man and a terrible enemy."

"Have you nothing but friends, then, Matiás? Is that why they offer twenty thousand *pesos* for your head?" He laughed again, filled with the purest pleasure of his own malice.

"Very good," Bordi said. "I shall not talk to you. You are not Juan Oro, but Juan Diablo tonight. It is all because I will not let you go to this poor American and kill him."

"That is a lie, and a black lie," declared Juan. "I shall never murder. No! For where is the pleasure in kneeling behind a man and shooting him through the back? As well shoot a pig, I say. But to stand before him, face to face, and to give him an equal chance with his weapons for his life . . . to put your own life into the game . . . ha, Matiás, what is there in the world like that? If all the tequila were poured into one barrel, and all the barrel were poured into one bottle, and all the bottle made into a single mouthful that had in it all the wildness and the joy of all the tequila in the world . . . why, even that, Matiás, is nothing compared with standing to a man face to face, and feeling his eyes on you, as they hunt for the place where he intends to send his bullet . . . through your head . . . through your heart . . . do you understand?"

"Is it that way to you, Juan? Is it such a wine to you?"

"And you, Matiás?"

"To me? No, no! I kill where Providence tells me to kill. But never for pleasure. But you, Juan . . . you will be a famous murderer one day."

"You lie," said Juan. "I shall always give the other man an even chance. Is that murder?"

"When you face a man, do you say to yourself . . . 'Is this man good? . . . Is this man bad?' "

"No, but I say . . . 'This is a man, therefore made to fight, therefore made to die, if I can finish him.' "

"Very good! Every wolf thinks as well as you do. And when you fight other men, they have against you the chance of the lamb against the wolf. Your gun is in your hand faster than the thought of a gun in the mind of another. You cannot miss, when you shoot. And why? Because you live to destroy. How many hundreds and hundreds of *pesos* worth of ammunition have you shot away, Juan? How many hours, like a cruel devil, have you practiced with your knife? And so I say that, against you, other men have only the chance of the lamb against the wolf!"

Upon this, Juan Oro meditated. But he could not meditate in silence. He was as restless as a young wildcat. And as the cat purrs in its content, so Juan Oro, as he sat in the shade of the great sabina tree, began to sing softly to himself.

"I shall do this," he said at the last. "I shall go to this *gringo* and take off my gun and my knife and fight him with my hands."

"Ha?" said Bordi.

"With my hands. Yes."

"Do you know what you say?"

"With my hands . . . yes!"

"You have never seen a *gringo* fight with his hands."

"They are men like other men."

"And you turn other men into weak things, when you put your hands on them. But listen to me, Juan. A *gringo* learns to strike with his hands as a hammer strikes on the face of the anvil. He practices that manner of fighting as we practice with a knife and a gun. Besides, he has learned how to wrestle. A *gringo* is a brute. He does not fight like a gentleman, with weapons, but like a mad bull. Those *gringos* love to rush together and beat at one another with their fists. Do you understand? With a blow, they crush bones. Besides, this Marshal is a big man. And you are not too large. But, first, tell me how you heard what *Señor* Maldonado said to me about the *gringo?*"

"I put my head close to the door. That was all."

"Ah, fox! Well, would you fight with this man really with your bare hands only?"

"Yes."

"You say that, but when the time came, when he had knocked you from him, and the taste of your own blood was in your mouth, you would snatch at a knife. I know you."

"I shall swear to you to leave knife and gun behind, when I meet him."

Bordi fell into a brown study. "Perhaps," he said, thinking aloud, "it would be very good for Juan Oro to be beaten once."

There came a cry from Juan — a cry of sheer joy. "I shall go, then?"

"You may go, Juan."

"*¡Diablo!* He is already a dead man!"

"Are you happy, then?"

"You are my friend, Matiás! Who would not hunt with you? All other men are dull. But you have teeth. I shall do this, Matiás. I shall go to the *Señor* Fontana and beg him to give back my oath again and set me free so that I do not have to kill you some fine day."

"That is well, Juan. But he will never give back your oath."

"He? He is kinder than a father. He is as gentle as a spring rain. You, Matiás, do not know him."

"Well, we shall see about that."

He could talk no more that night to Juan, for it was like talking to a storm wind. Juan Oro made the pace, as they started on again toward the mountains, and, while they rode, he sang one song after another, weird Indian chants, older than the last Montezuma, and more wild and sad because of the very softness of the voice that sang them.

Two marches brought them to their mountain rendezvous, and the next day Juan Oro prepared for his journey. For such an occasion he donned his best, and his best was guaranteed to turn the head of any Mexican girl between the Río and Yucatán. He put on boots as neatly fashioned to the foot with tailored care as any gloves ever fitted to the hand. They were of rich red leather, exquisite to the touch, and polished until they shone again. His tight-fitting trousers showed the ripple and leap of the long thigh muscles as he walked. They flared out like the pants of a sailor at the bottom, and down the outer seams they were loaded with rows of silver conchos, each button curiously engraved, sometimes with flowers, or with the heads of saints, or curled snakes, or running wolves.

There was a year's work for a cunning artist in the making of those conchos which adorned the trousers of Juan Oro. He wore a shirt of heavy white silk, open at the smooth, round throat and buttoned down the front with great, costly, pearl buttons. Around his waist was twisted a sash of scarlet silk, richly and curiously brocaded. Was it on a time an altar cloth, the product of loving and reverent labor? Because of that there would have been no scruples in the mind of Juan Oro. But he loved the flare of color and the whisper of the long fringe that hung below his knee as he walked. His tightly-fitted jacket was a mass of gold embroidery of the most mysteriously interwoven patterns. All in flowers and in dainty arabesques was the coat of Juan Oro embroidered. And the price of that jacket was almost beyond computation. For in the front, for instance, the buttons were carnelians, each a gem worthy of a place in a museum's showcase.

But even the coat was nothing compared with the crowning masterpiece — the sombrero. For all its weight — and there was a full pound and more of gold work upon it — it had a jaunty air, with the great brim curling up behind and elongated in front. But the gold work! Let others have mere golden medallions stamped out of the metal. Juan Oro's fancy was not to be so lightly pleased. The medallions themselves were linked together with a golden meshwork of a design so fancifully delicate that the taste of the most fantastic Moor must have been pleased by it. And, perhaps, that chain work had been done by some crafty Moorish goldsmith in the olden days when a quarter of the world looked to Cordova. But each medallion was a separate hand carving, and each carving represented a scene from the life of a saint. If that hat had blown from the head of Juan and tumbled roughly upon the rocks, ten thousand hours of labor would have been marred or ruined. And yet even the ruins would have been worthy of the inspection of a connoisseur.

Such were the clothes of Juan Oro. But still his outfit was not complete until he had thrust into his clothes a long knife with a hilt roughened with a mosaic of fine jewels, and two revolvers whose handles were finest pearl, set over with gold and with gems.

Thus equipped, at last, he presented himself before his companion. The grim Matiás sat cross-legged, smoking a cigarette and dreaming upon the mountain mists that filled the cañon before them, and listening to the hollow chanting of the river that rolled through the valley bottom, giving up now and again a broad flash of light as the sun sank to its surface.

He turned his head and smiled at the beauty of the youngster and the brilliancy of his attire. "Are you a man, Juan? Or are you a peacock?"

"I am myself," said Juan Oro, "and this is the proof of it."

The knife winked from his flashing hand, and the heavy blade sank half its length into the solid trunk of the pine against which Matiás Bordi leaned. There it quivered and sent a tremor down his back. The blade was not half an inch above his skull! And yet the bandit did not stir. If the thrill of death had shot through him the instant before, now he made himself meet the mocking eyes of Juan Oro. And he smiled with a broad glint of white teeth.

"You are yourself," he said. "But I think

that in those clothes they will take you for a general."

"That is not enough," said the boy, looking down at his finery with a fond eye.

"Or for a matador," said Matiás.

"That is much better," sighed Juan Oro. "These boots do not fit me." He poised himself on one foot and extended the other, as slim as the foot of a woman. "The dog, Pintachio, made them too big by an eighth of a size. He shall make me three pairs for nothing now, or else I shall cut his throat and burn his house!"

Matiás nodded and grinned. "Which horse do you ride?" he asked.

Juan waved his hand toward the little hollow nearby where half a dozen horses were cropping the rich grasses. Of all the horses which had been in the great band that had served Matiás and his crew, these were the chosen spirits. They were not all entirely Thoroughbred; perhaps there was a dash of five percent of wicked mustang blood in them that gave them an added toughness, and added ferocity and mental agility. But they were made with a beauty that told what they were — the fleetest creatures that walked the surface of the earth.

Yet Juan Oro, staring at them, shook his head. "They are a currish lot," he said. "I wish to the black devil, Matiás, that you would find me a horse, and a real horse."

Even the face of Matiás, accustomed as he was to the reckless talk of the boy, darkened a little. "What do you wish? Derby winners?" he asked. "Shall I import horses from France or England for you, Juan?"

"No, for they are too soft. But, someday, I shall have a horse."

"What will it be?"

"Black."

"Like your heart, Juan. Well, take the best of the herd."

He sat back to watch, filled with curiosity. He himself could not tell. He knew horses and loved them and had lived with them all his years of life, and yet he had not the keen insight of Juan Oro, who looked on them simply as so many machines for carrying him over the ground.

Now he saw Juan take his lariat of coiled, oil-suppled rawhide and walk, singing, across the hollow. The hobbled horses, with their ears flattened in fear and hatred, fled from him as well as they could. Far different from their actions when Matiás Bordi went out among them, for then they came with pricking ears to his call, and seemed to struggle with one another to offer themselves for his service on that day. But Juan

Oro laughed with a malicious pleasure as he saw them flee, and yet his laughter was as soft as a song.

"There is no kindness in him," sighed Matiás Bordi. "I shall never tame him. Nothing will ever tame him. To the end of his days, he will be all teeth. But which horse is the best? The bay! Ah, I knew it would be the bay . . . or it is the chestnut . . . tush. He is blind."

For it was the smallest and the youngest of the herd that Juan Oro made for. A dark-coated chestnut mare, beautifully limbed, indeed, but neither of a size nor with quarters that were after the heart of Bordi. Now she whirled before her pursuer and strove to escape, but at that instant, with an underhand flip, the lariat shot out as a snake strikes. A hemp rope floats through the air — swift as a bird on the wing, perhaps, but never like the rawhide that darts like powder-driven lead. The loop shot over the head of the mare. And now she stood trembling, dancing, shuddering at the thought of the cruel spurs that were to master her on this day.

Juan Oro brought her back, still singing.

"Is she the best?" asked Bordi.

"No," said Juan. "The bay is the best. But the fool is too filled with green grass today.

Besides, this one needs a lesson. See her throw her head. She will be wise enough by the time I ride her home again."

He brought out his best saddle, brilliant with new-polished silver, heavy with gleaming gold. A moment later he was on the back of the mare, controlling her easily with one hand, waving his cigarette with the other.

"Pray for me in the hands of the *gringo,* Matiás," he cried, and then, with a touch of the spurs, he fled like a winged thing down the slope until he reached the edge of the trees. But still his laughter hung upon the air behind him.

Chapter Fourteen

Out of the Mountains

What passed, then, in the mind of Juan Oro, as he rode down from the mountains, dipping from copse to copse like a great butterfly? What thoughts possessed him? Was he filled from the first with the savage lust for blood? No, that was not in him. Whatever purpose lay at the end of his ride, he had before him for the moment only the sights and sounds and odors of the mountains, and whatever entered his senses was good to them.

When he slipped into the rolling country, before midday, to the south, he headed for the first little mud village that was in his path. It was nearly noon. Here and there through the fields he could see the laborers, coming in for the second meal of the day, their straw sombreros bobbing, their white cotton trousers gleaming white with distance rather than with cleanliness.

He stopped to brush himself clean before he entered the town, for even in the eyes of these humble people he wished to appear at his grandest. The mare was already a little weary from the journey, for Juan Oro was a bitter taskmaster, when he was in the saddle. She would have preferred to go drooping in with downward head, but Juan Oro had another mind. A wicked and a cunning touch of the spurs goading her flanks, a pressure on the vicious curb, and what with fear and pain and anger she went into the little town like a festive dancer, all that Juan Oro might appear more knightly, sitting at ease in the saddle.

He was gaped after to his heart's content, before he dismounted at the inn. He saw her stabled and fed and paid a peon to rub her down — not that he cared for her own comfort, but he knew well enough that the rider who is careless of his horse is careless of himself. So he left her standing there with trembling flanks under the hands and the voice of the peon and went into the inn. It was a squalid little place, with a mud floor in the eating room, a few half-broken chairs, and goat skins everywhere for cushions or for extra seats. But Juan Oro found the place instantly to his mind, for there was a pretty girl to take his orders and rush with them to her fat, greasy mother in the kitchen. So, in a moment, there was a delicious odor of kid

roasting upon the spit in the kitchen —
there was fresh pulque set before him — and
tortillas with which to break the edge of his
hunger.

The girl, too, was instantly changed.
Somewhere — out of the thinnest air, it
seemed — she had plucked a crimson
blossom that now appeared thrust into her
hair above the right ear. A shining, amber
comb was now in her neatly piled coils. And
a red-and-yellow sash, drawn tight around
hips and waist, set off the tawdriness. Now
she smiled more boldly down on Juan, and
he smiled back on her, sure of his power,
conscious of the havoc which those brown
eyes of his worked upon female hearts, old
and young.

"*Señor,* we have not seen you passing
through before this day," she said.

"I may have come by night," said Juan.

"Ah, no. We should have known. We are
sad that we have not a finer room to seat the
señor."

"I am more comfortable," said Juan,
"than I would be in the house of my father."

"*¡Señor!*"

"It is you, *señorita.* You have smiled. The
air is filled with fragrance and with music."

But he laughed as he said it, and she grew
rosy, not knowing in how much he was mock-

ing her, or in how much he was serious.

"Only," she said, "you ride alone. And this country is dangerous. You should not do it, *señor*."

"And why?"

"There is that frightful Matiás Bordi. He leaps out of the mountains like a lion and strips rich travelers."

"But never the poor?"

"He will not bother them."

"I have heard that he gives to them, even."

"Have you heard that?" said she, beaming on him. "It is true. He scatters gold as if it were water, and he were a rain cloud. He is a good man."

"But he cuts a throat now and then?"

"Those throats that deserve cutting."

"Ah, *señorita!* You speak of it so easily that you frighten me."

He smiled at her again, but his bold, keen eyes searched hers steadily, so that she blushed again, and she answered, looking down: "Well, I am afraid that *you* are afraid of nothing, *señor*. Not even of the *Señor* Bordi. I begin to understand my mother. She is always saying . . . 'Ah, the men! The men!' . . . and shaking her head."

She shook her own head at Juan, and tipped it a bit to one side, smiling still on him.

"And what does your father say to that?" asked Juan.

"He? Oh, I have never seen him. He went away, when I was little. He was a very bad man!"

"No . . . no . . . for he left a rose behind him."

"Ah, *señor,* you are very kind."

"No, I am a truth-teller. And at this instant, my nose tells me that the kid is roasted."

She brought him a great platter heaped with tempting meat. And what flesh is more temptingly sweet than that of a roasted young kid? As he ate, still she talked.

"You must sit down," he said.

"I must stand, *señor.* My mother would never. . . ."

"Then I must stand, also."

"Well," she said, slipping into the opposite chair at the little table, "do you always have your way in the world?"

"I am one of those simple people," said Juan, "who love to look a man in the face. And I love music, *señorita,* with my dinner. What news is there?"

"You have heard of the giant who came to the city the other night?"

"What giant?"

"A monster who caught a gendarme and

whirled him in the air and hurled him into a ditch. He was at least seven feet high, the *policía* says, and his horse was as tall as a house."

"I hope that I shall never meet him," said Juan. "What is the shortest road from here to the house of *Señor* Fontana?" he added as he finished his meal.

She was covered with awe instantly. "You are his guest, then, *señor?*"

She led him to the door and pointed out the way. "Where the road branches, you keep to the left, and then to the right at the next crossing, and then straightway."

"A thousand thanks," said Juan Oro, and laid a piece of gold in her hand.

"My mother can never give you change," she cried.

"It is not too much," he said.

"*Señor,* we cannot take it."

As she looked up to him, he touched her lips with his.

"Now," said Juan, "I leave in your debt. I must come back, to pay you the rest. But what is your name when I ask for you?"

"Ah, the men, the men," quoted she, raising her hands to cover her blushes and her laughter. "My name is Rosa Cordelle."

Chapter Fifteen

<u>Released</u>

In the dusk he came into view of the *Hacienda* Fontana like a white ghost city among the hills, for the great house was surrounded by pleasant groups of outbuildings, and in the hollow at its feet was the village where the servants and the laborers on the farm lands lived. There, at the inn, he spent the night, sleeping in their best room surrounded by attentions, so that he could not help remembering how he had been when he was last at the *Hacienda* Fontana.

He rose early, from old habit, but far too early to go at once to the great house. So he dropped into the shoemaker's shop and chatted with the half-breed who was busy with his awl, patching a pair of cheap *huaraches*. He was a stranger, he said, in that part of the country. The shoemaker at once bubbled with chatter. He, too, had come to that country as a stranger, he said. But when he reached the *Hacienda* Fontana, he had found employment and had remained there ever since. As for the people in the great house, the *señor* had doubtless heard about all of them? No?

"As for the *Señor* Fontana," said the shoemaker, "we see very little of him. He is like a god living behind clouds. We hear of him now and then. Sometimes we see him, when he goes out hunting. But that is rare. And rarer than ever since his daughter died. She was a lover of the outdoors. Poor little thing. She was a pretty child, and very gay. There is a shadow in the *Hacienda* Fontana now, men say. Or there was, until the *señor*'s cousin, Dorotea, came."

"But who is she?" asked Juan.

"She, *señor*, is the one who will now inherit all of the lands of the don."

"Well, she will be very rich. Is she young?"

The shoemaker raised his head and looked about him. Then he waved his hand toward the open door. "She is like the morning, *señor!* She is goodness and grace and mercy. She comes like an angel into the town. There can be no unhappiness, after she has been here. She sweeps it all away before her, as a housewife cleans a floor. God bless her, the *Señorita* Dorotea."

"Well," said Juan, "it is easy for the rich to be happy."

Here the shoemaker pushed his spectacles

up onto his forehead and sighed. "No, *señor*," he said. "I, also, was once rich. I had fifteen hundred *pesos*. I won it gambling one great, wild night. When I had all that money, I felt that I was the king of the world. I sat down with it in my lap and stared at it. But when the next night came, I began to be afraid. I thought to myself . . . what if some robber saw me win this money? He will come, then, and take it from me . . . he will take my life, also. Or again, what am I to buy with this money? A farm? But on a farm I must then go to work. And why should I work, when I have this money, like a prince?

"For a year I remained wondering what I should do with my great fortune. I was very unhappy. It was the saddest year of my life. And then, at the end of the year, I opened my purse, and there was nothing in it! Yes, *señor*, you will wonder at it . . . that such a man as I now appear to be could have spent so much as fifteen hundred *pesos* in a single year. But the people of the village remember me very well in that great year. I had three suits of clothes. And I ate meat twice a day. Nothing but fine wine or brandy was good enough for me. The taste of the cigars I smoked, it is still on the roof of my mouth.

"But when I found that I had no money left, do you think that I was sad? No, *señor*. I felt that a great burden had been lifted from my shoulders. I began to be happy. I went out into the street, and who could keep me from laughing and singing? The sunshine was yellower and warmer than gold. I wanted to work. I was humble enough for any sort of work, then. For a year I had been in misery. I had hated and distrusted everyone. If a girl smiled at me . . . 'Ah,' I said, 'she has her eye on my purse, the sly devil!' But when my fortune was gone, I loved everyone. I shall never forget that day! I was like one who had come back from a great journey. No, no . . . do not say that riches make happiness!"

"Then perhaps even the *Señor* Fontana is not happy?"

The shoemaker shrugged his shoulders slowly as high as his ears. Then he leaned forward and whispered through the cup of his hand: "*¿Quién sabe? ¿Quién sabe, señor?* He has no heir of his own flesh and blood. And every time he looks on the lovely face of the *Señorita* Dorotea, does not his heart quake with the memory of his own girl?"

Juan Oro had heard enough. Besides, the sun was now high, and so he went out into the morning and rode toward the *Hacienda*

139

Fontana. When he topped the first hill, he paused and looked around him. He could trace the whole flashing semi-circle of the Río Fontana, now, as it half embraced the gardens and the village of the great house. Within the gleaming bounds of that river, no one dared to raise so much as an onion for food or for profit. But all was made garden or grove by the will of the don. His father, and his grandfather, and his great-grandfather in the beginning of the family tradition — not one of them had ever permitted useful products to be raised on the grounds surrounding the house. So a rich district of several square miles was devoted wholly to beauty. And beautiful it was.

Once, it was said, there had been nothing but the naked, gently rolling, grassy hills. But when that first Fontana received this estate from The Conqueror, with his own hand he had set out the rows of cypresses that now fringed the edge of the Río Fontana. Each of those cypresses was now a mighty tree. They towered up far higher than the hills. They were giants among a race of later pygmies. And there were other groves, although perhaps on a lesser scale. But never anything dense. They had been kept so carefully cleaned of underbrush — they were so steadily and regularly thinned

— that the eye passed easily through them. One gained changing glimpses of the country beyond, riding through this woodland at a walk. Only at a trot or a canter, the trees moved one into another swiftly enough to shut one in with a living and solid wall of greenery.

But interspersed among the groves, Juan Oro passed stretches of garden of incredible richness. Sometimes it was only an immense sweep of well-shaven lawn that stretched away over the open and under the trees. Again, there was a rioting blur of stocks, crowded one upon the other, or, through a cleft in the trees, he had a glimpse of a pergola, a little rest cottage, surrounded by a formal garden that would have delighted the heart and the eye of a French marquise.

To the eye of a boy, all that is beautiful is transformed to a miracle, however. And, whatever joy he felt in the things that were around him, they seemed to Juan Oro to have fallen sadly off from the beauties of the old days. The beauty was still there. The mystery was gone. It had been the work of giants and fairies in the old days. Now it was only the taste and the invention and the labor of men. And while his eye enjoyed what was before him, his judgment was saying: "How the devil can even a Fontana afford to keep up the army that must take care of these gardens?"

Here the road wound to another hill, and through a cleft in the trees his eye reached forth to the haze of a distant horizon. Here was the answer. As far as his eye could stretch — and it was a clear, dry day — all belonged to *Señor* Fontana. Beginning on the farther side of the Río Fontana, the green farm fields rolled in gentle waves toward the hills behind. In this immensity a nation could have been born prosperously, and grown to strength. He was looking down on sixty thousand cultivated acres.

No, more. This had to do only with the farm lands of the rolling grounds, but the hills beyond were covered with the yellow-green of the vineyards. Famous wines were made from the grapes that grew on those gravel hills. Red wines and white. The old vintages of Fontana were stored deep in the cellars of the *Hacienda* Fontana.

He went on again. Yes, the owner of these lands was an emperor — not a common man. And these gardens were only a tiny nook in his domains. It was only wonderful that he had not chosen to make them thrice as large.

Now the *Hacienda* Fontana itself was before him, and he circled around its great white façade, pierced with huge casements a dozen feet in height, until he came to the stables behind. There he dismounted. His horse was taken at once, without question. And Juan Oro strolled to the house itself.

He was growing more excited, now, with the passage of every moment. For he was about to see the man who had been a god to him. Would he, too, have changed with the house and the lands from a mystery to a man?

A grave-faced servant took his name. He was shown into a little waiting room and sank into cushions to wait. At length came a rapid, tapping step, and a thin little man with a tired face came up to Juan.

"I am Francisco Moreño," he said, "the secretary of the *Señor* Fontana. Will you tell me on what business you come to him?"

"My name is Juan Oro. Have you heard of that?"

And he waited, half smiling. But the face of the secretary remained a blank.

"Shall I take that name to the *Señor* Fontana?"

Juan nodded, and the little man hurried out again. A door opened in the distance. He heard a girl's voice singing, heard the song end abruptly. In another moment came light footsteps, still in the distance, the murmur of the girl's voice, and the deep tones of a man speaking a language that Juan Oro did not understand, except to know that it was English. And he did not need to be told who these were — the Lady Dorotea — the man, *Señor* Don Steven Marshal. He smiled to himself, filled with malice. That deep voice, if all went well, would not be heard again after the end of the day.

Moreño returned in another moment. The *Señor* Fontana would be very happy, he said, to know what affairs brought *Señor* Oro to the *Hacienda* Fontana — or what friend had commended him there?

Juan stood up, blinking with surprise. "Tell me, then," he said, "has he forgotten my name, even? Has he really forgotten my name?"

Moreño waved apologetic hands. "Names and faces," he responded, "run into every day of the don's life, and they run out again. You will forgive him, *señor*. The river cannot remember all the ships which have sailed upon it. The ocean cannot recall all the beaches that its waves wash."

Juan Oro stared in amazement. The very commission on which he was solemnly sent had been forgotten. His name was lost. He was a cipher in the life of the great man. And yet during almost ten years, with the passage of every day he had kept that burden in his mind. Now he was released. Matiás Bordi was safe for all of him!

"This is well," said Juan quietly. "I did not think that he would forget."

And he walked past Moreño, who was murmuring needless apologies, and through the great doorway, and down the steps to the open where the wind cooled his face.

Chapter Sixteen

The Westerner Rides the Outlaw

He arrived at the stable in time to find a scene going on that securely removed all attention from him. The stable boy ran at full speed to get his mare, and back again, handing him the reins in haste. For there was another center of attention, and Juan Oro, swinging into his saddle, reined back under the shadow of a tree. Here, he was removed from the confusion of the crowd, and yet could clearly oversee all that happened.

Nearly the entire household had gathered to watch the spectacle. That spectacle consisted of a tall, black stallion with the look of a devil in his eyes, now being controlled by a full half-dozen men, who had ropes attached to him. When he showed signs of plunging, twenty or thirty hands were instantly added to those ropes. Even so, they could hardly handle him, and he dragged them here and there as he pranced. One determined burst for freedom would give it to him, of course, but whether he was more angry or frightened, it was hard to tell.

Yonder stood none other than Fernando Guadal, now much older, much grayer, but quite recognizable to Juan Oro. He was directing the stable boys in their efforts to control the big animal. To the side, in front of the ranks of murmuring *mozos* who were there to enjoy the fun, there was a little central group of three. The one was *Señor* Don José Fontana in person. He was much altered from the day on which Juan had last seen him. He appeared no less aristocratic, but very much smaller, thinner, feebler. He was simply, from one aspect, a little pale man with a wearied expression in his eyes, as though it were impossible for him to find in the world anything better than utter boredom. Juan Oro devoured him with eager eyes. It was as he had feared. His god was transformed into a common man, and, if he owed a debt to the fellow, it was, perhaps, not such a very great debt, after all. The doctor, it seemed to Juan today, was perhaps more to be credited than *Señor* Fontana in person.

As for the other two, standing with the *señor,* he knew them at once. They were Dorotea and the *gringo,* Steven Marshal. To the girl he gave one glance, for that was enough. One flash of the landscape shows the whole, and Juan Oro, with a breathless lift of the heart, turned from her to the man with whom his grim business was to be transacted this day.

He was worthy, it seemed, of all that had been said about him. He was an inch or two above six feet in his height, and he was made with both care and amplitude — a big man without being necessarily a slow man. Juan could tell that by the lightness and poise with which the other stood. He could tell it by the clear, bright light of his eyes that speaks more from man to man than any knowledge of training or of poundage. Whether with weapons or with naked hands, this fellow was formidable. And Juan knew it, and rejoiced in his knowledge. He felt, indeed, for the first time in his life, a little thrill of fear, but that emotion was merely a sauce that added to the poignancy of his delight. And as he looked at the thick, round neck, like a column of stone, he thought of his thumbs buried in its hollow base. Such were the emotions in the gentle brain of Juan Oro.

Now the big man was settling the hat upon his head.

"*I* think it's foolish!" exclaimed

Dorotea. "You never can tell. He has a frightful name . . . the great beast! I think a treacherous demon like that should be killed and put under the ground, Steven."

"Do you think so?" said Steven Marshal. He smiled at her as though she were a child — as though her remarks needed no other answer than amusement. And Juan Oro flushed with astonishment. He looked again at the girl. Now he, for one, would never have been able to speak so lightly to her. Yet, she did not seem to mind the casual manner of Steven Marshal. She was even half laughing at him through all of her anxiety.

A trifle more of enthusiasm appeared in the pale face of the don. His eye began to flash. "Well, *Señor* Marshal," he said cheerfully, "I have tried to dissuade you . . . but if you insist upon going on with it, you have my bet that you will not ride the horse today!"

"I have your bet," said Marshal with perfect calm, "and I intend to win it. You know, we Americans will always risk our necks for the sake of a bet."

With this, he stepped suddenly forward with no other preamble and was instantly in the saddle. The ropes were loosed from the big black, which sank cowering a little toward the earth, his ears flattened. Juan Oro lighted a cigarette and smiled through the cloud of smoke that he blew forth. He was very willing to place his wager upon the black stallion, after what he had seen. He looked into the set face of the *gringo,* and still his mind was made up. The horse would win.

Half a dozen riders were now on horseback, their lariats ready, prepared to rope the stallion in case it should throw the rider and attempt to get away. And they had not long to wait. The black bolted into the air and came down on one stiff foreleg. The twisting snap at the end jarred the rider far over to the side. Before he could regain his balance, the horse was in the air again, and again he came down with a shock that made the ground tremble. Here he whirled like a flash, and the *gringo* lost a stirrup. Once more the stallion "fished for the sun," and this time Steven Marshal was snapped from the saddle as cleanly as though a club had struck him down.

He landed sprawling, but unhurt. In spite of the yell of the peons and the *mozos,* Juan could see that. But there was another danger. The stallion, finding himself free, did not take advantage of that freedom to dart away. Instead, he wheeled and lurched straight at the fallen form of his late rider.

He was a fifth part of a second too late. A pair of ropes, thrown by the watchful hands of the Fontana riders, darted over the neck of the black and tugged him back with the full force of two struggling mustangs.

Steven Marshal rose to his feet and dusted his hands together with a foolish smile. Dorotea was instantly beside him.

Juan heard her cry: "Now, thank the merciful Virgin that this is ended! We have had enough for the sake of a foolish bet. There has been enough, Steven!"

He only laughed at her. "Why," he said, "the fun is only beginning!"

And he was instantly in the saddle once more. The ropes were loosed, while a clamor of admiration rose from the crowd. Even Juan Oro nodded approval. And in another moment the battle was on again.

If the black had proved himself an expert fighter a moment before, he doubly proved it now. He weaved from side to side — he heaved his shining bulk like an arrow into the air. He landed with a sickening jar that snapped the head of Steven Marshal down upon his breast. He whirled and bucked again. He ran forward at full speed, sprang high, and came down on stiffened legs; and twice Marshal lost a stirrup, and twice by skill and luck he recovered it.

At length, he swayed his quirt above his head, and, while a yell of astonishment broke from the lips of the crowd, the black stallion felt the stinging cut of the lash. His answer was a squeal of pain and rage and surprise. Then, forgetful of all his skill in bucking, he leaped straight forward, as though he would see what speed could manage in working this burden from his back. And the whole number of the mounted men streamed after him to watch.

It was like trying to keep within tagging distance of a hurricane. The black reached the first fence, a lofty mass of stone, and cleared it with an immense bound that flung the hat from the head of the rider. Then he went on like the wind. The cow ponies, racing hard at first, were promptly distanced. Even Juan Oro, on his fleet mare, flagged far to the rear. But his weight was a good fifty pounds lighter in the saddle, and he knew that he would come up with his quarry at the last. So he rated his mare back to a fleet gallop and then kept her steadily at her work. The black, after a time, would wear himself down with this terrific sprint.

But the strength of a Thoroughbred was in the blood and the bone of the black, and the strength of the desert blood was in his heart, also. He flew like a winged thing through the scattering woods, and then away toward the flashing waters of the river. He swung again to the left and crossed the bridge with a brief thunder of pounding hoofs. Then the metal echoes clanged through the village and one or two cries of frightened children came tingling far back to where Juan Oro led the pursuit.

Through the village, and then on and on. He was dropping the men of the don behind him, as fast as the black was dropping him. And with every stride his wonder grew. What a king of horses that stallion was!

Again the great horse swerved to the left. Far away, Juan saw him turn toward the loftier hills. Behind Juan, in turn, the pursuit was out of sight. But now the killing pace, the great bulk of its rider, and the steep slope of the hills took quick toll from the struggling stallion. Its pace diminished, and Juan Oro began to gain.

But if I were in that saddle, said Juan to his swelling heart, *and the* gringo *in this, I would still be off on wings, and he would be rooted to the ground behind me.*

There was no doubt in his mind about what he would do now. When he took the life of Steven Marshal, he would take the black giant thereafter.

They passed the foothills. He was gaining

fast and faster, now. When he topped the first ridge, he looked down into the next hollow, and there he saw that the stallion was spent, indeed. It had ceased running. It had ceased trotting. It merely walked with downcast head and trailing hoofs.

"Now the whip," Juan said to himself. "To let the devil know that it is mastered."

Instead of that, the *gringo* was soothing the big animal with gentle touches of his hand, and talking, no doubt, all as gently. Juan Oro watched with amazement. It was a thing that he could not understand. It was a thing that he despised.

He let his own panting mare jog gently down into the easy hollow. There was the American dismounting, yes, and tethering the stallion to a tree with the lead rope. Now, with a wisp of dried grasses, he was wiping the sweat from the shining body of the great horse. And, with every heave of the stallion's working sides, ripples of light flashed back and forth.

Juan Oro studied this scene with increasing wonder, as he drew closer. Yes, it was plain that this *gringo* fool intended to complete his mastery of the animal by sheerest tenderness of speech and of actions. His hand was working at the neck of the stallion, and, under the stroking, the head of the black began to rise again, and his ears wavered a little forward at every touch.

Now the keen ears of Juan could hear the voice of the man, speaking English, to be sure, but in a tone that was easily translatable. Not a mother soothing an infant could have spoken more tenderly.

Juan Oro, indeed, came up unperceived behind the big man, and he had sat his saddle for some time before the other looked up and started.

"Well," said Steven Marshal, "how long have you been looking on, sir?"

And he ran his eyes over the bright costume of Juan Oro — surveying him, Juan felt, with a sort of hidden mirth. What was there in that costume to awaken mirth? Who laughs at gold, silver, and costliest silk? It could not be.

"I have been watching," Juan said and smiled in turn with all his broadest insolence.

But Steven Marshal was the height of good humor. "I have not pleased you with my handling of the horse?" he suggested.

Juan Oro nodded. "I shall tell you why," he said.

Chapter Seventeen

Juan and Sombra

The big man seemed amused again — not
broadly. One could see it more by an indefi-
nite wrinkling around his eyes, although the
smile never reached to his lips. His handsome
face remained, on the whole, quite impassive,
so that Juan Oro began to guess at a new
strength in the stranger — a strength of mind
that matched with the strength of his body.
All powers of body that Juan Oro admired
during his life had been the strength of the
tiger — a deft and swift hand, a supple body,
deceptive cunning, but for bull-like, down-
right power of hand he had little respect. Yet
in the bulldog, persistent strength of this big
man he had been forced to place some tribute
of admiration. And the powers of mind that
Juan Oro had always admired were sudden
flares of insight, passion, or hidden workings
of a calculating intelligence. But here was a
man who suggested a life complete in himself. Put him on a desert island, and he could
live quite contented. Isolation would not ruin

156

his existence. He would commune a little with himself. He would enjoy the scene even without a companion. He would find a stern joy in conquering nature.

Not that Juan framed all of these thoughts in words. It was something that required long pondering. But now a new star had swung into his heaven, and it startled him with the newness of its light. He began to be touched with a shade of awe.

First of all, he wondered what this man had found in Dorotea to be worth his effort? For the sort of wife that Juan Oro predicated for the big man would be a grave-faced, mature woman, thoughtful, solemn, strong in body and brain. Not a gay and childish flash of a creature like Dorotea, impalpable as a wisp of incense smoke, delightful as a strain of music. It was an anomaly.

He had been silent for an instant, looking gravely at the stranger. And Steven Marshal said: "Well, sir, you are to tell me what in my handling of the horse displeases you?"

"My horse," Juan explained, "is my slave . . . you treat that horse as if it were a friend. That, *señor,* is wrong."

"And why," asked the *gringo,* "is it wrong?"

Too many questions are irritating, when one is dealing with axiomatic truths which must be on their face self-evident.

"Because," said Juan coldly, "I say so!"

And he tensed himself a little, prepared for battle. An insult of a tithe of this strength, offered to one of his own kind, would have led to trouble. But the brows of Steven Marshal merely raised a trifle, and then he was as calm, as good-natured, as ever. Again Juan was amazed, but now there was a shadow of contempt in his amazement.

"Ah, well," the *gringo* said, "every man has his own way with a horse. What would you, my friend, do with this black devil?"

"I would crush him," Juan said, his brown eyes narrowing to blazing rays of light. "I would crush him until he trembled when he heard the sound of my voice. Do you understand?"

"I understand," said the big man, as calm as ever.

"But you, *señor,* give to the horse what you should give to a man. *Señor Americano,* if they treat horses like this in your country, how do they treat men?"

There was a thorn in every word that Juan Oro spoke, but the skin of the big stranger seemed much too thick to feel the prick of them. He countered by replying with question for question. "Are you Mexican, my friend?"

In the mind of Juan Oro there was no

doubt about his ancestry. He knew that his skin was paler than the skins of most Indians. He knew that his eyes and his hair were of a different color. And yet his heart was with the Yaquis, and for the rest he did not care to analyze the question. He chose to be Yaqui. If other men doubted, he would prove his point with the edge of his knife.

"I," he said, lifting his head a little, "am an Indian. I am Yaqui!"

At this, the American looked at the big brown eyes of Juan, the broad, smooth, high forehead, and the long hair, shining like dark gold where the sun struck it.

"Yaqui?" he said, and he smiled, sympathetic with this satirical touch.

It was rubbing the fur of the panther in the wrong direction, and the voice of Juan became a purring snarl. "You smile, *señor?*"

That smile was instantly banished from the face of the stranger. "By no means," he said. "You are, then, a Yaqui?"

"I am!"

"I have never seen a Yaqui with your hair and your eyes, that is all," he said quietly.

"Perhaps," said Juan with insufferable insolence, "you see too much, *señor!*"

Surely now the big man must turn against him. No, he merely smiled again. "Perhaps, I do."

Juan was amazed. He felt that he could hardly attribute fear to this giant. And yet what was it that made him hold back?

"As for the horse," said Steven Marshal, with a touch of mischief in his eyes, "he has recovered now. He is about as strong as ever. Perhaps you, my friend, will care to ride him?"

"This horse," said Juan, "is one who kills men?"

"I have heard that."

"When you mounted him, *señor,* there were many men standing around to make sure that you should not be hurt."

"That is true."

"Had it not been for them, you would have been broken to bits by him, when he first threw you."

"You were there, then?"

"I was there."

"However, his spirit has been tamed a bit. I think that it would be an easier thing to ride Sombra now. Perhaps you, *señor,* wish to try him?"

"Gladly," Juan said, and was instantly on the ground and, like a flash, into the saddle on the big black.

There was no doubt that the stallion had been rested by this halt. And he settled under the weight of his new rider with a shudder. Then his ears flicked back, and he hurled himself into the air.

In the old days, Juan Oro had sat on the backs of mustangs. He had learned to grip the unsaddled bare skin of a horse with knees and heels. He had felt beneath him the fiery energy of wild stallions, swift as the wind and strong as tigers. But they were like toys compared with Sombra. To see the great horse from a distance, fighting, was a wonderful sight, but to ride him as he bucked was like riding hurricane waves. A yell of startled wonder and of joy left the lips of Juan Oro. Up from his heart rose a hot fire. And in his hand he held not the reins, but the soul of the fighting beast.

If the horse was terrible, Juan Oro became instantly more terrible. If the stallion was a fighting tiger, Juan Oro was a fighting panther that has gained a death grip on the larger foe. And as a panther, exulting in his victory, would rake the side of the enemy with steel-sharp claws, so Juan Oro raked the flanks of the great horse with his spurs. His quirt whistled in the air and cut as a knife edge cuts when it landed — mercilessly.

Sombra, transformed into a demoniacal thing, struggled madly to escape. If he had fought the *gringo* before with fiery courage, he now fought like flame itself. He flung himself into the air. He hurled himself to the ground again and rolled to crush the rider. As well strive to catch a whirling dead leaf with a beating hand. For Juan was out of the saddle as the black monster rolled and into the stirrups again as he lurched to his feet.

And, in the middle of his ecstasy, with insane joy swelling in his heart, he began to sing. That Indian chant came screaming from his lips — torn short — mutilated by the twisting, plunging, rolling stallion — a song shrilling out in brief notes — disintegrated — but nevertheless a song.

From the distance, the voice of a man was shouting louder and louder. And Juan had glimpses of the *gringo* — yes, even glimpses of him with a gun in a hand, as he rushed forward, expostulating, commanding Juan to end the battle. But what the *gringo* said was nothing to Juan in his hysteria of battle. Who could take raw meat from the panther's jaws? His hat was off. His hair was flaring, flaming fire shaken against the sun. He had fought men, but never a man whose resistance filled his hands and his soul as the fight of this horse was doing. But then, suddenly, the great black staggered — reeled in the midst of a frantic effort, and stood suddenly still, his legs braced far apart, his head hanging down.

Then the voice of the *gringo* could be heard as he ran up, crying and cursing. "You devil," he groaned at Juan. "You have killed him!"

What were words to Juan? He was all Indian now. The grip of his knees crushed stronger upon the barrel of the black stallion; he threw up his hands to the sky, and, swaying from side to side in the saddle in the greatness of his ecstasy, he chanted madly — "The devil came down from the mountains. He wore the form of a black horse. He came to kill men. Fire was in his eyes . . . his teeth were steel . . . his hoofs were beaten iron . . . in his legs was the strength of the four winds. Men died before him. Men trembled and shrank from him. Men feared him. And then came I, Juan Oro. I came like flame that runs over the fields. I found the black horse. We looked in the eyes of each other. We both knew fear. But I leaped upon him. Fire fought fire. At last he weakened. I took him in my hands. I bent him like a slave . . . and he was my slave. I struck with my whip, and he cowered. He came like a king . . . now he is nothing . . . he is the dirt under my feet. I, Juan Oro, have done it! I, Juan Oro, am speaking!"

He ended, and, as his ecstasy departed, he heard a sharp voice break in upon him. He looked, and there was a leveled gun in the hand of the *gringo,* and the voice of the gringo was saying: "You bloodthirsty devil, get down from that horse! You've killed a thing that's worth more than you and all your tribe!"

Chapter Eighteen

Men and Beast Recover

What Juan Oro noticed, as his wild passion left him, was that, although the body of the big man quivered and shook with rage, the hand that held the gun was as steady as the very rocks. By this token, if by none other, Juan Oro knew that he had to do with a man, indeed. And Juan slipped to the ground.

There he could see his work in detail. The dripping flanks of the black horse were ripped across and across by the biting rowels of his last rider. His chest and his neck were covered with lather. His head hung down. His dead eyes looked only to the ground. His sagging knees seemed, every moment, lowering his weight to the earth from which it would never be lifted again by his own strength. All of these things Juan Oro did see. And he saw, moreover, that the *gringo* was still white with a furious passion, stronger, perhaps, than the very ecstasy of Juan himself had been the moment before.

He did not care for the *gringo*, however, or his thoughts. What he cared for was the condition of the stallion. He had crushed the great horse, to be sure, but, indeed, it seemed that he had killed it, and woe rose up in the heart of Juan. Not pity for the death of the great horse after two such struggles as it had been through in the one day, but a rage of grief to think that, having commanded this lion-like strength, this speed of the wind for one long moment, he, Juan Oro, could not leave the *gringo* dead on the ground and canter away on the back of Sombra.

And he was instantly at work. A little mountain stream worked its noisy way down the hollow a short distance from them. To it ran Juan Oro and returned again carrying with him his canteen filled with the cold water. With that water they soaked the cooling places of the body of the big horse where the great arteries were distended and swollen with blood just under the surface of the skin.

He gave that work to Steven Marshal to do. He stripped off his fine jacket and his shirt; not because he feared to spoil all his priceless finery — for, indeed, he merely threw the garments on the rocks — but because he wished to be free to use his strength. He appeared naked to the waist — with a skin, indeed, sunburned as dark as the skin of any Indian brave. But now his muscles, all his powers of hand and arm were unshackled, and he devoted himself steadily to his labors.

He rubbed down the body of Sombra. Many a time he had done it before, under the skillful tuition of Matiás Bordi. And, many a time, he had been able to bring back an exhausted horse to supple usefulness again. Also, there was the stimulus of the rubbing which kept up the circulation of the weary animal, that was falling away apace. He paused to open the mouth of the tired horse and poured a great drink of brandy down its throat. Then he continued the rubbing. Steven Marshal followed his example. One on one side of the great horse, and one on the other, for more than the space of an hour they worked until they were drugged and drunk with exhaustion. But when, at length, they dropped helplessly into the shadow of the tree, they had their reward. The head of the black was raised a little. His knees no longer shook. But though he was far, far spent, there was great hope that he would now recover. No stable-raised horse could have rallied from such a condition, but Sombra had both the demon and the strength of wildness in him.

The two men lay side by side. Steven Marshal, following the lead of his companion, had thrown off coat and shirt. Naked to the waist, they drank up the coolness of the shade beneath the tree. They closed their eyes. The wind touching their drenched skins cooled them. Their breathing was hoarse as the breathing of a windbroken horse, for every breath was a groan.

But Juan Oro, in a moment, rolled from the shadow into the burning sun. Only his face he left in shadow, but the sun bathed all the rest of his body, burned it, seared it, blackened his chest. He rejoiced in its ardent strength. The bite of its strength was a joy to him. And he felt the tremor depart from his muscles. The blood ceased to pound in his temples. He breathed without irritation, and the joy of that new conquest came back to him.

But what of the big man? He, Juan Oro, was already restored. He was like the horse — wild-bred and, therefore, able to recuperate from what would have been a day's exhaustion for any normal man. Steven Marshal was far from average, but he had been badly spent, and now, as Juan turned and sat up, he saw the big fellow lying like a hulk, his great arms distended, with the long, prominent muscles of the forearms quivering and jumping. His face was blotched crimson and purple. They had kneaded every one of the iron-hard muscles of the stallion, those big fingers of the *gringo*, and now he paid the price of his effort. Suppose, now, that Juan Oro flung himself upon the American?

That cruel purpose gleamed for an instant in the eyes of Juan Oro. But, instead, he rolled a cigarette and lighted it. He went to the stallion and offered a wisp of grass. The big horse flattened his ears, but he nibbled feebly, disinterestedly at the food. It was enough. He was recovering fast. In another hour, Sombra could take the road with a man on his back. Juan Oro knew. He had seen mustangs brought to the very point of death by exhaustion before this day, and he had seen them recover to do another fifty miles before the twenty-four hours ended.

So, squatting in the shadow with his back against the tree, he said to Steven Marshal: "*¡Señor!*"

There was an inarticulate groan from the *gringo*.

"*Señor* Marshal!"

"Well?" gasped the weary man.

"It is time for you to begin to think of sitting up."

Marshal passed a shaking hand across his forehead. "Let me be!" he insisted. "I've been as spent as this before. In another half hour, I'll be as fit as ever."

"Hurry to recover, *señor,* for fear lest I should grow weary of waiting and ride away on Sombra while you still sleep."

This jerked open the closed eyes of the exhausted man. He propped himself up on arms that shuddered.

"What in the name of the devil are you saying?"

"I speak in the name of Juan Oro. My good friend, the devil has nothing to do with it."

"Ah, well," said Marshal, "you are joking, Oro. You are a wild fellow, but a good one at heart, or you would never have helped me to bring Sombra through the pinch. But is he saved?"

"He is saved. Ah, yes!"

"He is!" said Marshal with great emotion. "I thought he was a dead thing. I would not have given a dollar for his chance of recovering. Why, man, what made you ride him as you did?"

Anger darkened the face of Juan Oro. "Do you ask me that?"

"I do. I saw a wildcat, once, drop on the back of a young fawn from a tree. It tore the poor thing hardly any more than you tore that horse."

"Will you tell me, *señor*, how Sombra fought me?"

"As wildly as you fought him, of course. But, if you had been gentle, he would have been gentle."

Juan Oro chuckled softly. That voice as golden and beautiful as his shining hair made answer: "To you, *señor*, gentleness may be of some use. But to me, it is nothing. There is no amusement in it."

In spite of the thundering of the blood inside his temples, Marshal peered intently at the face of the younger man. He was beginning to be more interested in the conversation than in the condition either of himself or of the horse.

"Why," he said, "tell me this . . . do you believe that gentleness is never worthwhile?"

"No, no," said Juan. "Why should it be?"

"So?" said Marshal, smiling a little as he mopped his face. He was beginning to breathe more easily, and the color in his forehead was clearing. "But how would you have a young man, let us say, treat an old woman?"

"Treat her with silence," said Juan, "for fear she should talk."

"What is that?"

"I had rather," said Juan, "hear the rattle of a snake that is about to strike at me, than the rattling of an old woman who is about to speak and tell a long story. About what? About how she was making tortillas on the day that her neighbor came in to tell her how her cousin found a mine in . . . ah, bah, old women are old fools! When I am near them, what do I do?"

"Well, and what do you do?"

"This, simply. When they begin talking, I point my finger at them . . . 'Woman,' I say, 'this is your warning. Do not speak again. I have eyes. I understand signs. But my ears are very delicate. The least sound hurts them. Ah?' " He ended on the last word with a little intonation of the voice that was half snarl and half purr, and which made the blood of the *gringo* run cold.

"After that you have no trouble?" he suggested.

"They become lambs," said the youngster.

"But can you talk like that to young girls?" asked the American. "Tell me that, Juan. Can you talk like this to young girls?"

"Young girls," said Juan, "do not interest me. I pay little attention to them."

"What, man, have you never had a sweetheart? And at your age!"

He glanced askance at the gold-worked clothes of Juan that still lay flashing in the sun on the rocks where they had been thrown carelessly.

"Oh," said Juan, "as for the girls who are pretty enough to be bothered with, I sometimes pay them a little attention."

"But tell me frankly . . . do you dare to be rough with them, if you wish to have their favor?"

"Do I dare?" echoed Juan with lifted brows. "*Señor*, I dare anything! I am Juan Oro!"

The American bit his lip. "Very well," he said. "But I should like to watch your method, Juan. I have watched five hundred men making fools of themselves around girls, but I have never yet seen one use roughness *before* he was married."

"It is true," mused Juan, "that most men are fools, when they are near women. But not all. And I am one. For, *señor*, I understand them."

Once more the American bit his lip, and Juan, studying his face with the eye of a lynx, knew that there was a smile on it, but could not for all his keenness detect it.

"This is remarkable," said Steven Marshal in a serious voice. "I have heard old men throw up their hands and admit that the older and the wiser they grew, the less they could understand the ladies."

"I have heard the same thing," said Juan. "Well, I shall tell you why it is . . . women are so simple that men are afraid to see them as they are. Is it not true? If you have a wife . . . if you have a mother . . . you are ashamed of letting another man call her a fool. So you are also ashamed to admit to yourself all the truth about her. For it cuts very deep. If one's mother is a fool, may there not be the blood of folly in one's own veins?"

"Well, Juan Oro, this is a new viewpoint."

"It is all the truth. Now, *señor*, you, like most other men, go through the world with a mist before your eyes, do you not? And through the mist you see the women. Through the mist they are surrounded with flaming lights. A halo is over their heads. Ah, bah!"

"And you, *señor?*"

"I open my eyes. I see the truth."

"But does that give you success with them?"

"Why, there is no doubt of that. I simply let them know that I understand them."

"And . . . ?"

"And they at once fear me."

"Continue, *señor.*"

"Do you not understand?"

"Not as yet. First, you make the girl who is to love you feel fear?"

"I do, and feeling fear, she is bound to feel love, if I choose to have it so."

"That sounds to me like a very great riddle."

"It is as simple and as clear as the light of this yellow sun, *señor*. Will you not consider that, when I have shown her that I know her, and after I have filled her with fear of me, she will be grateful, if I do not reveal her foolishness to the rest of the world? Besides, since all men are fools around women, I, who see the truth, seem a rare and a strange creature to them. And women are like deer . . . they cannot resist coming close to stare at a new thing . . . even if it is no more than the rifle of the hunter raised above the grass to attract them."

"Juan Oro, I sit at your feet and learn about women. Continue."

"That is all."

"But when you show them that you know, do they simply throw themselves into your arms?"

"No . . . it requires more cruelty. It is easier to show you, than to tell you about it. But suppose that I have first shown her scorn and frightened her . . . then one day I stand and smile on her and look right into her eyes and seem about to speak and yet say nothing. That does a certain thing inside their foolish hearts . . . I do not know what. Then, again, on the next day when I pass them, I see them blush a little. She is nervous, when I come near. But on that day, I yawn in her face and go past her.

" 'Ah, brute!' she will say. But she does not think it. She is melting. She is becoming ready to be a slave. On the next day, I come to her and look in her eyes again. I say nothing. I put my arms about her and take her close to me. I look down in her foolish eyes, like the eyes of a lost cow. Suddenly she melts. Tiny diamond points appear in her eyes. She is mine!"

Chapter Nineteen

The Challenge

Thus spoke Juan Oro, the Yaqui, to Steven Marshal, the American, and, as he ended, he smiled slowly with half-closed eyes, watching the other, and seeing amusement, wonder, and just a trifle of horror or disgust in the *gringo*.

"You do not like that," said Juan Oro.

"Every man," said Steven Marshal, "has his own way with women, I suppose. But my experience is that all ways are bad."

"And what, *Señor* Marshal," Juan asked, "is the best way to win the heart of a girl?"

"I shall tell you, Oro. In my country a man opens his own heart to a girl, if he loves her, and tries to let her see the truth about himself, and then he hopes that she will find something in him to care about."

So Juan Oro sneered and shrugged his eloquent shoulders.

"Have you never failed?" asked Marshal, with more curiosity than repugnance.

"Never, *señor!*"

"That is strange."

"How can they help but do, as you might say, what they are commanded to do?"

"But you, Oro, dressed in such fine clothes as yours, could turn the head of any woman."

Once more, upon the face of the *gringo,* it seemed to Juan Oro that he could detect the elements of a smile, but again he could not be sure.

"It is true," Juan Oro said with his usual immense self-assurance, "that I look well in the eyes of a woman. Because *I* am handsome, they cannot help but look at me."

Señor Marshal bowed his head and coughed violently into his hand. But the face that looked up to the Yaqui a moment later was perfectly calm and grave.

"And after they look," went on Juan Oro, "they see my fine clothes. That is enough. They say to themselves . . . 'He is handsome, and he is rich! I shall marry him, if I can.' " Here Juan Oro paused and smiled, then he yawned broadly. "You are more rested, *señor?*"

The big man stood up and stretched himself. He looked like a giant, viewed in that position with his arms outstretched and the thick, ropy muscles standing out on them.

"I am myself again," admitted Marshal.

"However," he went on, reverting to the theme of their conversation, "you must admit that you have yourself said that among women you are caught by a pretty face."

"Why not?" answered this surprising youth. "There is nothing but their surface. Put a sack over the heads of them all, and from under the sacks the same sounds come . . . chatter, chatter, chatter. I had rather listen to hens cackling in a yard. One may eat a hen, on a hungry day. Well, it is so with the women. But what fools they are to look at a handsome man. What is a face to a man?"

"Well, very little, perhaps."

"And when," Juan went on, "I appear to them not only in fine clothes but riding such a great horse as Sombra, it will be no more of a matter than the snapping of my fingers. I shall simply beckon, and they will come. Ah, yes."

Here he ended, and dropped his chin upon his fist, staring at big Steven Marshal with the contented and mysterious smile of a sphinx. With the nameless malice, the nameless cruelty of a sphinx, also. So that Marshal had to shrug his shoulders in spite of himself, such a tremor of cold sweat went through him.

"Very well," he said. "You are to ride away upon the black horse?"

"I am," said the Yaqui.

"Because I have thrown away my belt with my gun," said Marshal, "you intend to take an advantage of me?" He smiled as he said it, but his smile was a feeble thing, for in his mind there was forming the great black of a shadow of doubt.

Juan Oro, however, stretched forth both his hands and smiled. And his eyes half closed as he smiled, and the white of his teeth flashed at the man. "Ah, *amigo, amigo,*" sighed Juan. "Do you think that I could do such a thing? It is true that I intend to leave you dead here. It is true that I intend to ride off upon the black stallion. But take advantage of you? No . . . no . . . never!"

Here, in spite of a considerable effort on the part of Steven Marshal, his smile went out, and he found himself staring glumly down at the slender-bodied boy who sat cross-legged before him, blowing forth a thin cloud of smoke and smiling up at him through the smoke. After all, there is a cat's smile when it sees game before it.

"For you observe," said Juan Oro, with his white teeth still showing while he smiled, "that there is no pleasure in a woman, *señor,* except in the winning of her." He paused, for he remembered at that instant the great dark eyes of Dorotea as she watched her lover fight with the black stallion. He ended rather abruptly: "And there is no pleasure, surely, in killing a man, except in the fight that comes before the end."

"Very well," said Steven Marshal, recovering his composure. "We are to fight upon equal terms?"

"Perfectly equal, *señor.*"

"Is this a Mexican jest, Juan Oro?"

"I was never so serious, or so happy."

"Now tell me, Juan, because I think I see enough devil in you to make me think that you *are* serious . . . tell me, then, why you should wish my life?"

"Perhaps it is only because I wish the black horse," said Juan Oro, half closing his eyes as he stared at the big man.

"That is not it," said the other calmly.

"Perhaps it is because of the mere pleasure of the fight."

"You could find ten thousand men to fight you, but you have made a long journey to find me."

"How can you tell that I have made a long journey?"

"Well, a man like you is soon known for a great distance. But as for this fight . . . is it to be with knives?"

"You do not like knives, *señor?*"

"No. I'd rather not use the detestable things. I'd rather be a dog and fight like a dog with my teeth, I think."

"So, so, so," smiled Juan. "The *gringos* are all like that. They do not like to be tickled with steel. Well, if you must know, the fight is not to be with knives."

"Good," sighed the big man, still frowning at his young enemy. "You will restore my revolver, then?"

"Guns? Guns? Why should I murder you? I said a fight . . . not a murder."

"Would it be murder, then?" smiled the big man.

"You will see. There is a little white stone on the ground near your foot. Will you throw it into the air?"

Marshal obediently picked up the stone and tossed it high in the air. As for the young Yaqui, as he chose to consider himself, he waited with his head raised, indolently watching the stone fly up until it hung at the height of its rise, twinkling like a winking light. Then his hand moved with the oiled ease and the breathless speed of a flying piston head. Out came a revolver and exploded. The little white stone was snuffed out and disappeared from the air.

Marshal remained with his own head

raised for a time, staring rather stupidly. "The devil!" he said at last.

"No," said Juan. "Only Juan Oro! It is not to be guns, then?"

"You are right," muttered Marshal. "I could never choose guns against you. But what's left?"

"The best of all," said Juan Oro. "Ourselves!"

He stripped off his own gun belt and tossed it away with knife and all. Then he leaped up and stood before Marshal. The latter recoiled a little.

"Youngster," he said with frowning wonder, "do you mean that you would stand up to me hand to hand?"

"*Señor*, you are kind enough to understand."

"Well, Juan Oro, you are a brave young madman. Do you realize that I outweigh you by fifty pounds?"

"I realize," Juan Oro said calmly.

"And you will kill me," went on Marshal, shuddering a little, "with your bare hands?"

"I shall do my best. No man can do more."

Señor Marshal smiled and shook his head. "I see how it is, Juan. You have come against some of your own countrymen . . . big fellows as large as I am . . . and you have been fast enough and clever enough to tear them to bits. You have given me some fair warnings. I'm in honor bound to warn you. I am a trained man, Juan. I have boxed and wrestled all my life. And I do it, frankly, rather well."

"*Señor*, you are modest, and you are kind. I shall be sorry to do the thing that I must do . . . for the sake of Sombra. But I, too, have seen some training. I have boxed many months with a very rough man, *señor*, who went afterward to fight in the prize ring. I think that I may know enough. But if I were *sure* to beat you, would there be any pleasure in the fight?"

Still Marshal shook his head. "I don't know," he replied, "how people in your own land look on an affair like this, but in my country, Juan Oro, a man fifty pounds larger than another would be called a coward and a bully, if he fought with him."

"*Señor*, I beg you!"

"Don't be an ass, Juan. There is really nothing at all for us to fight about."

"If I were to go to other men and say that the courage of *Señor* Marshal was. . . ."

"I am vain enough to say that my courage does not need proving."

"Will nothing do?"

"Nothing. But I can tell you that this is

the first time I have ever been forced to re-fuse to fight."

"This may help you to change." Juan Oro's hand flashed out and his four fingers made a bright red pattern on the cheek of the *gringo*.

Chapter Twenty

The Battle Is On

It was touching the proverbial match to the proverbial powder, and the first danger that flew in the direction of Juan was a ponderous arm and fist that moved with the speed of a lashing snake's head. He ducked under the driving danger, but as the elbow shot across, it struck his own shoulder and sent him reeling half a dozen strides.

"You young jackass!" exclaimed Steven Marshal, making no attempt to follow up his advantage, but merely caressing his cheek where the fingers of Juan had smitten him. "Do you want me to break you in two?"

"If you can," Juan taunted. "For I intend to learn a great deal, or else to teach you something, *amigo!*"

And he came again, cautiously, for the bear's paw had grazed this active panther and taught him clearly the ponderous might with which he had to deal. He came cautiously, but with a flame of joy in his eyes. He was drunk with excitement, and Steven

Marshal, fighting man though he was, watched in amazement. But there was no denying that the smaller man intended to attack. He poised his heavy hands and warned the other away.

"If I land on you, it may do you some damage, Juan. I tell you again, keep back from me."

"Good, *señor!*" And as he spoke, he darted in. Under the guard of big Steven Marshal, he found the ribs of the *gringo* with all his force — it was like striking against an oaken barrel. But, when he struck his left fist up between the beam-like forearms of Marshal, that blow went home against the jawbone of the *gringo* and made him reel with a gasp of astonishment. Juan Oro, snarling with joy, followed, only to have two great arms reach out and gather him into a clinch that half stifled him, again like the grip of a bear.

He slipped away from that hug, and, as he jumped back, a flying danger overtook him. Those driving knuckles landed beneath his eye, split the flesh like a knife edge, and made the blood spurt out. The weight of the blow snapped his head far back on his shoulders and rolled him on the ground. Had he been coming toward that stroke, it would have been the end of the battle at once. But he was backing away, so the blow merely lifted him and flung him off. He landed on his back, but he twisted nimbly to his feet in time to leap aside from the plunge of the big man.

There was no question of further parleying, so far as Steven Marshal was concerned. He had felt the fist of this slender youth, with such cutting, jarring power behind it, that his brain had been curtained with darkness for an instant. He had saved himself by floundering into a clinch until his brain luckily cleared. Now, with all his senses about him, he started furiously to end the fight with a single charge. That first charge failed. He wheeled and lurched in again, struck at a weaving shadow that evaded his straight-driving arms, and took in return a slashing blow across the mouth. He spat and wheeled again to find Juan Oro now transfigured by a great, black lump that was swelling rapidly beneath his eye.

"A taste apiece," Juan said, "but the next taste will be mine . . . so!"

He leaped in, swerved outside the shooting fist of Marshal, and whipped him across the jaw with a swinging punch that flung another shadow over the wits of the American. But men will fight instinctively, if they have been trained well enough. So the big man struck through a mist, and his fist jarred against the ribs of Juan Oro. It knocked the smaller man away, gasping. Once more Marshal charged — and stumbled foolishly over a figure that dropped suddenly at his feet.

An instant later, he was caught by a leg and toppled to the ground and a tearing, gripping wildcat was on top of him. A hand like the hand of fire reached for his throat and drove a gaggling thumb into the hollow where the breastbone makes a V-shaped cleft. He tore that hand away, with the fingers raking the flesh raw, so frightful was their pressure. With all his might he twisted, whirled over, and found himself on top.

It was like lying on a serpent. Before he knew it, Juan Oro was out from under, and Marshal, lurching to his feet, was met with a cutting, staggering shower of blows. He gave back, bewildered, half blinded. Every punch stung, and they came faster than hailstones. When he struck in return, his ponderous strokes, which would have broken Juan in two, plunged into the thin air, while the dancing shadow slipped closer and struck with a hand that was a sword of fire. Again, and yet again, shadows leaped over the shocked, battered brain of Steven Marshal. And only a flame of utter shame served to clear his wits again. For here was he, a giant, and yonder was a comparative pygmy. He rallied with a groan and started a lifting stroke with all his might centered in the wrist of his right arm. He saw Juan Oro start to dodge — but he slipped on a round pebble, and, instead of avoiding the danger, his head dropped straight against it.

Fairly beneath the chin the knuckles of Marshal landed. He felt a huge lifting strain on his arm, his shoulder, his back, as the blow came home, and Juan Oro left his feet and was jerked into the air. He landed inert. Neither would the senses come back to this tigerish youth for some moments, at least. All in a crumbled heap he lay.

Steven Marshal paused to wipe the perspiration from his forehead and to fumble at his bruised, bleeding throat. Then he found that he was shaking from head to foot. Truly it had been a nightmare and a miracle combined. His knees were weak, and they were weak with fear. For, only a little more, and he would have gone down for the end. Luck, then, had enabled him to plant this finishing blow. And the wildcat was stunned.

But if he had missed it — he saw himself floundering through a storm of blows. He saw himself grappling with an oiled body, that twisted like a serpent from his grasp, and then fingers of steel catching at his throat. And he gasped at the mere thought of it.

Then he trussed Juan Oro over one arm. How light, how wonderfully light that youngster was. Hot shame swept over Marshal. But he remembered, in his football days, how a certain halfback, blue-stockinged, had come leaping through his position in the line, come like a slender child, and struck with the weight of a pile driver and broken through — once, twice, again, to a touchdown. Yes, it was true that the victory was not always to the big in brawn.

He carried the boy to the curling stream and dipped him into it to the waist. Then he laid him, dripping, on the bank. It was only an instant. Juan Oro sat up, and his hands leaped halfway to the throat of the *gringo*. Then realization of what had come to him rushed over his brain. He looked down for a moment on his wet, gleaming body, then he dropped his head into his arms, while his fingers were buried in his hair.

Now Steven Marshal was accustomed of old to fights. He had beaten, and he had been beaten. He felt the Anglo-Saxon's sturdy love of battle — and honest willingness to admit the superiority of the better man — without soul-burning malice.

191

He stared down at the quivering body of Juan Oro in amazement. As suddenly as he had curled himself into a knot, Juan Oro straightened again. The effort made him white, but he managed to look calmly into the face of Steven Marshal.

"*Señor,*" he said, "why did you not kill me, when I was in your hands?"

"Do you wish to know, Juan?"

"Aye, with all my heart."

"For three large reasons. In the first place, in my land people do not fight to kill . . . except with guns . . . and then only when they're drunk with alcohol or hate. In the second place, it was only a lucky blow that dropped you."

There was one flash of savage satisfaction in the eyes of Juan Oro, but he banished it at once.

"The third reason," said the big fellow, laying a hand on the naked shoulder of Juan, "is that I'm fairly certain that you, Juan, are one of my people."

"Did you think that?" said Juan. "It is not true."

"What are your father and mother, then?"

"I never knew them."

"Ah? I knew it! I knew it! You fought like a white man, Juan. No one else handles his fists as you did."

"I am no damned *gringo*," Juan snapped savagely. "And besides, I had rather cut my throat than be one. A *gringo?* Pah! I hate them, *señor!*"

"You can't insult me, Juan," smiled Marshal.

Black despair settled upon the face of Juan Oro — such despair, indeed, that as it looked forth upon Steven Marshal, he felt his heart changed in him.

"It is true," Juan said huskily. "I have become a dog. I have been beaten. I have been held in another man's hand." He leaped to his feet. "Dog of a *gringo!*" he cried. "I shall never rest until you and I have fought again . . . now. . . ."

Steven Marshal did not rise. About his hips, by this time, his gun had been belted. If fight there must be, it would be with that weapon — with anything rather than hand to hand against this incarnate fiend. Now, full of bewilderment, he watched the other in a gloomy silence. But the agonies of shame in Juan Oro would not let his mind cling to one thought long enough to persist in a purpose. His tensed hands fell to his sides again.

"You are right, *señor*," he said bitterly. "I am not worthy of it. I have been beaten once . . . like a dog . . . like a dog. As I have beaten others, so I have been beaten today."

He struck his hands against his bruised and swollen face. A new stream of crimson started out beneath his eye and trickled down his face. It was too much for Steven Marshal. He stood up and put his hand once more on the shoulder of Juan.

"Listen to me, lad," he said. "I have heard enough of it from you. Let me tell you that I was already more than half beaten, when I struck you a lucky blow. Do you hear me, Juan? I confess to you that in spite of my size, my training, my strength, you are a better man than I am, Juan."

Chapter Twenty-One

<u>Strange Talk</u>

To Juan Oro, it was more strange than the singing of any fabled sirens from a rock in the sea, charming sea-bound mariners, for to him humility was a word without meaning, and frankness was an undiscovered country. So he stared hopelessly, wondering at the *gringo*. He felt, at first, that it must be a very cunning sham, a mockery, but there is a certain bell-like ring to truth, and, when it really comes from the lips of a man, it cannot be mistaken. Neither could Juan mistake the sincerity of the American now. He passed a hand across his eyes and looked again.

"Well," he said at last, "this is strange talk, *señor*. What is to come now?"

"The next thing that I wish to come is your friendship, Juan."

The hot blood rushed through the face of Juan. He trembled with anger, for this, certainly, was the rarest mockery. But yet the expression of the *gringo* was one of the most open frankness.

"*¡Diablo!*" muttered Juan. "I am in a deep sleep, and I dream. None of this is true! You have struck me down . . . you have beaten the wits out of my head. And now you ask me to be your friend?" He laughed without mirth.

"If you had won, would it have been possible then?" asked Marshal.

"Ah, well," Juan said. "Why should we talk of what has not happened?"

"Let me tell you, then, that in my country a man fights without malice, if he fights at all."

"*Señor, señor,* you speak good Spanish, and yet I do not understand."

"In the States, Juan, if a man has a great enemy whom he hates, he calls in the law and lets the law fight for him. If he fights with his hands, he admits by fighting in that way that it is possible for him to become the friend of the very man he is fighting."

"I have not heard it," Juan said blankly. And he looked at Marshal as a child looks at a long problem in mathematics.

"Let me tell you in another way, Juan Oro. You have tried to make yourself out a very grim sort of a fellow. But I don't believe it. You have been telling me words to the effect that you want to have my heart's blood. And yet, Juan, you are a white man. I would trust

196

you completely. Do you see?"

He unbuckled his gun belt and tossed it to the ground. Juan Oro, instinctively, leaped upon it like an eagle, stooping at rich game. It was in his hands before he recalled himself and dropped belt and gun with a groan.

"I cannot do it," sighed Juan.

"Why not?"

"Am I a beggar and a coward? Do I take an advantage that is given to me?"

"Well, call it that, if you wish. I tell you, Juan, there is a certain bond between us. Answer me frankly. Do you not begin to understand me?"

Juan Oro, in spite of himself, drew a step or two nearer. "I cannot tell what it is," he muttered. "But it seems to me that I have known you for a very long, long time, *señor!*"

"Of course, you have. Because our blood is the same. You will learn, one of these days, that the same *gringo* stock that you have hated so much is in you. I shall be glad, when that time comes. Why, Juan Oro, perhaps we shall see much of one another. Who can tell?"

He said this with such a smile of frank good nature that Juan Oro, utterly baffled, shook his head and sighed again.

"It is true," he groaned at last. "I could be your friend, *señor*. Who can tell? There is such a thing as witchcraft in this world."

He swept up his clothes and leaped suddenly into the saddle upon the mare. Marshal called eagerly: "Wait one moment, Juan. You have not heard everything."

"I have heard too much," Juan stated. "Do you wish to talk me out of my country and my blood? *¡Adiós!* We shall meet again, *señor* . . . by day or night, we shall meet again, *señor*."

And with that grave warning, he spurred the mare furiously down the hollow. The deep, excited voice of Steven Marshal pursued him, but he kept headlong on his way. For he half feared that, if he listened to the call of the big man, he would be forced to turn and ride back, and, if he rode back once more into the influence of that grave, persuasive man — what might be done? He hardly dared to think. But he knew that in five minutes the big American had planted the seeds of many doubts and many sad discontents in his heart. His skin was not the skin of a Yaqui. That he knew. Neither was his skin nor were his features those of a Mexican peon. He had known these things before without thinking of them. He admitted them most unwillingly into his mind, now.

He halted in the shelter of the first trees

and put on his shirt and jacket slowly. Looking back through the branches into the little valley, he could see the big man, walking back toward the direction of the *hacienda,* leading the black stallion behind him — a weary and a humble horse, indeed. Yet, although a little time before, Juan had looked upon the black as upon a mine of gold, he now considered the animal without a second thought. All his attention was for the big *gringo.*

It was more than a miracle that had been accomplished in the eyes of Juan Oro. He had been beaten. He had gone through the greatest humiliation of his life, for the war with the little Garcilasso was only a thing between boys. Yet, now, he looked into his mind in vain to find bitterness. He looked into his very soul in vain to find any real hatred of the *gringo.* Instead, a certain warmth of emotion was growing in him. He had never felt anything like it before. But, indeed, in the heart of Juan Oro there was a great impulse drawing him back toward Steven Marshal.

He shook his head and closed that thought from his mind. For, surely, it would never do to follow a man who wished to wean him away from his country. But in spite of that decision, when he rode on again, his brain was clouded with doubts and a miserable uncertainty. Suppose, then, that the man was right? Suppose that he himself was actually a *gringo* and belonged, therefore, in the vast land north of the Río Grande — a land in which people swarmed by uncounted tens of millions — a land in which cities of stone were built to the skies — a land where the droves of cattle made the face of the ground seem a living, working thing — where the sheep covered the hills like snow — where money flowed more plentifully than water flows through the parched highlands of Mexico. And, north of the Río Grande, as all men know, there is no poor man, there is no sickness, there is no trouble. All men are big; all women are happy. Contentment rings like a bell in every home.

And yet, who would give up his country even to become a citizen in heaven itself? So felt Juan as he came out of the forest and looked suddenly across a valley which opened through the hills a vast trench, with sides a thousand feet high, of solid, polished stone. Now it flamed in the sun of midday, and up and down the ravine wild colors were burning, a crimson streak, a yellow smear, soft purples like mountain mist, and yonder a cliff of talc, a broad face of white.

Juan Oro gazed sadly upon all this beauty, for he felt as if he were already half stolen away from it. He felt as if he were already snatched away and put down in the hurry and the turmoil of that huge and unmeasured land north of the Río Grande where men live for the sake of money only and chase round dollars, and catch them, and put them in their pockets, and think — poor fools! — that they have captured happiness itself.

So deep became the emotion of Juan Oro that he said aloud: "I shall not go! I shall die first!"

Like a deeper echo, another voice spoke behind him: "Be true to yourself, Juan. Never listen to the *gringos!* They are wiser than snakes. No man can follow the twistings of their thoughts."

He turned and saw Matiás Bordi, sitting in the shadow of the trees.

"How does it come that you have followed me and that I have not seen it?" asked Juan, by way of a gloomy greeting.

"Would it be hard," the bandit asked, "to stalk a bat at midday? You were as blind as that. Your heart was so full, Juan, that there was no room in you to think of noises . . . your eyes were blind. You were seeing only your own thoughts. Perhaps you will never again be yourself . . . perhaps you will never again have the eye of a hawk and the hand of a puma, striking."

"Perhaps not," Juan responded with a black look. "You have seen the fight, then?"

"With the *gringo?* Ah, Juan, what do I care for the blows that the *gringo* strikes with his hand? The blows that he strikes with his tongue are all that I dread."

Chapter Twenty-Two

Will Bordi Escape?

It came so pat upon the very fears that had been crowding into the brain of Juan Oro that he could not restrain a cry of wonder. "Matiás, Matiás! How could you know that?"

There was a gleam of triumph in the outlaw's eye. "You have laughed at me many times," he said, "when I say that the voice of Providence descends into me and speaks. But I heard Him this day while you stood yonder speaking with the *gringo*."

"Why did you not shoot him down, then?" asked Juan fiercely. "He has made me unhappy forever."

"Providence did not tell me to shoot," said the other anxiously. "What has he done to you, Juan?"

Perhaps this question should have revealed to Juan that his companion was not entirely illumined by the divine presence. However, he was not in a logical humor, and he allowed the slip to pass unnoticed. He only answered sadly: "He has tried to steal

203

my country away from me, Matiás. Ah, Matiás, he has tried to tell me that I am a *gringo* myself. That I belong yonder, where they live in cities of stone and where the noise of the street is worse than the yelling of a hurricane or worse than the trampling of fifty thousand cattle, stampeding. He has tried to tell me that I am a *gringo,* Matiás, but you, *amigo,* can prove to me that he is a liar."

Here Matiás Bordi, glancing into the eager eyes and watching the quivering lips of Juan Oro, felt his heart suddenly swell and, as suddenly, contract again. For he remembered that, after all, Juan Oro was only a boy, and it was a disconcerting reflection.

"If you were to discover that you are a *gringo* . . . you see, I talk as if the American fool were right . . . what would you do, Juan?"

Juan Oro cast out his arms with a cry toward the splendor of that painted ravine beneath him, and toward the yellow, soundless river that plunged through its heart, and toward the farther mountains robed in black pines to the shoulders, with brown granite throats above and heads of eternal white.

"I should do only one thing . . . I should take this knife, so, and stab myself in the heart, Matiás Bordi."

"Ha? Would you do that, Juan? No, don't talk like a child and a fool. Tell me, seriously, what would you do?"

"I have told you," Juan replied, very sad, very stern.

"Listen, boy. Do you hate this Steven Marshal?"

"Hate him? Yes!"

"You did not drive your knife into *his* heart," said Matiás with a dreadful certainty and logic.

"No," admitted Juan. "I wished to hear him talk. He was like no man I have ever heard. And I was afraid . . . perhaps he was telling me the truth. But he lied, Matiás! Did he not lie?"

Matiás Bordi cast a somewhat wild glance around, but he managed to muster a ferocious scowl as he answered in a loud voice: "He lied, of course! All *gringos* always lie, Juan Oro. But you know that, my son . . . do you not?"

"I know it," Juan sighed in a most inconclusive fashion. For he was remembering the straight-looking eyes of Steven Marshal, and they shook his confidence to the ground.

Something of what was passing in him was guessed at by Matiás Bordi, for he now added: "As to this American dog, I wish that I had sent you to him with a gun, and not with your bare hands. We have been too generous and too kind and too gentle."

Here Juan sent a chill through his companion by shaking his head slowly. "You do not know that man," he stated. "And you can never know him. But I begin to guess at many things in him. How do I guess it, Matías, unless my blood is like his blood? Why do I feel a kindness for him? Consider, Matías, that he shamed me as I was never before shamed, and as I shall never be shamed again . . . and yet, before I left him, he had rubbed the shame away . . . he spoke to me, I swear to you, as a brother speaks to a brother."

"It is *gringo* cunning. Ah, they are snakes!" cried Bordi.

Juan was silent.

Bordi considered him for an anxious moment. "Well, Juan," he began, "I have made plans. I have gathered five good men to follow me again. You shall ride with me. I shall show you such things as you would never see, if you were living north of the Río Grande."

Juan shuddered. "I shall ride off by myself," he said. "I wish to be alone. But in ten days I shall meet you at the house of

Fontana . . . do you know that house?"

"I know that house," admitted the other. "But is it wise, Juan, to go off by yourself and dream over this thing and let the poison of the *gringo* work in your heart? Come with me. I shall show you happiness."

"My mind is made up," said Juan. "We must not talk about it any longer, *amigo*."

By the edge of the cañon he left his friend and turned to the west. Matiás Bordi stared after him for a long time and then rode in the opposite direction, as one who knows when an irresistible force has been met which cannot be overcome.

As for Juan, he spent the lonely days that followed living like some beast of prey in the highlands. He descended into a small village before night, bought rough clothes, left his finery safely behind him, and then dipped away into the peaks. His rifle gave him food — there was salt in his pouch — there was water from cold, clear, mountain springs for his drink. And he lived from day to day with no thought of what was coming on the morrow. And, indeed, he fought against thought, feeling that behind him lay danger, and that, if he meditated upon what he was and what he must become, there would be only misery before him.

In the meantime, the wounds on his face

closed and healed with all the rapidity with which the wounds in a wild beast's flesh close over, leaving no scar. The swellings reduced in a day. The cuts joined their edges. The purple shadows disappeared. At the end of the ninth day he studied himself in the unvexed surface of a pool and was satisfied. There was hardly a trace of the wild battle that he had fought against the crushing fists of big Steven Marshal.

Then he turned back toward the lowlands. In the little sleepy town where he had left his finery, he paused and donned his splendor once more. He put on the trousers and looked down to the broad flashing of the silver conchos. He girded the shining red sash around his waist. He handled again the costly revolvers. He weighed in his hand the ponderous sombrero and turned it so that the images of the saints wheeled by him, some kneeling, some hanging from sad crosses, some raining admonishing fingers as they caught the empty air. And, as he stared, he chuckled to himself. The weight of his worries dropped from him, and, when he descended to the street and mounted the mare, he was once more the splendid butterfly.

As a bird wings straight through the air, so rode Juan Oro, careless of the mountains in his way, twisting around their sides by dizzy trails where even the mountain goats would have trembled to walk, dropping down the sheer sides of ravines as fast as an eagle stoops at a quarry. So he came to the little white village and dismounted at the inn.

From Rosa Cordelle, when he entered, he received one flashing side glance and a smile that told plainly that she had not forgotten. But she was busy serving two young gallants, and she paid little further attention to Juan until the pair had swaggered through the doorway. Then she came to Juan and sat, uninvited, at his table.

"Which," he asked, "will you marry?"

She did not even smile. She merely said: "If I marry for the sake of money, I shall take an old, wise man in this town. He has no bad habits. He will not live ten years. And he is a fool about me. You, *señor*, have ridden a long distance since I saw you last. You have found much excitement at the house of your friend, the *Señor* Fontana?"

"I did not even go there," said Juan. "I changed my mind on the way and rode to another place."

"Ah," she sighed, "then you cannot explain it all to me."

"All of what?" asked Juan.

"The thing of which everyone is speaking."

"I have not talked with anyone. I have

209

waited to hear the news from you, Rosa."

"Who would believe you?" smiled the girl, letting her dark eyes soften upon him. "Who would wish to believe you?" she added, and laughed tenderly.

"You must not look at me like that," said Juan through the smoke of his cigarette. "You turn me into a calf and make me sad." His smile denied his words neatly.

"What am I to tell you, then, *señor?*"

"The thing of which everyone is speaking, of course . . . what happened at the house of Fontana?"

"It is all too strange. No *gringo, señor,* could be so brave or so terrible as Matiás Bordi, eh?"

A flash of premonition crossed the mind of Juan Oro. "Except by witchcraft," he said.

"That is it. There was a spell cast over that brave *Señor* Bordi. Everyone knows it and speaks about it, *señor.*"

"What *gringo?*"

"*Señor* Marshal. They met alone. Matiás Bordi was struck across the head by a bullet. He was taken to the jail. And there he is to this day. That was seven days ago, and still he is there, and has not escaped. But when he goes out of the jail, men say that he will take this Steven Marshal and burn him slowly over a fire. Do you think that he will do such a terrible thing?"

"But will Matiás Bordi escape?"

"Do you ask me that to laugh at me? He was never born to die at the end of a rope. Every child in Mexico knows that! He will die like a hero, fighting bravely, *señor*. But you know it very well. Do you not?"

"Ah, well," said Juan Oro, "perhaps Steven Marshal will flee to his own country, and so he will escape."

"If lightning were aimed at me, I should rather try to escape from it than from Matiás Bordi. And you, *señor*, do you know that?" She added the last words with a special meaning.

"Why do you say that," he asked frankly, "as though you saw another face behind my face?"

"You have not heard, then," she said, "of a young man who has ridden with Matiás Bordi? He is never far away, when a raid is made. Some men say that his hair is like gold when the sun strikes on it."

"Men talk like children," yawned Juan Oro, and he filled a glass for her.

Here her eyes flashed across the room to the doors, to the windows, as though to make sure that no one was near. She leaned a little toward him, and her voice was a whisper.

"There is *much* talk, *señor!*"

"Well?"

"And in our land, talk turns into knives and bullets very quickly. Is there not a Mexican magic?"

"Perhaps," he said. "But I am a man of peace. I do not love fighting."

He stood up and stretched himself, like a cat before a fire. She rose with him, still whispering: "If you go to him, let no man see you. They have put a whole company of soldiers to guard the jail. Men ride a hundred leagues for the sake of seeing the great Bordi in jail and looking at his face. Men do not talk of any other thing except . . . how can he escape? And if he does escape, there will be a hanging among those soldiers. Yes, and they know it, and will be honest for the sake of their necks."

"If you, *señorita,* were a man, what would you do?"

"I would die with him, or I would save him."

Juan Oro smiled on her. "I," he said, "was born a man, by chance. *¡Adiós!*"

She followed him to the stable yard to see him mounted. There she stood, worshipping him with her eyes.

"What is the town?" he asked her.

"It is the town of Fontana. He is in the jail

there. He has been tried there."

"Have they tried him so soon?"

"What was the need of a long trial? Besides, he admitted everything."

"Ah?"

"Is not that like him, being a hero? They came to him and said . . . 'You are Matías Bordi . . . on a certain day, you did such and such a thing.' At that, he smiled and said . . . 'I am Matías Bordi. I did that thing!' "

"¡*Diablo!*" muttered Juan. "That is strange."

"Well," she said, "when a man is in danger of hanging, might he not as well hang for his own crimes as well as for those of ten other men? They have put a hundred murders on his shoulders, and, when they asked him, he still shrugged his shoulders and smiled and said . . . 'It is true! I have done those things!' "

"Why do they not hang him, then?"

"They have more and still more foolish things to ask of him. And still he will smile and say . . . 'Yes!' Is it not sad and brave, *señor?*"

"Perhaps it is. *Adiós* once more."

"God save you and help you, Juan Oro."

Chapter Twenty-Three

Steven and Dorotea

Where the river swung lazily down from the hills and came flashing into view of the *Hacienda* Fontana on the distant height, and then pooled itself quietly on a broad, clear lake, the images of the great cypress trees stood far out on the placid face of the water. And by the edge of the water, sitting on one loop of a huge root that issued from the ground and dipped into it again like the single fold of a giant python, writhing through the earth, were Steven Marshal and his lady, Dorotea Fontana.

He had a handful of pebbles from which he extracted with care one bright bit of the quartz from the other and tossed them far off into the lake, aiming at a bit of rock that thrust its shining head above the waters. And the sound of the pebbles as they plumped into the still waters was like a faint, far chime of music. His face was placid, but the face of Dorotea was darkened by a frown.

She said at the last: "I have waited a long time, Steven."

"For what?" he asked gently, without turning his head toward her again.

"To learn why you have brought me down here."

"What better could we possibly have done?"

"We could have gone for a ride. You have not been on the back of Sombra for a week. Not since that day of Matiás Bordi."

"They are to hang him in another day, they tell me."

"What do I care for Matiás Bordi?"

"All the world has a care for every brave man in it. He is brave, this poor Matiás."

"Why do you speak of him still? Was it for that you brought me down here?"

"No. But so that we could be quiet together."

"You have not spoken six words. I wish you would throw all those pebbles away."

He let them slip in a shining shower over the ends of his fingers, and they tinkled against the ground beside his foot.

"Do you wish me to talk?" he said rather sadly.

"Is that a strange wish?"

"I thought that to be silent together would be the most pleasant thing. If I talked, I should only argue."

"Argue, argue, argue, then! But when you sit here so moody and so silent. . . ."

"No. I have been quite happy."

"Ah, Steven," she said with a sudden passion, "you are breaking my heart, and you know it."

He looked not at her, but up through the giant branches of the tree to the sun-paled sky far above their heads.

"When you say that," he said, "my heart stirs again. I have a foolish new hope. If I were to look at you now, I should say some foolish thing."

"Look at me, then, Steven. I *want* you to be foolish. And when you speak, speak in English."

He shook his head. "It is better this way. The Spanish seems to draw me a little closer to you. Do you understand? English is a harsh tongue in Mexico."

She broke in: "What was that which stirred in the brush?"

"Where?"

"Yonder. It may be one of Fontana's spies. He will never let us be alone together, if he can help it."

"It is nothing. Only the wind. Some of the leaves are dead and dry. You do not love Don José?"

"Love him? Does one love a man made of stone?"

"Do you like him better, then, than you like the new man?"

"What new man?"

"Pedro Maldonado, of course."

"Steven! I have forbidden you to speak his name!"

"Why?"

"It is horrible! I shall be sad, now, until night."

"Do not say that. Since you are to marry him, you will have many years to think of him."

"Have I chosen him? Has it not been forced upon me?"

"A strange sort of force, Dorotea."

"What could I do? Could I see the *Hacienda* Fontana be given away or sold to strangers, or presented to the Church? That is what would have happened, if I had not come to take it as the heiress. What is my life and my happiness compared with such a great thing as this? Oh, a nothing."

"Well, I can never understand."

"But you can, and you will. It is like a kingdom. If a woman gave up her kingdom for the sake of her own foolish little happiness, would she not be a base, low creature?"

"Do you think so?"

"Do you not?"

"I am only a man," said the American. "I could not even do the thinking for another man . . . far less for a woman."

At this, she looked darkly upon him and said nothing. And he turned to her, at last, saying: "Well, my dear Dorotea, tell me, have I made you very angry?"

"Not very," she said. "Only a little . . . you never make me very angry."

"And never very happy."

"Perhaps not."

There was a trifling pause between them. He had automatically begun to re-gather the fallen pebbles, and now he resumed the random business of tossing them toward the jutting rock. They once more plumped musically into the still water.

"This begins to be a little serious," he said. "I had hoped to go through these last few days that I am to have with you without really angering you. And now I see that you are worse than angry . . . you are seriously displeased."

"Why should you think that?"

"I don't pretend to understand women, but, when they are silent, I have always felt that they are most to be dreaded."

"Ah, well," she said. "I wish that you

would open your heart to me for one instant."

"I have, Dorotea. I have opened it five hundred times, and five hundred times I have told you that there was nothing in it but the love of you."

"I am not so simple as to believe that. There are a thousand other things . . . your work . . . your riding . . . your horses . . . your dogs . . . your many friends . . . they are all in your heart, to say nothing of your family."

He confessed at once: "Yes, they are all there. But they can go with a great love, can they not?"

"I won't ask you. But if you were I, Steven, would you let this great Fontana place pass on to the blood of strangers?"

"If I were you?"

"Yes."

"I shouldn't make an answer, but the temptation is too great. Well, my dear, if I were a woman, I would never dream of marrying a man, except for love."

"Oh, this is talk out of a book. We are dealing with life . . . not with words, Steven."

"I tell you, there would be no reason for love, and I would never give myself to a man, if I were a woman, unless my love for him were so great that I could not get him out of my mind . . . unless he haunted me . . . unless I were on fire at the thought of him."

At this, she threw up both her hands and raised her face. "You have said the thing for me! I have not been cruel enough to say it, but you have said it for me. I am like you, Steven. I have yearned all my life with all my heart, not for some dull, stupid marriage of convenience, arranged by the family, but for a wild passion that would carry me away with it. And if I loved you in that way, Steven, do you think that I would hesitate for an instant? No, if the *Hacienda* Fontana were a king's palace, I would turn my back on it and run away and never think of it again . . . never, never, never!"

He passed his hand over his face and drew a great breath. But, at last, he said in the same calm voice with which he had spoken before: "That, really, is what I have been waiting to hear. It isn't really necessary for me to wait much longer after today. Of course, I've guessed it before. But a man can't act on guesses in such things."

At this, she put her head a little to one side and considered him as though in a new light.

"After this," she said, "if I were to say that I'm willing to marry you . . . without such a very great love . . . what would you say?"

Steven Marshal smiled faintly. "I should

like to be tempted," he said.

She mused: "There was a time when just a word from you would have been enough . . . just the crooking of a finger."

"How long ago?"

"Seven days."

"You mean . . . ?"

"After you had met that terrible Matiás Bordi single-handed, and taken him a prisoner, and turned him over to the authorities. I was a little excited then, Steven."

"I thought you were," he said.

She lifted her head suddenly. "Then why didn't you speak?"

"Why, I thought it would be unfair to take an advantage, when you were feeling as you normally would *not* feel toward me. So I waited. And today gives me the correct answer."

"At least I'm glad," she said, "that you don't pretend your heart will be broken by my refusal."

There was something a little pettish in her voice that made the big man bite his lip, and he did not look at her, but threw another aimless pebble toward the water as he answered: "I'll manage to salvage my heart, perhaps. I can use it on other things, as you suggest . . . my friends, my work, and what not. Eventually, I'll recover. Perhaps some

221

other woman will one day come along as you did and crook her finger, and then I'll follow her as I've followed you. Perhaps . . . but I really rather doubt it."

"Come, come, Steven. Are you prophesying a long, lonely, dreary life?"

"Not at all. I mean that some day I'll probably go back to my own land and find a pleasant girl. She'll marry me because she wants a home, and children, and such stuff. I'll marry her because I want a companion."

"Frightful!" cried the girl.

"I'm not an idealist," he said. "Life is a business with me. I've tried to capture a star. I've failed. Now I'll simply try to light a candle and stumble along in that way. My heart doesn't control my life enough to make me food for a poet. And yet I tell you frankly that I'm rather glad . . . philosophically speaking . . . that I've missed you."

"Is there a compliment hidden under that?"

"Not at all. I mean it seriously. I think our marriage would have been a tragedy."

"Will you tell me why?"

"Some day a man might have come along and found you at the same moment that you found him. And then there would have been an end."

"Do you mean, Steven, that I could have

been untrue to you . . . or to any man . . . or to myself?"

"I don't want to put it too bluntly. But I think, Dorotea, that, when the right man comes by, he'll simply put out his hand and take you with him, and you'll leave the *Hacienda* Fontana as if it were a peasant's shack."

"Steven!"

"The truth is rarely beautiful."

She sprang to her feet. "I'm going back to the house alone."

"Don't be childish," he said, rising in haste.

"I suppose I am . . . but I'm too angry to speak with you just now. I *want* to go alone."

"Very well, then. By all means."

Chapter Twenty-Four

The Pseudo-Indian

He watched her with a white face until she had passed from view among the trees. Then he felt the mysterious probing of eyes and a thrill in the small of his back. He whirled about to find the slender form of a ragged Indian, leaning against the cedar trunk. A young Indian with black hair streaming past his cheeks, ill confined by a band of dirty white cotton. He was the poorest of the poor. His feet were bare, even *huaraches* seemed beyond the reach of his purpose. He had on ragged trousers and a sort of shirt without sleeves. His bare, brown arms were folded, and a cigarette hung from his lips.

"How long have you been here?" asked Steven Marshal sharply.

The Indian shrugged his shoulders.

"Why, you rascal!" cried Marshal, "has *Señor* Fontana sent you here?"

The Indian smiled, and rage rose in the breast of the American.

"Come here to me," Marshal commanded.

224

The Indian removed the cigarette leisurely from his lips and then blew a lazy cloud of smoke toward the white man.

"You confounded, insolent rascal!" Marshal spit, his teeth set in most disproportionate disapproval.

At this, the youngster tilted back his throat, and from his lips there flowed out a sort of crooning laughter of content.

"I've seen you before," frowned Marshal. "Who the devil may you be?"

"Ah, *señor*, a humble friend. Will this help you to remember?"

He scooped up a rock and tossed it into the air while his hand twitched forth from some mysterious hiding place a long-barreled Colt that exploded with no obvious aim taken. The rock dissolved in the empty air. Far off, there was a faint sound of tiny fragments showering into the still lake.

"Juan Oro!" cried Marshal.

And the echo of the gun came back across the water like a loud echo of the name.

"It is I," admitted Juan Oro.

"You have made yourself into an Indian."

"I have become my real self," Juan said, shrugging his shoulders.

Steven Marshal looked at him again, with an odd mixture of amusement and disgust.

Yet, there was a genuine gladness in his face as he held out his hand. The slender, strong hand of Juan Oro closed over it.

"I am sorry to hear your name tied up with Matiás Bordi," he said. "I suppose that you've taken this disguise on account of that trouble?"

"Some traitor has talked about me," said Juan Oro. "I have found the man."

"And who is he?"

"His name does not matter. They will know it in purgatory when he has gone with a new mouth made in his throat." He drew an eloquent forefinger across his throat and made the Colt disappear into his clothes as mysteriously and as suddenly as he had first produced it.

"But, Juan, there is a devilish lot of danger in coming among people like this. What has brought you here?"

"I have come like a good friend, Don Steven, to help you."

"With what?"

"Advice."

"Ah? And about what, if you please?"

"That," said Juan, and hooked over his shoulder an irreverent thumb in the direction in which the girl had disappeared the moment before. Marshal flushed a deep red. However, he smiled a moment later.

"You were rather close, I suppose?" Marshal asked.

"Oh, yes. I heard everything."

"Very well, Don Juan, and what is your advice?"

"I have told you before that there is only one way with a horse . . . the whip and the spur. And with women, the same thing. The whip, *señor*, the whip."

Marshal, at the thought, shuddered, and then he laughed again. Juan Oro placed his own interpretation upon the laugh.

"You have been tempted, too," he said. "You should have done it. Now, you see, she has gone to another man."

"A man she has never seen," sighed Marshal. "It is true. Well, Juan, it is too late now for all your good advice."

He could not help smiling at the enthusiasm of the youngster who was now exclaiming: "She has never even seen him?"

"A pure contract of convenience. You know so much that it can do no harm to have you know more. In fact, even Fontana has never seen the man. It was arranged, my friend, through Fontana and *Señor* Maldonado, the elder. And there you are."

"You are a mild man, *señor*," said Juan with a rather visible touch of contempt.

"What would you do, Juan?"

"If there is nothing else . . . a mask for the face, a meeting with Maldonado . . . a bullet through the head . . . and then the lady once more. It could all be arranged very smoothly."

"Juan, you make all things appear easy."

"Ah, well," said Juan, "one may lead a horse to the water, but one cannot make it drink. But did you say, Don Steven, that no one has seen this Maldonado?"

"There is a wicked imp in your eyes, Juan. What is in your mind?"

"A little, small thing," said Juan, grinning broadly. "Does no one know him here?"

"How could anyone know him, then? He has only come back a few weeks ago from Europe. He lives a long distance from this house. It is long since he has been in the country. No, his face is not known."

"Not even a picture for the lady?"

"I have heard her ask for it. There is a painting that is being sent for. Why do you ask all of this?"

"As I have said . . . it is a small thing."

"Very well, Juan."

"I have come, then, for another thing, also."

"And what is that?"

"To tell you that Matiás Bordi. . . ."

"Hangs tomorrow. I know that."

228

"I have come to tell you that the plans have been changed."

"In honor of the coming of *Señor* Maldonado on his visit? They do not wish to use the gallows on that day?"

"In fact, it is decided that he must go free."

Marshal looked steadily at the other. Then he nodded. "I understand," he said. "You have a scheme for liberating him. Have you come for my help, Juan?"

"No, no, *señor!* I could not ask you to help. But I have come to warn you that tonight a great enemy of yours will be free . . . be on your guard. *Señor* Bordi is a brave man . . . but there are times when he strikes his foes like a puma rather than a lion. Do you understand me, *señor?*"

"Perfectly," smiled Marshal. "You are a kind fellow, Juan. However, what I worry about is not myself. This scheme of yours . . . is it safe?"

"It is one chance in ten chances."

"Juan, they will have your life."

"I owe him a life already. That would be payment for a debt due. It is all!"

Marshal, greatly moved, caught his arm. "Juan," he said, "the man is a confessed murderer. Is it right for you to risk so much?"

"*Señor,* the thing is decided. Besides, it is a game. I would not miss the playing of that game for much money!" He added: "But for the lady . . . what do you do? Do you leave her?"

"I leave her."

"Stay, *señor,* until the coming of this tomorrow night."

"I cannot do that."

"Stay, *señor,* and I swear to you that I shall prove her so light and so worthless that you will thank the kind God, who kept you from marriage with her."

"Juan," said the American gravely, "there are ways and ways of talk. And this is one way that I don't like."

"I ask you ten thousand pardons. But give me your promise."

"You have some wild plan?" Marshal asked, full of curiosity.

"It is not very wild."

"It is some harm planned for Maldonado?"

"Not a hair of his head shall be touched . . . if you stay."

"I shall stay, then. I am too curious to leave, as a matter of fact. But Maldonado is to be safe?"

"Perfectly!"

"Very well. It is a bargain."

Juan Oro struck his hands together. "The thing is already done. And I must live through the rescue of Bordi to do it. *¡Adiós, señor!*"

"*Adiós,* Juan. There is another thing that you and I must talk about, however. That is a plan I have of taking you back to my own land when I go. Would you listen to that?"

A shadow passed over the face of Juan. But then he banished it, and, drawing himself up with dignity, he answered: "I should listen to whatever you have to say to me, and at any time, of course. *Adiós* once more."

"*Adiós,* Juan."

He watched the pseudo-Indian draw back among the brush. Then, by black magic, Juan Oro disappeared, and there was only the wind, waving the tops of the shrubs. Still, Marshal watched, and finally he saw a man in the distance, jogging down the hill and toward the bridge that arched the river — an Indian's run, smooth, swift, effortless. He crossed the bridge and ran lightly up the farther slope. Only, when he reached the next hill, he paused, turned, and waved a hand. Then he disappeared beyond the crest. Steven Marshal walked back toward the *Hacienda* Fontana, but he was smiling faintly as he walked.

Chapter Twenty-Five

The Thundering Herd

Merely to march Matiás Bordi from the jail to the gallows was surely not enough. He, who had taken the burden of so many crimes upon his shoulders, surely needed a more carefully considered punishment, and a clever mind had hatched a sufficient scheme.

At midnight of that day, when the bell from the *Hacienda* Fontana on the hills above was casting silver waves of sound across the valley, the captain of the company that the military had placed at the disposal of the civilian powers to guard their famous prisoner, received word that his men were needed. They fell in, therefore, in the street before the jail, while the midnight bell was still sounding — its notes echoed from across the river by an occasional bellowing of the bulls in a great herd that was being driven down the valley. From upper windows in the town, people could see the dark stream of cattle moving, and the pale light of a young moon gleamed on their stirring

232

horns. Perhaps they were being rushed for the coast for a sudden shipment by Don Fontana.

The soldiers stood at attention. They were drawn up in a hollow square, filling the narrow street, and into the center of the hollow square there advanced from the door of the jail half a dozen gendarmes — three before and three behind — with Matiás Bordi striding between their ranks with his hands bound behind him. His head was bare, but it was carried high, and his whole air was extremely jaunty. He smiled upon the gendarmes before him and behind, with their gold and silver flashing in the dull moonshine. The captain gave the word — the hollow square began to move forward with a slow step.

By now a crowd had gathered. All of these preparations could not be made without some noise, and there had been a constant lighting of lamps in the village and an out-pouring of men first, then ragged boys, and women at the last. They hung, chattering before and behind the soldiers, and advanced with them, a living screen up the street until they had all climbed the little eminence that rose in the exact center of the one main street. There stood the tall, gaunt form of the gallows, black against the moonlit sky. And under the rope that dangled from it, they halted Matiás Bordi.

He raised his head and looked calmly upon it. "You wish me to die under the stars, then, my friends?"

A priest came toward him through the crowd.

"I have brought the good father for the sake of your soul, Bordi," said the captain.

"I do not need him," said Matiás. "I hear the voice of Providence more plainly than he can. I have lived in the mountains, my friends, where He is often near those whose eyes and ears are open to receive Him."

"Matiás Bordi," the good priest said gently, "I am a humble worker, and yet do not despise my offices. God performs great works through weak heads, and through me, even, he may recall you to repentance. Think, man, how close you stand to eternity."

Bordi shook his head. "It is still too far from me," he said.

The priest was enough moved to point above his head to the rope, dangling in the wind like the body of a serpent. "Is this not a sign?" he asked.

"It is not a sign," said Bordi. "When my time is near, I shall know it."

"There is no reprieve," said the priest.

"Bordi, I conjure you, do not let your soul perish with your body. Receive my words, and let your heart be softened, and repent!"

"Father," said the brigand, "I know you for a good man and a kind man . . . but to-night I shall not listen to you. Help will come to me in time."

"There is no use in exchanging words with him," said the captain to the priest. "Stand back, Father, and let us go to our business."

The priest, with a sigh, drew back into the crowd, that made reverent way for him. Two tall men, masked in black, approached Matías Bordi, laid hands upon him, and fitted the noose of the rope about his neck.

"This is a frightful thing," said the priest, drawing the captain aside. "Shall this man be hanged in the middle of the darkness of the night?"

"No," whispered the captain in return. "These are our orders, however, to keep him in suspense until the daylight comes, and then to see that he is properly executed."

"It is a cruel punishment," said the priest with a shudder.

"It may break his strength and make him readier to receive you, Father," said the captain.

"True, true," said the man of God. "And

yet he was right . . . he knew that his time had not yet come. Listen."

Matías Bordi was calmly requesting one of the gendarmes to place a lighted cigarette between his lips, and it was done. He smoked it contentedly and, when it was a butt, blew it from his lips, leaving a hanging trail of sparks in the air.

The captain returned to his side. "Tell me, Bordi, how you can possibly be rescued from this danger that you are in? Have you enough friends to rush us and break the ranks of my men?" — and he pointed to them.

"They are picked men," Bordi said courteously, "and their commander is a picked man, also. They have done me too much honor to appoint such a guard for poor Matías Bordi. However, my fate is in the hands of Providence, not of men. As to how I shall be saved, I cannot tell."

The captain laughed softly. "Take the rope from his neck," he commanded. "We will give him another moment for the ordering of his mind."

"You are very kind," said Bordi, but there was no emotion in his voice.

In the meantime, the lowing of the cattle had been approaching nearer with the passing of the moments, and their shambling hoofs were making a low, rapid thunder as they trailed in packed masses across the bridge that arched the river, and now they were proceeding toward the town. The captain grew a trifle angry.

"Go tell the fools who are driving that herd toward the town," he said, "that the street is blocked, and that they cannot pass this way. Hurry, that the herd may be turned in time."

The messenger leaped on a horse and disappeared. He was back presently with an answer.

"They do not intend to drive the cattle straight through the town," he informed the captain. "They take the turn to the left and follow that trail without passing through."

"The left trail? The left trail?" echoed the captain. "The devil fly off with me! Where does that trail lead, except straight up the hills toward the *Hacienda* Fontana? Do the idiots intend to pasture tonight on the lawns of their master's house? However, that is their concern and not mine, and, if *Señor* Fontana chooses to employ blockheads, that is his affair."

The herd had been advancing slowly, but now it rolled forward with a sudden increase of speed, and a front of tossing horns and heaving bodies appeared through the moonlight at the end of the street.

"Son of a pig!" screamed the captain to the messenger who had just returned. "Did I not say it? Go back to them, dog, and find them. . . ."

He stopped, half choking with a torrent of oaths, as he watched. For now four or five shadowy forms of horsemen were seen working among the cattle, and their shrill cries tingled up the street. They were doubtless doing their best to cut the living stream away from the street's mouth, and yet the cattle already had such untoward headway that the efforts of the herders seemed only to urge them on. They had merely served to thin out the herd and turn back the rearward masses. But some two hundred cattle were now surging up the narrow street. The captain fell into a mighty fury. He was so enraged by this clumsiness on the part of the herders that he vowed he would live to hang them all for a set of idiots.

Then he screamed to his line of soldiers on the lower side of the square to turn about and level their rifles at the advancing mass. "Stop them!" commanded the captain. "If this costs the don a score or two of beefs, he will only consider this street his slaughtering house and will not care. Shoot at their legs, *amigos*. But if you happen to hit one of the herders, why the *señor* will thank you for taking one fool out of his service."

The soldiers, half laughing, scattered a line across the narrow street; they waited until the herd rolled still closer; then, at the word of command, their rifles blazed. There was a snorting and a groaning from the herd as it wavered, stopped, sagged back from this wall of darting fires.

The herders themselves appeared to have fallen into the wildest panic. They rode straight toward the head of the column of beefs, yelling, waving their hats like madmen, and screaming to the soldiers not to shoot — that they would turn the cattle without any further harm being done. And the soldiers, now roaring with laughter, leaned on their rifles to watch.

But what happened was extremely strange. One would have said that the riders were goring the sides of the cattle with their spurs as they passed. One would have said that the foolish waving of the hats was really to urge the frightened beasts forward. For suddenly, with a great snorting, the leading bulls lunged headlong out of the cloud of boiling dust that had gathered in a dense fog over them. With a mighty bellowing and with the knife-like screeching of the herders in their ears, they stormed down the street in a solid wall.

The soldiers did not pause to fire again. Who cares to send a bullet into a sweeping tidal wave? For an instant they wavered, dumb with astonishment. Then they leaped like cats for places of safety.

Chapter Twenty-Six

A Turn and Turnabout

Even now, no one understood what was happening except the captain. He was brought to his hysteria of anger by a cold and stabbing flash of mental illumination, and, as he jumped into a doorway, he shrilled at the top of his voice: "Guard Bordi with your lives! Guard Bordi! It is his plot! Oh, ten thousand devils, I have been made a fool! Oh, Lord, keep him safe!"

So shouted the brave captain, falling back through the doorway as his first line of men leaped on every side for other doors, for the narrow interstices between the house walls, and even dove through open windows. But here was a living wall of horns that tossed and hoofs that stamped and eyes that gleamed red with terror and with anger. That solid column washed the street clean of every living thing in the twinkling of an eye. Behind the more solid mass in front, there followed a looser stream behind, that still made the street extremely dangerous.

What saved Matiás Bordi was his own quickness of eye and speed of foot. He leaped through a doorway and into a jam of the frightened soldiers just as a keen point of a horn grazed his shoulder blades.

Two of the captain's men had presence of mind enough to take his arms and hold them fast as the herd thundered past — but the suddenness of that brute charge, the roar of hoofs, the screaming of many voices in the crowded hut had already unnerved them, when there leaped through the doorway into the filled room a newcomer who seemed to have been thrown among them from the very midst of the herd itself.

There was enough firelight for them to see his face. It was a ragged, young Indian boy with long black hair, falling about his face — hair loosely confined by a band of dirty cotton cloth around his forehead. He had been seen loafing around the town recently, a harmless, mild-eyed wanderer.

But now he was transformed into a young panther, with a revolver in either hand, and each revolver spitting fire as he ran in — spitting fire in their very faces, so it seemed. For if those shots were aimed rather at the ceiling than at them, how could they be expected to guess it in that moment of wild confusion? Moreover, behind the young tiger rushed three more armed men whose guns were working.

There was one wild cry — "The men of Bordi!" — and the brave soldiers became so much helpless pulp, jammed breathlessly in the rush of their companions toward the rear wall of the little house. Only Bordi himself leaped forward, wrenching his arms easily free from the hands that held him. A knife touch freed those hands of his. He caught a gun from the nearest man — and all four were back in the street, where a fifth man held their horses. Five horses — and an extra horse for Matiás Bordi, young, strong, and swift as the wind. No wonder, then, that as he twined his legs around it and lifted it into full speed with a yell, the cry of his lips was: "The will of Providence!"

For it was like a miracle, indeed, this sudden snatching of his life from beneath the gallows.

The captain was already back in the street, screaming for horses and firing a revolver as fast as his finger could press the trigger. Others of his soldiers raced out and, jerking their rifles to their shoulders, blazed away. They were excellent shots, these men, but he, who has just faced a stampede and escaped with his life by a fraction of an inch, is not fitted to find a target that is composed of a racing horse, disappearing in a faintly moonlit cloud of dust.

The six riders streamed down the farther slope from the village and turned unharmed into the fields beyond. In another twinkling, they had gained the bridge, raised upon it a brief thunder, and now they were winging away to safety. Fifty men rode behind them, but six chosen riders and six chosen horses made the pace and dropped the pursuit dizzily behind them.

Up through the hills into the cool shadows of the pines they pressed, however, without abating their pace, until they were finally more than an hour of hard riding from the town. There they found before them the glimmer of a fire among the trees, and Bordi proposed that they should circle it.

"You will find a friend at it," Juan Oro said, so they pushed on until they came to a little clearing in the center of which was a broad-built fire, now burned down to coals.

The fragrance of roast meat and coffee lay in the air, and the cook squatted on his heels, caring for his pots and pans. He looked up with a grin illumined by the fire's glow. And Matiás Bordi began to laugh out of sheer joy.

"Now," he said, "I know that I am free, for

I begin to taste it! Who has done this thing? Whose thought prepared this food for us? Who was so sure of our delivery that he planned this for me? It was you, Cristóbal! I know your mind. There is a meal at the end of every trail, for you."

Cristóbal was a fellow with a face like a pirate's, and, as he grinned now, the deep hollows of his cheeks were filled with wrinkles. "It was Juan Oro," he said.

Here the leader turned sharply upon Juan, but he said not a word.

They fell to upon the most delicious food — roasted flesh of young kids, tortillas in place of forks, coffee made by an artist's hand, and plenty of good brandy to spice the flavor of the food.

"I have not eaten," said Bordi, when at last he leaned his contented back against a broad tree and lighted a cigarette, "I have not eaten since I was taken and put into that sty. And now I am out!"

He looked up through the branches of the trees to the moon that stood almost at her zenith, making all the heavens the deep blue-gray of polished steel.

"Now, dear friends," he said, still with his happy eyes wandering through the branches above him, "tell me what man among you conceived it and planned it. Or did it leap all at once out of your brains?"

There was no answer at once, and, glancing down at them in surprise, he found that all their bright, black eyes were at once upon Juan Oro.

"*¡Diablo!*" murmured the chief. "Is it he, also? Is it all from his mind?"

"It was he," admitted Cristóbal, "although he needed our hands to help him. I thought that the boy was a fool, at the first. But then he showed me how it might be done. We went unwillingly. We thought that it would be running our heads into nooses. However, that chance was worth one risk, and we took the risk. When the cattle went boiling down the street, I thought that we had already been successful. But when the guns of the soldiers stopped the cows, then I thought we were lost. I tell you, in that minute I smelled the mold and the damp of a dungeon . . . I was sick . . . I was weak. But Juan Oro poured some of the devil in him into the cattle. We began to gouge them with our spurs and shout . . . so they jumped ahead at last. I hoped for a moment that they would catch the soldiers and grind them to bits, but those dogs, they were active, were they not? Well, it was all Juan Oro. Thank him, Matías."

Matiás merely shrugged his athletic shoulders. "A turn and turnabout," he said solemnly, gravely. "Is it not, Juan?"

"It is very true," admitted Juan. "We have crossed off all debts, Matiás. I am free, am I not?"

"It is the will of Providence," said the chief.

Around the circle of his companions the wink and the smile of understanding passed covertly. It was an old feeling among the crew that their captain, brilliant in all else, was a little twisted from sanity in this respect alone.

By that campfire they rolled down their blankets, but, while the others were curled up in sleep, Matiás Bordi and Juan Oro sat close, side by side.

"And now," said Matiás, "that the score is cleared between us, am I to expect a knife between my ribs, Juan?"

"The Don Fontana has forgotten that there is such a man as I," said Juan Oro. "He has even forgotten my name. And, therefore, do I owe him my promise still?"

"We are true to one another, then, Juan?"

"With one promise from you, Matiás . . . that this *gringo* . . . this Steven Marshal shall not be touched by you."

The bandit shook his head. "If he lives,

Juan, all men will say that he has beaten me, and, therefore, I fear him."

"Is it not true?"

"The devil! Can you believe that?"

"I have asked you, *amigo*."

"I have answered you." Matiás sighed. "I am no longer so young," he said, "and this *gringo* fights like a flash of lightning. I would need all your own speed even to stand against him, Juan. However, I shall let him be, if you wish. Besides," he chuckled, "do I need the money and the influence of the young Maldonado so long as I have you, Juan?"

"Tell me," said Juan Oro suddenly, "if this Maldonado is not my size and height?"

"Why do you ask that?"

"I have a little reason."

"I think he is very close to it. But heavier, Juan. Perhaps heavier."

"I seem lighter than I am."

"What is the point of this?"

"Tomorrow you and your men ride with me, will you not?"

"To the end of the earth, my son."

"Good."

"And then . . . ?"

"We sleep now. Tomorrow we ride."

There was no more talk that night. Juan Oro twisted himself instantly in a blanket, rolled himself a little closer to the fire, and was asleep as soon as he had closed his eyes. But Matiás Bordi remained awake for some time longer, sitting cross-legged, his hands folded in his lap, his face raised, listening to the night winds as they stirred the trees into covert whispers.

Chapter Twenty-Seven

<u>Juan Holds Up the Cavalcade</u>

Señor Don Pedro Maldonado could have ridden to the railroad and could have slid southward in a few hours to a point close enough to the *Hacienda* Fontana, but such a means of travel did not appeal to him. He was a romantic fellow, and he decided that, when he went to see and to woo his bride to be, he must go as a knight would have gone in the old days. So he mounted his best horse and took the road.

Not that he went alone. By no means. For companions, and perhaps for guards also, although he was brave enough, he took with him four men from his estate, four men of a social position high enough to appear at his side, and low enough to serve him as a master — four men of proven courage and proven skill with weapons. When he had done this, there were still other preparations to be made. Five men cannot ride alone on a two-day journey without some preparations, unless they are prepared to go most roughly, and, although the *Señor* Maldonado journeyed as a traveler, at the end of the trip it was necessary that he appear as a bridegroom to be. Therefore, he needed equipment for that purpose.

The cavalcade of five, accordingly, rode in the lead, jauntily sweeping over hill and dale, but, when they halted, they were forced to await the coming of their provision train. Behind them toiled three peons who drove five pack mules, and each of those packs contained, besides enough food and cooking utensils for the trip, ample clothes to furnish forth all five gallants at the end of it.

They had ended their first day's journey, and they had begun the second in the highest spirits because all had gone so smoothly. Indeed, the ground was covered so fast, that they expected to arrive at the *Hacienda* Fontana before the darkness came. They now approached a rise of the road where it wound around the hip of a mountain from the side of which they should be able to look forth to the *Hacienda* Fontana itself. And here they planned to dismount, change from their traveling clothes to their finery for the reception at the *Hacienda* Fontana, and then start forward again.

It was the golden middle of the afternoon. The mountain air was cool and pure. Fragrances breathed forth from the pine shadows along the slopes, and the hearts of the riders were high, indeed. So when one started forward at full speed to gain the first glimpse of the *Hacienda* Fontana, the others set out in hot pursuit. It was determined beforehand who should win that race. For the noble Maldonado bestrode a dark chestnut Thoroughbred worth all of the five thousand dollars that it had cost — a horse like a prince — fleet enough to have run on the track and schooled like an educated man. That stout runner broke away from the others and widened the gap between him and them with every stride that he made. Up the slope whirled *Señor* Maldonado, shouting back his mockeries to the other four.

He swept to the curve of the road as it climbed the mountain and dipped around its side, and so, far in advance, he shot into the presence of three masked villains with ready rifles leveled in their hands. There was no question of resistance. He could only tug on his reins with a groan and bring his horse to a halt at the same time that he caught a glimpse, far off, of the broad red roof of the *Hacienda* Fontana, high on its own hills, embowered among the trees.

"*Amigos*," Maldonado exclaimed, furious, "you do not know what you do! I am the *Señor*. . . ."

"*Señor* Fool!" exclaimed a brutal voice. "Keep your hands high, or your life is not worth a *peso*. Ride straight before me into the trees."

So, with a groan, he was forced to the side of the road, where his hands were instantly bound behind him. Now the other four rounded the turn with no less velocity, and, before them, they found new enemies. Three more brigands had come up out of the shadows with their rifles, and against this battery of steadied guns there was no possibility of fighting back. The excellent followers of Maldonado straightway halted their panting horses and pushed their hands high in the air.

They were tied, and tied with unnecessary rigor. They were herded down the road, along a narrow trail, and then through the unpathed forest until they came to an opening in the woods, a pleasant little dell through which a brook wandered, talking busily to itself. And birds sang above them, unheard by the unlucky Maldonado.

He was saying: "I am Pedro Maldonado, as you perhaps know."

"*Señor,*" said a gruff voice, "it is ten thousand pleasures for me to meet you. For the sake of meeting you, I was forced to stop you on the road. But not for the sake of hearing you talk."

"Friend," said Maldonado, "how long are we to be kept here?"

"A matter of a few days only."

"A few days?" shouted Maldonado. "I am ruined, unless I can ride on today!"

"*Señor,* you cover me with grief," mocked the ruffian.

"If you wish to hold me for ransom, I can give you now an order for money and send you back with it faster than I could possibly overtake you. But I must be set free."

"Ah?" said the other. "This begins to sound like good sense."

But here a musical voice of one of the brigands commanded: "Gag that fool and stop his tongue. And the rest will be silent, also. Herd them back into the trees. Keep them out of sight. And if they move, remember that lives are cheaper than dirt! They cannot hang us twenty times for twenty murders."

"As you will, Juan," answered the other. "If you will not listen, neither shall I."

So straightway, poor Maldonado was gagged, and with his friends he was driven back into the trees. There they were forced to sit in a row against the stump of an old fallen giant of the forest, while before them stood a man with a rifle dropped significantly over the hook of his left arm and a finger constantly upon the trigger.

This had hardly been accomplished, when three of the bandits returned to the high road above and presently bagged and brought back with them the pack mules and their muleteers. The latter were sent to join their masters under the muzzle of the rifle. The mules were instantly stripped of their packs by the expert hands of the outlaws.

Bordi, in the meantime, had withdrawn to the edge of the clearing, where he amused himself, watching, certain that his share of the spoils would not be stolen. The overhauling of the capture was managed under the entire supervision of Juan Oro. It was a rich capture. The mere price of the jewels and the gold watches was a rich capture, not to speak of the worth of the horses that had fallen into their hands, and, above all, this, there was a tidy sum of cash. In addition, hardly less prized, there were gala costumes and evening clothes neatly folded in the commodious packs.

The clothes, Juan Oro carefully laid aside. Only first he stripped off his own jacket and then tried on one coat after another until, at length, he slipped into one that fitted him with glove-like exactness. At that point he permitted himself to sigh with relief.

Next he went to the dolorous line of captives and surveyed their faces, one by one, until he selected one of the muleteers above the rest — a grim-faced man, who scowled back at him with a savage meaning. Him he beckoned to and led apart among the trees.

"*Amigo,*" he said, "you are not bred for the muleteer's trade."

The other was silent.

"I said," muttered Juan, "that you were not bred to the muleteer's trade."

"My friends are gagged or under a rifle. They may not speak, and I *will* not," said the fellow gloomily.

Juan Oro's eyes, behind his mask, turned tigerish with cruel purpose. "In the twinkling of an eye," he said, "I can have a fire started. Will roasted feet help you to talk, *amigo?*"

"Try me," said the other calmly. "I have spoken my last word, even if you tear me to pieces and burn the little bits that are left."

"So?" Juan said, and his voice changed adroitly. "I knew, by the first glance at you, that you were a man, and not a slave. Why else did I select you from the rest? I could have taken that fat-faced fool who sat on your right, yellow and trembling. He would have talked. I should have showed him the edge of this knife, and he would have turned his mind inside out for me as I can turn my coat. He would have emptied every pocket of his memory. But we, *amigo,* do not hunt slaves. We want men. Men of courage, and men with steady hands and skillful in the use of weapons."

Here curiosity forced the other to break through his silence. "Who could tell you that I use guns?" he asked.

Juan Oro stepped up to him and extracted a revolver that was slung inside his loose jacket, under the pit of the arm. He showed it to the other and examined it for a moment, noting the perfect condition of the weapon.

"I shall tell a good marksman by the face of his gun," said Juan, "and yours is clean. You have practiced many and many hours with this Colt, my friend."

"*San Miguel,*" murmured the other, in a sulky admiration. "Your eye is sharp."

"However," went on Juan Oro, "I do not need to look at your gun to know that you are an expert marksman. We know more of you than you dream, some of us. We have had our eyes upon you. We have been wondering at what season you would be ripe to become one of us, Miguel."

"*¡Diablo!*" exclaimed the other. "Do you know my name, also?"

"I know that," Juan said in a voice full of meaning, "and I could tell you other things that might surprise you."

"It is not true," said the other, though he flinched a little. "I am new in this country. No one can know anything about me. As for my name, you guessed it because I ex- claimed upon the blessed *San Miguel*."

"Are you so sure of that?" smiled Juan Oro. "Well, Miguel, I do not wish to frighten you, but I might tell you more . . . a great deal more than I have already said."

"That is a great lie!" snarled the muleteer, beginning to tremble a little.

Juan Oro stepped closer to him, first glancing behind him and next upon either side. Then he said significantly: "Good friend, Miguel, let me whisper it . . . come closer. Miguel, I could tell you why it is that you are forced to keep that gun with you and practice with it so constantly."

Chapter Twenty-Eight

Juan's Wild Plan

The face of Miguel grew livid. "God stand with me!" he gasped at last. "But it was not true! They accused me falsely! I shall swear to the judge...."

"Tush, man," said Juan Oro, "you need never see the face of a judge. You will stay with us and become a man and live like a man. Do you not think that they would have found you out while you were in the service of this Maldonado? Would he have been a shield to you? No, Miguel. He would have given you up to the wolves the instant that they called for you."

"How did you know?" asked Miguel humbly.

"I shall tell you. Come with me."

He led him back to the clearing, where the spoils were being carefully appraised by the bandits.

"Here is the man, Miguel, of whom I told you," he said in a meaning voice.

"I remember," said Matiás Bordi. "I remember, of course."

"Will you show him your face?"

"As you please."

Bordi removed the mask, and the effect upon even the firm-nerved Miguel was magical.

"It is Matiás Bordi!" he cried.

"Come," said Juan Oro, "you must go back with me. We have still more to talk over."

Miguel went like a lamb, thoroughly subdued.

"Now," Juan said, when they were apart again, "you may make your choice. In spite of what you have seen and heard of us, you may go back to your fellows and stay with them, unharmed by us. Or, if you choose, you are one of us."

"I?" Miguel asked in a hushed voice. "One of the men of the Bordi? I?"

"I have said it."

"I would rather be one of you," said the other with a fierce joy, "than have a gift of a million *pesos*. For if I am one of you, I am a free man."

"You are, indeed."

"*Señor*, is it you whom I must thank?"

"You will thank no one. Your first service is a dangerous one, and may bring you to the hangman's rope. But you are a man of courage, Miguel."

"Try me," said Miguel, in a voice that Juan had heard with admiration before. "And tell me first what my part is to be?"

"I must learn other things from you. But in the meantime. . . ."

He drew his knife and with a touch of its razor edge he set the hands of the muleteer free. The latter recovered the use of them with an instinctive lurch forward, as though he would fly at the throat of the other, but he recalled himself at once and took the hand with which Juan extended toward him with a great grip. His whole body was trembling with joy.

"I could sing!" gasped Miguel. "Lord, Lord! I am born again, and above the fear of the law."

"It is true. You will take an oath to Bordi, next. But now you talk with me . . . you are one of us . . . I open my mind to you because I trust you, Miguel."

"Ah, *señor,* will you not find me one who never forgets? And will you tell me your name, since you know mine?"

"I am Juan Oro."

"So? So?" murmured the other, and he scanned the face of Juan as the latter removed the mask from it. "Then the stories we have heard of the new man in the riders of Matiás Bordi are true. It is you who ride like a pigeon and strike like a hawk!"

Juan waved this compliment aside. "First," he said, "tell me what you know of this journey of Maldonado to the *Hacienda* Fontana."

"He rides to see his lady. That is all I know."

"Recollect, Miguel. You are not a muleteer or a fugitive, now. You are a man whose ears must be as keen as the ears of a squirrel and whose eyes must be sharper than the eyes of a cat. You must remember everything. Out of a whisper you must read a whole story. I give you five minutes, Miguel. Sit by yourself. Smoke a cigarette. Remember everything that has come to your ears or to your eyes since first you started out on this journey."

The other nodded, puckering his brow. And Juan Oro sat down and smoked his own cigarette through before he resumed his questions. At length, he tossed it away.

"First," he said, "what are the names of those who ride with Maldonado?"

"I know only three. They are . . . Oñate, d'Arragon, and Gonzales."

"They are gentlemen?"

"They are friends of Maldonado."

"And not servants?"

"When Maldonado rides, they ride with him. They will fight for him. They will obey him. Still, they say that they are not servants." His lip curled. "They say that they are free men, *señor*. I, because I killed one man, one small man, was made a man who was afraid of the light of day. But, *señor*, I was happier and freer than they."

"It is true," Juan said gravely. "Now, Miguel, do the people at the *Hacienda* Fontana know these men?"

"I cannot tell."

Juan Oro thought for a moment. "Do they know, then, that he is riding with several friends?"

"Yes. They know that much. I have heard *Señor* Maldonado speak of a letter he wrote to the don. They will expect these men, and they will know their names."

"Ah, Miguel, and you do not remember the names of the other men? But we can have their names from them, if we will."

"If they lied and gave false names?" suggested Miguel with lifted brows.

"That is true," sighed Juan Oro. "It would ruin all that I have planned. I intend to walk, if I can, on the edge of a cliff. Do you understand? I intend that you and I and, perhaps, others shall walk on the edge of a cliff ready to fall into a great danger."

Miguel snapped his fingers and grinned. "Who," he said, "will not do more for the sake of a game than for the sake of money, or a safe neck?"

This made Juan Oro smile in turn, very well pleased. "In their talk, did you hear any of them speak of the *Hacienda* Fontana?"

"Yes."

"*¡Diablo!*" Juan hissed. "Then some of them are known in the house. How did they speak of it?"

"They spoke of the hundreds of thousands of *pesos* that had been spent in building it."

"Did any of them speak of what was inside the house?"

"I do not remember."

"Did you hear them name Don José Fontana?"

"As a very rich man, of course."

"But as a friend?"

"No."

"And the lady, Dorotea? Did they speak of her?"

"Very much, *señor.*"

"Ah, then, perhaps, some of them are known to her?"

"No, *señor.* Of that I am sure. For from their voices, I knew that they had not seen her, but that they wished much to see her."

"Ah, ah," chuckled Juan Oro. "It would be a sad thing, if they were disappointed. Stay here. I shall call for you after a moment. I wish to tell my friends that you have consented to be one of us. And, for that purpose, we must have their consents. If one of them bears a grudge against you, he will speak out, and then you will be sent away. For we all must live together as brothers."

"That is very wise," said the muleteer. "Whatever your plan may be, luck go with it, *Señor* Oro."

So Juan went back to his comrades in the little clearing. There he stood, surveying the four men who stood by the plunder.

"*Amigos,*" he said, "what ones among you can be fitted with these clothes?"

They took up the coats and tried them. To one tall, thick-shouldered villain, all of the clothes were quite unsuited. But three of the others were tolerably well-dressed in the rest. They held up the trousers beside them.

"Well?" said Cristóbal, who, after Juan Oro, held the second place under Bordi. "What is it for?"

"They are tickets of admission," said Juan.

"The devil!"

"To what?" asked another.

"To *La Hacienda* Fontana!"

"Ha?"

"Do you hear me, *amigos?* We are to go together to the *Hacienda* Fontana and. . . ."

"Have our necks stretched with ropes! There is not treasure enough in the world to tempt me!" exclaimed Cristóbal. "There are armies of *mozos* there!"

"What are armies of *mozos* to four *men?* Besides, we do not go for plunder."

"For what, then, in heaven's name?"

"For the pleasure, *amigos,* of walking through the fine rooms of the *hacienda.*"

"Juan, you have had too much brandy."

"And of sitting at his table. . . ."

"Ha?"

"And drinking his toasts."

"Juan, you are mad!"

"Tell me," Juan asked, "if you fear to go? For, if you do, I shall go alone."

"Juan, what is to be gained?"

"We will have the pleasure, I tell you, of seeing the inside of the finest house in Mexico, will we not?"

"Aye, that is true. But I have the finest neck in Mexico, and I do not wish to have it wrung."

"Ah, cold heart. But consider that we will sit at the table and eat food cooked by a Frenchman, an artist, a man who receives for his cooking more than we, friends, rob in a year!"

"Is it possible? Well, I might go for the sake of stealing his money," answered one, "but I would never go for the sake of eating his food. Roasted kid and brandy is food enough for me."

"We will have at our fingertips," Juan Oro said persuasively, "the finest wines in the world. I have seen them in the cellars of the great house. One walks a mile . . . yes, a mile, through the old passages. There are wines hidden in that cellar coated with cobwebs inches deep. There are wines there, dear friends, so old that their names have been forgotten. There are wines so old, so delicious, that men cross the seas to taste of them."

"Ah," cried Cristóbal in the voice of a bull, "that is enough! I am ready. I shall go with you, madman. I am ready. Let us be off."

"Wines," broke in Juan Oro, "that, when they are opened, fill a room with fragrance like the breath of evening wind over a bed of roses. Wines of France . . . I have tasted them . . . wonderful clarets from the Médoc . . . Burgundies to speak of which is to speak of heaven . . . champagnes that are diamond-set nectar . . . thick, rich, heavy wines of Spain . . . ah, shall I forget the taste of the deep Oporto, like blood with a blue shadow in it. And the Madeira. . . ."

"Enough!" Cristóbal shouted, his eyes rolling in his head, while his hands clutched his throat. "Say no more . . . for my throat is filled with sand and ashes. I choke . . . I die of thirst!"

"You, swine," said one of his companions, "live for the sake of the bottle. Shall I risk throat, belly, head, and all for the sake of swilling down some wine, old or new?"

"You, Alonso, must hear me speak still further. The treasures of the *Hacienda* Fontana are countless. But you will see the great man himself . . . the richest man in Mexico . . . perhaps the richest man in the world!"

"I have seen him already," muttered Alonso. "The pale-faced devil looks like a *gringo*. I have seen him, and I would not turn and glance over my shoulder for the sake of seeing him again."

"True, true. But is he all? No, no, Alonso, *amigo mío!* For you will see in the *Hacienda* Fontana the lovely *Señorita* Dorotea!"

"The daughters of all rich men are beautiful . . . when newspapers speak of them. But when one's eyes. . . ."

"Hear me, Alonso. Here is my throat. You shall cut it freely if, when you see her, you do not say . . . 'It is an angel from heaven!' "

"Angels," said Alonso, "are fair enough. But I will not talk with a cold woman."

"Cold? Cold? I, Alonso, have not been a stranger with pretty girls. But I swear to you, dear friend, that I would walk barefoot a hundred leagues over the thorns for the sake of taking one glance at her beauty."

"Is it true?"

"Her voice is a hand plucking at the heart in your bosom."

"Ah, Juan, I have dreamed of such a voice."

"To look into her eyes is to fall into a sea of delight."

"*¡Caramba!*" Alonso moaned in ecstasy. "Who shall keep me from her? To horse, Juan! To horse!"

"To horse!" cried the other pair, equally enthusiastic.

"Peace," Juan said, stepping back and breathing hard from the efforts of that little oration. "There are other things that we must provide for first."

Chapter Twenty-Nine

When Outlaws Disagree

"Consider," Juan Oro said, grinning at his companions, "that we must now become gentlemen."

"Ha?" questioned the exquisite Alonso. "Gentlemen? We are to *become* gentlemen?"

The grin of Juan Oro did not falter. "Can we be gentlemen, if we are not dressed as those men are dressed? We must have riding boots and whipcord trousers and crops and English saddles."

"*¡Diablo!*" Gregorio exclaimed, opening his mouth wide. "I would rather sit on a greased rock on the edge of a cliff than on a piece of pigskin no bigger than the palm of your hand! It is inviting a horse to throw you over his head!"

"We must ride on them, nevertheless," said Juan Oro. "Turn the five out of their clothes and see what we can find to suit us. But the *Señor* Maldonado has extra riding clothes in his pack, so I shall be suited."

It was done. Poor Maldonado and his

friends lost their clothes in the twinkling of an eye. There followed a wriggling into glove-fitted riding breeches, and into shoes too small for the feet. They giggled at one another like a crew of self-conscious girls, but, in the end, each man looked down upon himself with an unquestionable approval.

Gregorio had been a barber, and he was the umpire who knew everything that was to be known about society and social affairs. While with a jabbing forefinger and an excited voice he corrected the other two in their dressing, he sat Juan down on a stump and proceeded to trim short his bronze locks. They fell in a rapid shower around him, and, when the trimming was ended, Alonso submitted to the shears, while Juan ran to look at himself in the pool.

They heard his voice calling out happily: "*¡Diablo! Amigos,* I am more handsome than ever!"

There was a roar of laughter in response to this, but they were accustomed to the perfectly frank vanity of the youngster. He came running back to them with a lighted face, running a hand lightly over his head, from which the thick tresses had been shorn.

"Look!" he exclaimed. "Is it not true? I

was a boy . . . the shears of Gregorio have made me a man!"

"How old are you, Juan?" asked the amused voice of Matías Bordi.

"I? I forget," Juan responded, pretending to study. "Let me see . . . I am twenty . . . nearly twenty-one, am I not, Matías?"

And he began to shed his clothes and then step adroitly into the new costume. The new things that the others fumbled at were nothing to Juan, it seemed. And they were still working over details when he was all equipped.

But the struggles of the outlaws and the advice of the ex-barber had not been wasted. They had been dashing fellows in the saddle in their picturesque rags of banditry. They were just as dashing in another sense when the razor had passed over their faces and they were garbed like a more quietly civilized race. Gregorio himself was the least presentable of the lot. And Cristóbal's hollow cheeks and deep-shadowed eyes were perhaps a little too strikingly in contrast with his costume. But handsome young Alonso and Juan Oro were perfectly in place.

"I shall introduce you to your new self," Juan offered. "Cristóbal, I present you to *Señor* Oñate."

"*Señor* Oñate" — grinned Cristóbal — "it is a real delight to know myself."

"Alonso, know yourself as *Señor* Gonzales."

"A poor name," Alonso said doubtingly. "But I'll wear it as well as any man."

"And you, Gregorio, are *Señor* d'Arragon."

"Ah," groaned Alonso, "why couldn't such a name as that be found for me? A woman would hear such a name as that."

"Peace," Juan Oro said. "You are now my henchmen. You are my devoted followers."

"*¡Diablo!*" Gregorio shouted. "I shall follow no man in the world except Matiás Bordi, and him only so long as he has good luck with him."

"You blockhead," answered Juan. "Will you play your part, or will you not?"

"I shall play my part," Gregorio sighed, "but I shall hold it against you the rest of your life that men have seen me as your follower."

"You are devoted to me, all three. You are rough fellows . . . but for a journey like this you have insisted upon going along with me. And I have taken you . . . to humor you."

"You," said Cristóbal, striking his thumb against his own chest, "you, Juan Oro, humor me, Cristóbal, by allowing me to ride as your guard? Ha! That is a thing to make a man laugh . . . yes, laugh until his throat splits wide open."

"Cristóbal, you are a jealous fool. I expected you to show more sense than that Gregorio. But you are worse . . . you are a child. Do you not see that it is all a game?"

"A stupid game," muttered Cristóbal, and he twisted the end of the great mustache that had been hewed and sheared by the expert fingers of Gregorio into a more fashionable and fragmentary decoration for his ugly face.

"Wait," Alonso stated. "You will present us as rough men, then?"

"So that you may be yourselves. You will not have to ape the grand gentleman. You will be yourselves and at ease. Is not that the best?"

"That," said Gregorio, "is really very well."

"That is sense," Cristóbal agreed, nodding vigorously. "I would rather choke myself with my own hands than give myself airs."

Alonso, in the meantime, had remained silent, but it was the silence of the approaching storm that now broke and roared about their heads. He cast a glance down his neatly clad body; he raised himself to his full height.

"*You,* then, are to be the gentleman?" he asked Juan.

"I am Pedro Maldonado, my friend," Juan confirmed, still smiling in the face of this black thunder.

"You are Pedro Maldonado?" sneered Alonso. "You are the betrothed of the *Señorita* Dorotea?"

"I am. And you have been a companion of mine. You have traveled to Paris with me, among other things. That will explain your knowledge of French."

"And what," Alonso asked savagely, "will explain your *lack* of that knowledge?"

"Ten thousand devils!" Juan gasped, taken fiercely aback by this suggestion.

"Ah?" Alonso sneered. "Are you such a perfect gentleman, after all?"

"She will not use French, unless *I* use it," Juan stated. "Or unless one of you starts it. Spanish will be enough for her."

"But this Maldonado speaks English, also, and so does she . . . and there is an American, a *gringo* dog, in the house. Is it not he who struck down our dear friend, Matías?"

"As for the *gringo,*" Juan explained, "I shall manage him so that his tongue will never embarrass me. You, as I was saying, have been my companion, Alonso. Do you

275

understand? It will be you who takes her aside and pours out sweet talk about me in her ear!"

"So?" snarled Alonso.

"Exactly as I say. For twenty-five years, you and I have been. . . ."

"Twenty-five years! That is the age of the Maldonado, but is it your age, Juan?"

Juan Oro actually shrank from this blow.

"You have the eye of an eagle to find the faults of another man, Alonso," he said bitterly.

"Well," said Alonso, "this is very clear. There is one here whose age *is* five-and-twenty years. There is one here who speaks French in such a manner that Paris opens its arms to him. There is one here who speaks English, well enough. There is one here with a gentleman's education, now wasted riding with the robbers and ruffians. Who is that man? It is I!"

"Ah, modest Alonso," Juan said through his teeth.

"It is I," said Alonso, "who must take the part of the Maldonado. It is I who must be followed by the rest of you. Speak to me, if it is not true?"

"There is better sense in that," admitted Cristóbal.

"There is," murmured Gregorio.

"It is the matter of the years," Cristóbal agreed. "Juan Oro would never pass for a boy of twenty . . . let alone for a man of twenty-five."

"Is it so?" Juan asked, with the gentleness of exquisite rage.

"Confess," said Alonso, "that what I have said to you now is only just."

"What knowledge have you of my plans, when we get to the house?"

"Knowledge? Do I need knowledge? We enter the house as guests. We drink the fine wines, eat the good food, dance with the lovely girls, and in the middle of the night . . . waken, steal from our beds, gut the great *Hacienda* Fontana of all that is worth carrying away . . . and then depart, perhaps, taking with us the don himself for ransom later on . . . and perhaps the Lady Dorotea herself." He ended by turning to his companions with an appealing gesture of both hands. Then he wheeled back upon Juan. "You have heard me speak," he said. "In what is your plan different from that?"

"Whatever the differences," Juan said, "it was I who planned the scheme, was it not?"

"Well, and what of that?"

"Should I not lead it, then?"

"That is the talk of a child. One man has a brain for scheming. Another man has a brain for action . . . like me. Come, come, Juan, admit that I am right and that you are wrong. Admit that I am better fitted for this little thing than you. You are years too young . . . and you look it. Why, you will appear younger than the girl herself."

"It is false! She is only a child."

"Eh? How old is this child, then?"

"Only seventeen, or eighteen," Juan admitted, flushing a little as he saw that he had trapped himself.

"Seventeen or eighteen? And are you much older? Juan, Juan, you are brave as a lion and wise as a snake, but now admit that Alonso is the man made and intended for such work as this."

"I cannot admit it."

"Will you tell me what your arguments may be, then?"

"There are three," said Juan Oro.

"I shall be glad to hear them."

"You may do better. They are so plain that you may see them. The first is this."

He flicked a hunting knife from his clothes, seeming to snatch it by the hilt out of the empty air, and hurled it so that it sank, humming, into the ground just between the feet of Alonso. And, after that, two Colts glided forth into his slender hands. He held them, drooping from his knees.

278

"Do you see my thoughts?" Juan Oro asked.

The face of Alonso was a strange study. There was very manifest reluctance in his expression, but there was immense pride that might have driven him into battle in another instant. But here Matiás Bordi rose and stepped between them.

He said in a soft undertone as he passed the ear of Alonso: "You are a fool. The devil will kill you." He said aloud to Juan: "Is this the way you handle my lions, Juan? Is this the way? You will have to learn better."

"They are not worth learning," Juan responded, white with rage. "They would steal a thought out of a man's mind. They are not lions. They are starved dogs. Do not lay your hand on your knife, Cristóbal! Let not a hand move, or I shall be among you, I, Juan Oro! Do you hear me?"

He was wavering on his feet, swaying from side to side with a venomous fury, like a furious cobra, weaving before it strikes.

"Juan!" shouted Matiás Bordi. "You speak like a man with no sense! These are our friends, our comrades, our dear friends, Juan. Do you wish to make three enemies in one stroke? No, it is not too late. Go quickly to them. Ask them to forgive you."

The suspense was drawn like a violin

string, vibrating the sense of danger, and the twitching fingers of the three were already near their weapons. What did Juan Oro do then? The tiger disappeared suddenly from his face. He went to Cristóbal and took his hand.

"Cristóbal," he said, "I curse myself for a fool. Forgive me, my friend."

"Ah, well," said Cristóbal, sighing with relief, "you would have killed two of us, but the third would have finished you. For my part, I think I would have been the third man, but let it go . . . let it go. I forgive you, Juan."

"And you, Gregorio?"

"Juan, we have been brothers . . . we bear with one another . . . it is forgotten."

"Alonso, you shall do as you plan," Juan said. "Perhaps it will be wiser. But let Matías decide between us. Is that well?"

The trouble disappeared from the face of Alonso. "Speak, Matías," he said.

"Why," said Matías Bordi, "you will all come to wreck, because you start like strange dogs, growling at one another. But since the scheme came from Juan first, let him lead you through it, if he can."

Chapter Thirty

Señor "Maldonado" Arrives

There was only one pair of eyes in the *Hacienda* Fontana that Juan Oro feared, and those were the eyes that first encountered him when his cavalcade drew up to the great house with the four cavaliers riding in front, and in the rear the honest Miguel laboring over the pack mules, assisted by a recruit from among the old members of the band — that is to say, Gabriel Donato, who was not too proud to exercise his old calling for a single day for the sake of the fun that might grow out of it, to say nothing of the money that was apt to flow, also. But there came to receive them, the active little secretary of the great Don José Fontana, Francisco Moreño himself.

His pale, busy eyes stopped their shifting and weary searching for a moment to dwell upon Juan Oro. For the least part of a breathing space those eyes grew cold with suspicion and fixed in eager anxiety. And the heart of Juan Oro stood still in him.

After all, it was not so many days before that he had stood under the eyes of this very man. He could only trust that the violent change in his costume and the difference in his manner might close the eyes of the secretary to the truth.

So he walked straight up to the little man.

"I am *Señor* Maldonado," he announced, "as I suppose that you have guessed . . . and you are Francisco Moreño?"

The first shock of the little man's surprise was quite swallowed by this second blow.

"Is it possible," he said, "that you can know me, *Señor* Maldonado? Is it possible?"

"My dear *Señor* Moreño," Juan Oro said with a certain condescending affability that he had noticed before in the rich and the fashionable, "how could I help but know you? All Mexico knows you, *señor,* as well as they know *Señor* Fontana. It is known that you are his right hand."

Señor Moreño choked. The thrill of his flattered vanity clouded his eyes. Instead of seeing in the handsome youth before him a possible pretender, he was blinded by self-esteem and began to tell himself that this man was, indeed, both polite and penetrating. In fact, he was probably a man worthy of being the heir to the millions of the *Señor* Fontana.

He heard the names of the companions of Maldonado. He acknowledged these introductions with little jerky bows that were hardly more than nods and clutches of his hand, like the gripping claw of a bird, cold and hard. He summoned servants by striking his hands together, and at once there appeared a whole myriad of them — enough to take charge of all the baggage, all the horses, all the mules, and, besides, a specially assigned body servant for each of the guests.

They were brought into the house, and Moreño carried his explanations with him. He was covered with mortification and regret, he declared, because the *Señor* Fontana had not expected his guests so soon. He had not believed that they would arrive, indeed, until the dusk of the day, they were riding so far in two long marches. Therefore, he was taking a short *siesta*. He, Francisco Moreño, would have hastened to waken his master, of course, were it not that unfortunately sleep was the greatest necessity of the *Señor* Fontana in the present failing state of his health, and, therefore, the doctor's order was that the great man should never be disturbed — with an alarm for fire, even, so long as he could sleep. Would *Señor* Maldonado understand?

Señor Maldonado would understand. In the meantime, Moreño begged them to retire to their rooms, discover if there was anything that could be added for their comfort, and instantly make him happy by letting him know. If they cared to bathe and rest after the ardors of the journey, the *Señor* Fontana would soon be awakened.

Of course, Juan saw through the little scene of diplomacy. *Señor* Fontana wished to be apprised of the character of his guests before he met them face to face, and, therefore, the eagle had sent the hawk before him to observe before his coming. They were led to their chambers, and the secretary, of course, fled instantly to the rooms of his master.

He found the don languidly enjoying the gentle warmth of the late afternoon on the roof garden that opened from his private suite. There, reclining on a couch beneath a vine-wreathed pergola, he listened to the play of the wind in the leaves and the delicious showering of a fountain that rose and fell with a pulsing rhythm in the center of the garden spot.

Francisco Moreño, before he entered, abated his excitement and his haste, so that he was able to go calmly before the great don with his report. He stood quietly in the heat of the sun, waiting for *Señor* Fontana to open his closed eyes — eyes which, he knew, had been purposely closed to annoy him, Moreño, when the great man heard his coming step.

At length *Señor* Fontana looked up. "So, Moreño," he said, "you have come at last? And they are here? I have slept," he added with a sigh of weariness.

"That is a great mercy, *señor*," murmured the solicitous Moreño, and he brought into his eyes his most affectionate and humble glance. Behind that simulated light he detested his master with all his soul. But when one has spent years in frightful servitude, one does not throw them away with a single gesture; instead, one controls one's thoughts and waits. Perhaps only a few years more, and then death would come to the don. And when that death came, surely it would be strange if Moreño were not remembered in the will of the rich man. "That is a great mercy," Moreño said. "I trust it has refreshed you."

"My body, yes," said *Señor* Fontana. "My soul . . . no! And to a man like me, what is repose of the body, when the soul still suffers? In a dreary and a barren world, Moreño, the mind still lives when the body sleeps. Ah, will the mind still live when the body is dead?"

"Assuredly," said the ready Moreño.

The don simulated a yawn. He stretched forth his pale hand and plucked a leaf from the climbing vine. "Ah, well," he said, "the end will come, one day."

"May many, many years lie between us and that dreadful day."

"You are kind," said the rich man dryly. "But now, Francisco, you may speak of them." He settled himself among the cushions and with a wave of his hand gave a second permission.

"I have seen them all," Moreño relayed. "There are not five, but four."

"And what has become of the fifth man? I hope it is not Maldonado, certainly."

"Certainly not he. I was not told why only four arrived, when five were expected."

"Well? Begin with the companions. We read the master by his men."

Moreño cleared his throat.

"You may speak frankly," said *Señor* Fontana, with a flashing side glance.

"In that case," the secretary said readily, "I can only say that they are strange men."

"You have said something and nothing."

"I mean, *señor*, that they are dressed properly in clothes that do not fit. Their clothes are entirely English . . . their air is entirely Mexican. They walked through the hall, gaping at what they saw around them."

"There is enough in the *Hacienda* Fontana, I hope," the master said coldly, "to make even men of culture stare."

"That is very true," said the secretary humbly.

"Continue, then."

"They were well-mounted. Since the *Señor* Maldonado chose to travel in this singular fashion, they were followed by ample packs. Though what is in the packs on the mules I cannot, of course, discover."

"That will be learned in time."

"In time, *señor*, yes. Neither was there time to learn what was in the minds of these companions of *Señor* Maldonado, but by the covers of the books, *señor*, I beg that you will pardon me if I guess that they contain rough reading."

"Rough reading?" echoed the don. "But in what would that interest me?"

"As you yourself have said . . . by the companions we judge of the master."

"Perhaps, perhaps! Is he like them, then? Rough like these followers, Francisco?"

Moreño sighed, so deep was his concentration upon this matter. *"Señor,"* he continued, "it has been my work to attempt to read men for your service and for mine. But in this case, the text is obscure. He is a very handsome man, *señor*. His voice is soft. . . ."

"A sign of culture," declared the don. "I detest a man with lungs of brass."

"But rather a natural than an acquired softness. His manner is graceful."

"Still better, for grace is more than a moral virtue. It will make even a fool agreeable."

"The grace, too, I should say, is nature, and not instruction."

"In short, Moreño, you do not approve of this man?"

"No, *señor*, merely that I do not understand him. There is more to him than what meets the ear or the eye. Of that I am sure."

"Would you prefer him shallow?"

"I thought that I had seen his face before."

"The face of every man with brains is a face that must seem to be familiar."

"He seems, for instance, far less than the twenty-five years which *Señor* Maldonado is said to have."

The don lifted his head and stared at the secretary. "Moreño," he said sharply, "do you suspect the *identity* of the man?"

"It is a great deal to say," murmured Moreño. "No, I cannot say it, *señor*. But my thoughts. . . ."

"Ah," sighed the don, sinking back among

his cushions once more, "how often must I tell you that, though you are my eyes and my ears, you cannot serve as my brains? Tell me what you see, what you know . . . but let me do the thinking, Francisco, if you please."

Chapter Thirty-One
The Don Is Impressed

The *Hacienda* Fontana was built after an eccentric pattern. The lower story was far larger than the upper and was still further extended by large, spacious verandahs whose roofs were upborne by ponderous colonnades, facing upon the great inner patio of the building. The upper story, although large, indeed, was still far from corresponding with the great dimensions of the lower, and the peripheral space around it was made up by a beautiful roof garden, part of which was enclosed in low walls for the privacy of *Señor* Fontana, but the rest of which ran completely around the building.

Here, in the cool, dim dusk of the day, the four from the band of Matiás Bordi took their places, lounging in comfortable chairs. They had discarded the riding clothes, and, now, as they waited for dinner and their presentation to the household, they wore dinner jackets after the habit which decorum in the house of Fontana prescribed.

Only Gregorio was at ease in these clothes. Cristóbal cursed at every turn the sharp edges of the collar that cut at his fat throat. Alonso groaned, for, when he looked down to survey the peculiar dignity of his new attire, his collar, in turn, choked off his wind. Juan Oro was like a splendid, sulky cat, scowling at them all and looking very grand.

"In a thing like this," he explained, "could a man bend or dodge or swerve from a flying knife, say? It is an invention of the devil, patronized by fools!" And he tapped the stiff bosom of his shirt sharply, so that it gave forth a hollow sound.

"You will manage well enough," said Gregorio, their tutor in polite etiquette, "and so will Alonso, if the blockhead will only stop craning his neck to look at himself. But Cristóbal is like a bear in a cage. He sweats with torture."

They were interrupted by a servant, bringing little glasses of water-colored tequila on a tray. They took them in turn, but Cristóbal called for the bottle himself.

"Look," he said to the *mozo*. "Is this drop of water enough to pour on a desert? And I am a desert, man. I am dry to the roots. Liquor has never reached to the bottom of me! Is this drop enough? No . . . you see!" He opened his mouth and tossed the contents of the glass into it. "Did you hear it hiss on the sand? Bring me the bottle, and I shall call you a friend."

"*Señor*," the fellow said, biting his lip to keep back the smile, "it shall be as you wish."

Gregorio fell heavily upon Cristóbal the instant that the servant was gone.

"You will betray us all!" groaned Gregorio. "Are you a mule, Cristóbal? Are you drinking muddy water and eating thistles on the desert? No, you are in the house of the Don José Fontana, and here one must take what is given and offered, not what is desired. More will be given, poor Cristóbal, than you have ever dreamed of before."

The servant here returned and placed the bottle at the elbow of Cristóbal. He had no sooner turned his back, while Cristóbal was in the act of pouring his drink, than the hand of Juan Oro darted out, seized upon the bottle, and cast it to the flagged floor of the roof, where it crashed into hundreds of pieces. The *mozo* came hurrying back at the very instant that Cristóbal, with a snarl, reached for a hidden knife. But the smile of Juan Oro was as ready as the hat of a beggar.

"Your hands are slippery, Cristóbal," he said, "and now it will be bad luck for you to drink before dinner. That is too bad. . . ."

There was nothing for Cristóbal to do except to sit back and swallow his wrath until the fragments were removed and the servant gone. Then, without a word, he whirled and leaped at the throat of Juan Oro. As well might he have leaped at a cat. Juan Oro slipped from his path and then laughed at him behind his back as he turned.

"Peace, Cristóbal," he commanded. "It was not to make a fight or spoil your drink, but because we need our own heads on our shoulders tonight. If you begin with tequila at this hour, you will be helpless to enjoy the good wines at dinner."

Cristóbal struck his hands together. "It is true!" he exclaimed. "I am a double fool to have forgotten. Ah, Juan, if I had made my tongue thick with this filth and missed the fragrance of the old clarets . . . how should I have forgiven myself, ever? I should have gone mad with sorrow and spite. Juan, you are my best of friends . . . but if you do such a thing to me again, I shall bury a knife in the hollow of your throat."

Juan Oro smiled down upon them all. "Dear friends," he said, "I am the man in the circus cage. I am among three great tigers. While my eye is upon them, all is well, but so soon as my back is turned, may not a great paw go out and tear me in two? However, I love the work, and will not give it up."

"At least not until we have our hands on some of the treasures of the house," said Gregorio.

"Or something worth more than gold?" suggested Juan.

"What may that be?"

"You must guess later. I cannot tell you."

The dusk had died away to thickest twilight, with the first stars beginning to come out like little yellow candles in the clouded west, and, looking down to the hollow through the tops of distant trees, they could see the double row of lights where the village stood, all its houses quite lost to view in the thickness of the evening mist of blue. And up and down the rooms that opened on the garden, the windows and the glass doors turned pale gold with radiance from within.

A dozen peons, returning late from the fields, were singing somewhere on the faint horizon of the ear — a sound no louder than a thought, one might say, but inexpressibly sweet. And then it was that they were asked to come down to meet the Fontana. Before they left the garden, Juan Oro gave them a last warning.

"Friends," he cautioned, "I have not told you that the little man with the pale eyes . . .

the secretary, Moreño . . . has seen my face before. It may be that on this day he recognized me. If so, we all are gone. There is no saving us. They will have called for the soldiers long ago. Or it may be that we are only under suspicion. In any case, one wrong step may ruin us all, for we are being watched, you may be sure. Cristóbal, I speak to you, above all. The wine may turn you into an old woman and make you talk. Now, let us go."

But Cristóbal took the warning lightly, and he was humming as they left the room and started down, for he was full of a thirsty joy. So they passed down the great, slowly turning stairway into the lofty hall beneath and so into a library, full of a hushed dignity, where the sound of steps disappeared on thick-napped rugs.

There rose to meet them the languid form of *Señor* Fontana. Near him, the stalwart American, Steven Marshal. And here was little Moreño to introduce them. Those introductions Juan overlooked with an anxious eye. He heard the voice of Cristóbal, far too loud in answer. He saw Gregorio take the hand of the great man in a grip that made him wince. He witnessed Alonso choke against his collar. But it was ended, at last, and he himself, having met and touched the hand of the don, turned to Steven Marshal.

There was no surprise on the face of the *gringo*. There was only a faintly discernible narrowing of the eyes as he repeated clearly: "*Señor* . . . Maldonado!"

But in the little swirl of talk that followed, Juan had a chance to say a few words to him.

"Juan," said the American, "what inexpressible deviltry are you up to now?"

"I only beg you to wait, *señor*, until the end."

"But my duty to the don. . . ."

"If I harm him," said Juan Oro, "by taking so much as the worth of a single *peso* above the cost of his food and his drink, call me a dog, and I shall smile."

"It is your word!"

"I have given you my word, *señor*."

"Very well," nodded Marshal. "It is quite enough."

But here the don drew Juan a little apart. "You have only one thought," he said. "I also was once young, and, therefore, I know. You have only an eye for *Señorita* Dorotea. But, *Señor* Maldonado, I must tell you that in seeing you, a strange picture has been brought to me."

"Of what?" murmured Juan.

"Of a small boy, half naked, with long,

copper-colored hair, skin brown as the skin of an Indian, torn to pieces with bullet wounds, but never letting a murmur of pain to escape him . . . what do you think of such a picture, *señor?*"

His eyes hung keenly upon the face of Juan Oro. As for the latter, with deliberate thought he ironed out from his features every trace of expression. It was a shrewd shock and a most unexpected one. But he was able to say: "Do you mean that I remind you of that boy, *señor?*"

"That, in fact, was my very thought."

"It is strange!"

"As strange, *señor,* as the lightness with which you bear your twenty-five years."

"Ah," sighed Juan, "it is the curse of my life. When I was twenty, I still looked like a boy of fifteen. I have tried to grow a mustache. But it made me look like a child with something pasted on my upper lip." And he laughed with such perfect good nature that most of the sudden cloud disappeared from the brow of the don. "But," Juan continued, "is it not possible that the *Señorita* Dorotea will consider me a child, also?"

"She has come to answer for herself," answered *Señor* Fontana. "Here is Dorotea."

Chapter Thirty-Two

Cristóbal, a Great Man

But, for that matter, Juan Oro could have guessed that it was she. From the corner of his eye he saw Alonso, now talking with Steven Marshal, straighten and stiffen, and Marshal himself changed as though a light had been kindled behind his eyes. He turned, and there she was.

"Look, look," muttered Juan Oro to his host, while the wild-faced Cristóbal was taking the hand of the smiling girl. "It is a frightful thing to mark Oñate among civilized people. And the rest . . . they are all rough . . . all very rough, *señor.*"

"I have not noticed," smiled the don appreciatively. "But is your country so wild, *señor?*"

"As quiet, as gentle as anything I have seen in Mexico, except the old trees and the green lawns of the *Hacienda* Fontana," answered Juan. "But my father loved stern, strong men. And when he left me his lands, he left me the men who were living on them.

They were attached to him, as knights were attached to kings, *señor*. And if I had ridden on this journey without them, they would have been cut to the quick. You will remember that I said that I was coming with four men?"

"I remember your letter."

"But I found that, if I took the fourth man, I should offend two others who felt that they had an equal right with him. So I brought only the three."

"Yours is a feudal state, Maldonado," said the great man. And he smiled with just the necessary touch of superiority. And Juan Oro laughed back at him quite frankly, as though he admitted that the whole thing was very ridiculous. On the whole, the don approved of this man. There was something bright, cheerful, gallant about him, and he seemed to have a talent for laughing at himself and yet taking *Señor* Fontana very seriously. All of this was intensely pleasing to the great man.

There was time for only this one flash of conversation before the girl stood before Juan Oro, and he was bowing to her, while *Señor* Fontana was murmuring the introduction. She was as cold as ice. Her smile was gone almost as soon as it came.

She said: "As the time drew nearer and

299

nearer, I was afraid that I should not have the pleasure of seeing my husband before the wedding day."

"Dorotea!" her uncle said sharply.

"Ah, *señor,*" broke in Juan Oro, deftly intervening between her and the wrath of her uncle, "I see at once that we are to make a happy family."

"And how is that?" asked *Señor* Fontana, smiling in spite of himself.

"A thousand pardons to *Señorita* Dorotea," said Juan, "but it is a secret that I can give to your ear only."

Yonder, a domestic bowed in the doorway.

"It is dinner," said the don, and, giving his arm to Dorotea, he led the way toward the dining room.

He murmured as they went: "What do you think of this husband of yours, Dorotea?"

"*Señor,*" said the girl, "I have never seen such assurance."

Señor Fontana rubbed his hands together with a singularly vicious enjoyment. "At least," he said, "you will not lead a dull life in your first year. Am I not right?"

"You have read my mind," said Dorotea.

But when she sat at the right of the don at the table, with Juan Oro opposite her, she found it hard to keep the cloud on her brow. She had determined in the first instant that out of this marriage, if she gained nothing else, she should at least secure the upper hand, and she had decided to waste no time but start establishing her supremacy from the first moment. But Juan Oro was like a happy boy, bearing no malice against anyone. Besides, the gallant Alonso was at her elbow, maintaining the burden of what was to him a most polite conversation, and farther down the table it was wonderful to see the execution which the worthy Cristóbal was making in the wine drinking.

The don was drawing out Maldonado to speak of his estate and of his people. He received only light answers.

"Ah, *Señor* Fontana," Juan said at last, "why should you ask me to speak of an old life after it is dead? And today it died."

The don laughed. Everything about this youth pleased him. He reverted to a thought that had come to him once before on that evening. It was of a copper-haired youngster, handsome as a young god, wild as a young tiger, who had been brought in from the Yaquis years ago. But the same note may be struck in two different songs.

"Are you a hunter?" the don asked.

"All the days of my life," Juan replied.

"How long is it since I have sat in a saddle? Ten months at least. But I shall have to try the stirrups again. With you, my dear Don Pedro, I feel my spirits rise. I feel them rise. You have stolen some years from my shoulders. Tomorrow, my friend, we will ride out and find what we can find, we two."

He looked about him with a brighter eye and then, suddenly, down to his plate in disgust. The chief interest of the *Señor* Fontana, for some years, had been his own failing health, and because of the attention which he paid to it, of course, it had been failing all the more rapidly — at least, in his own estimation. There are always doctors who will find an illness to fit the mental requirements of everyone. So it had been with the don. He had been limited to one small dish of meat in a day, water or milk for a beverage, rice and bread for his staple. So, in his great house, with his millions, he lived like an anchorite. But now, as he saw Juan Oro assail a liberal portion of roasted pheasant, a sudden appetite came to the don. He looked down to his naked plate, as has been said, in disgust and called for meat. It was smoking before him in a twinkling. And with the first mouthful of the game the limpid glass of water at his hand sent a shudder through him.

"Is there no wine?" he demanded. "I remember some Château Yquem that I imported myself eleven years ago. Let a bottle be brought. Pheasant and water is sacrilege! Let a bottle be brought!"

It was brought with the speed of light. Gently borne upon a basket, lying tilted upon its side, the musty bottle was first exhibited to him, and then a dark crimson stream filled his glass. He tilted, tasted, and then swallowed half the glass. The very fragrance of it intoxicated the don.

"My dear uncle!" exclaimed Dorotea. "What would the doctor say to that?"

"The devil, who is the patron of doctors," said the don, "fly away with the doctor and all his tribe. I feel that I have raised myself halfway from the tomb already. The beauty of the old years rolls back upon me. Look yonder at that Oñate, staring at the claret. Bring more bottles. This is not a hermit's meal. Fill the glass of Oñate. I shall drink to the rascal and his wicked eye."

A whisper of wonder, lighter than the stir that a moth's wings makes in a silent room, passed through the chamber — no more, let us say, than the rapid interchange of glances among the servants who, all in their proper liveries, stood in the shadows near the wall.

"To you, *Señor* Oñate!" toasted the don.

303

"Señor!" Cristóbal chimed in a vibrant voice, and drained his goblet at a draft.

"I see," chuckled the don, "that yonder Oñate is a man of might. He must remain here with you, Maldonado. You must not let him escape from us back to your dreary north country. For I have cellars where he can wander farther in ten minutes, I dare say, than he has ever traveled in all his life. What, Oñate? You shall walk through my cellars and transport yourself to Spain, to Italy, to Portugal, to Austria, to the Médoc, to the Rhine . . . you shall fly from land to land, as the bottled sunshine of each passes your lips!"

"Ah, *señor*," grinned Cristóbal, "the Church frowns upon magic, but I shall let you touch me with your wand." He turned in his chair. "Hither, donkey!" he said to one of the domestics. "Stand behind my chair and watch my glass. If it grows empty. . . ." Here his eye acknowledged the sharp challenge of the glance of Juan Oro, and he paused.

"Let him be, Don Pedro," the don broke in. "Everything that I hear and see from you and your men delights me. Let him ask for what he will, and let him have it."

Here the rosy lips of Dorotea parted as she framed to Juan the words: "How have you done this to my uncle?"

He merely smiled back upon her.

"But you, Pedro," cried the don, "have not touched your glass. What is wrong?"

"I am bewitched." Juan Oro smiled charmingly.

It was the merriest dinner that could be remembered within the *Hacienda* Fontana.

"You are not the only one who is bewitched," the don confirmed, with a side glance at the handsome Alonso. "See *Señor* Alonso. Is it not true? He is like a man with a fever."

But, when Dorotea had withdrawn, wine had not so utterly beclouded the memory of the don that he did not ask: "What was the assurance, Maldonado, that made you know you would find happiness with Dorotea?"

"There is a saying in our house," answered Juan, "that it is a poor horse which does not need the curb."

The don leaned back in his chair with his laughter. "Ah, well," he said, "*Señor* Marshal has sat for an hour without a single smile. And yet he has drunk as much as the rest of us. That is your American . . . he grows sad as he drinks."

He turned to Cristóbal. "Do you hear me, Oñate?"

"I would rise from the grave at your voice,

señor," vowed Cristóbal, still grinning broadly.

"There is a tale that my father told me, of his uncle, Don Fernando. The good man was a mighty drinker in his day. Bring the Valencia goblet!" ordered the don.

A priceless flagon of silver, worked with gold and brilliant at the handle with gems, was laid before the *señor*. He raised it and turned it in the soft lamplight.

"Look, my dear friends, at this goblet. A whole bottle of wine may be poured into it. But I tell you, and there was an oath sworn to make it good, that Don Fernando is said to have drained that flagon at one draft . . . one mighty draft and in twelve seconds' time!"

He struck his hand lightly upon the table to emphasize his point. Whereat Cristóbal struck the table with his balled fist so that there was given back to him a musical shivering of glass as it stirred on the polished wood.

"As for me," Cristóbal said, "if I could not drink with any man that ever walked under the stars, may I turn into a horse and eat hay! *Señor* Fontana, I defy your ancestor. I defy Don Fernando!"

"His ghost" — smiled the don — "will grow angry at the very thought. However . . .

since the goblet is here, and since my watch is in my hand . . . fill for *Señor* Oñate!"

The great flagon was, accordingly, filled to the very brim with rich old claret and presented to Oñate. He rose to perform the feat and held up the mighty cup by both its handles.

"I drink," he said, already a little fumbling in his talk from his recent potations, "to the *señor,* and to every man who has ever ridden with me under the stars . . . to take purses!"

A twisting thrill of cold went through the blood of Juan Oro, but the don had merely tilted back his head and roared with appreciative laughter. Indeed, this foolish, cheerful dinner seemed to have turned back the clock of his life and changed him completely into a hearty man.

"Drink!" echoed the don.

Forthwith the cup tilted, the lights flashing on the polished silver, and the head of Cristóbal went back and farther back. The whole body of the man swayed a little and, in rhythm, the bottom of the cup bobbed up and down, slowly. And so, staggering back, he turned the cup upside down and clapped his mouth upon the top of the table — and only a feeble trickle of crimson ran from it — he had drained it quite dry. Now, gasping, laughing through his wine-

307

stained lips, he shouted: "The time, *señor?*"

"By heaven and earth!" cried the don. "This is a great man, for he has drunk the cup in ten short seconds!"

Chapter Thirty-Three

<u>Inviting Disaster</u>

For Cristóbal, all that followed during that evening was obscured by a rosy haze; it was not wine alone, for the strength of his head and the capacity of his stomach were a miracle. But the special favor which was shown to him by *Señor* Fontana made him fairly giddy. It made him feel as if the entire world were wonderful.

How well was it for Cristóbal, then, that he did not overhear the conversation between Steven Marshal and *Señor* Fontana himself, as they sat withdrawn to a corner of the library, through the door of which they could look into the music room and there see Dorotea seated at the piano, accompanying the ex-barber, Gregorio, as he sang. There was the relic of a voice in Gregorio, and he had had enough of wine to make him feel that better than his palmiest days had come back to him. Now he sang with infinite feeling, with operatic gestures, passing up and down beside the piano more like a duelist in pantomime than a singer, while his voice swelled huge in volume, but frightfully flat, frightfully rough.

To one other than himself it was the sweetest music — and that was Cristóbal, who rose after every song and swore that this was music fit for the gods and that he would pistol whip any man who dared to deny it. Yes, he would pistol whip Gregorio himself, if that music did not continue.

Señor Fontana sat at his ease and smiled upon the scene from the distance, and clapped a polite applause and nodded and waved Dorotea on, when she turned toward him on the piano bench at the conclusion of each maudlin song.

"What does it all mean?" asked *Señor* Fontana. "You, Don Steven, are a cold-blooded fellow without much warmth to cloud your eyes. To you we are all a little ridiculous . . . except Dorotea and her pretty face."

"*¡Señor!*"

"Well, you are polite. However, tell me what you make of this Maldonado and his men?"

To this question thus put point-blank Marshal hardly knew what answer to make. A score of times he had cursed Juan Oro for the very confidence which that rascal had placed in him, for he felt that it was his duty to his host to protect him, but his promise bound him. Yet he feared that before the evening was ended, there might be some serious result.

"They are, indeed, a rather rough lot, those three friends of Maldonado," he admitted.

"Rough?" chuckled *Señor* Fontana. "My poor Moreño is in an agony. He has never seen such behavior in the *Hacienda* Fontana. That Oñate is very well. Wine will make a fool of any man. But d'Arragon sings like a wild bull. And there is Gonzales, turning the music for Dorotea and ogling her like a sick calf. I begin to be suspicious."

"Of what, *señor?*"

"I cannot say. A ridiculous thought has come into my mind. I cannot utter it. But I could wish that I knew Maldonado better. I have never seen him before this evening, as you know."

"Do you wish that I should talk with him and learn what I can?"

"An excellent idea. But tell me, Don Steven . . . is he a gentleman?"

"He seems at ease," said Marshal, avoiding the question as well as he could by this half answer.

"A tiger is at ease, also," countered Don

José. "Behind the bars of a cage, even, it is at ease."

"A tiger?" Marshal said, wondering at such penetration in such an indolent mind. "He seems a very gentle young man."

"Does he seem so to you? You do not know the Mexicans. This Maldonado is what I tell you, be sure. Go talk with him, Marshal. I'll bring the others into the garden. The moon is out, and that shall be my excuse. But I cannot endure any more of these bawling songs! I would rather listen to a roundup!"

So Steven Marshal found Juan Oro in a corner of the next room and opened his mind to him at once.

"This joke," he said, "has been a very clever one, Juan. But it has gone far enough. *Señor* Fontana himself has grown suspicious, and he is sending me to find out what I can about you. The devil take you, Juan, for making me your confidant."

Juan Oro looked upon him without emotion, but smiled slowly, so that his even, white teeth glinted in the lamplight.

"What is wrong?" he asked. "What is wrong with me and with my friends?"

"If it were you alone, I think that there would be no questions. He likes you. But the other three. . . ."

"Well? It is the drinking of Cristóbal?"

"It is only partly that, but the ogling idiot beside the *señorita*. . . ."

"I shall put a knife between his ribs before the night is an hour older," Juan said calmly.

Señor Fontana was now breaking up the musical party and carrying everyone with him into the garden.

"And the singing of that ass, Gonzales."

"I shall gag him. The fool sings like a braying mule on a mountain top. He would drown a waterfall. However, they have done me a mischief, do you say?"

"A very great one, and it may turn out to be even greater than I think. There is no telling what our friend, Don José, may do. We have taken him for a fool. Tonight he seems to have wakened, and he uses the wits of a man."

"Keep Don José with you," said Juan Oro.

"Do you mean, Juan, that you are not leaving, secretly, as soon as possible?"

"Is it so dangerous to stay?"

"Within five minutes Don José can draw five hundred armed men around the house! I have seen him do it merely for his amusement."

"Five hundred armed scarecrows!" Juan scoffed. "I still have not talked with the girl."

"What of that?"

"I do not know whether to hate her or to adore her. I must find out."

Marshal brooded over him with a deep wonder. "Tell me this," he urged. "You have lived among rough fellows all your life. How have you learned the ways of a polite household?"

"I was a prisoner in this same house. I watched them, then. And I have been in many places since. A man has his eyes, Don Steven."

"But you have had no opportunity for schooling. . . ."

"Why, what do you suppose that I have done with my time when the winter evenings were at their longest? When the others played dice until they were ready to cut the throats of one another? I was not fool enough to do that. And I had books to kill the time . . . plenty of books, always. I keep them in my saddlebags. Can a man lie under a tree for three hours and count the leaves? Or go mad waiting? I, at least, could not. So I have read as much as the next man . . . but studied nothing. This is the whole truth about me. But because I talk easily of many things, it does not mean that I have gained an education."

"Perhaps more than you think." Marshal

nodded. "Schoolteachers are as great a curse as a blessing. But listen to me, Juan. Your very life is now in danger in this house. I admit your courage. I admit that it has been enough. But, you must go!"

"Not if there were ten guns pointed at me. I have not had the prize of the game, yet. I must talk with her alone."

"Then go at once and find her in the garden. Manage to draw her aside, if you can. But it is really madness, Juan."

Juan Oro dropped a light hand upon the shoulder of his friend. "If you, Don Steven, had a hope, would you not risk for her as much as I am risking now?"

Steven Marshal pondered that question, biting his lip. Then he shrugged his heavy shoulders. "I cannot say, no, honestly. Go on, then, and take your chance. The devil be kind to you. But I expect to see you swinging by the neck from the gallows in the morning."

"I have had the same thought," Juan Oro said, fingering his throat thoughtfully. "However, this is worth the risk. Do you wish me good fortune?"

"With all my heart."

"*Adiós,* then!"

But he paused in front of the mirror to straighten his tie, smooth his hair, and dust the sleeves of his coat, all the time turning restlessly and viewing himself from many angles.

"If there is moon enough for her to see me clearly," Juan Oro said, "she should be half won, before I so much as speak. Should she not, Don Steven?"

"You vain scoundrel," grinned Marshal. "She will laugh in your handsome face!"

Chapter Thirty-Four

Juan Exacts a Promise

He found Dorotea walking a little apart from the others with the handsome Alonso Gonzales, while Gregorio was insisting, in the distance, on entertaining Don José with another song, even unaccompanied. Alonso favored his friend with a stare as fierce as the stare of a bull, but there was nothing left for him except to retreat, and Juan Oro found himself alone, at last, with the lady.

He had planned half a dozen ways of opening the conversation, but now he saw that none of them would do. She was too keen not to detect the rehearsal of a planned speech, and nothing could have made him submit to becoming ridiculous in her eyes. So a pause came between them.

"Well," she said at last, "after so much thought I expect a brilliant thing from you, *Señor* Maldonado."

"I am not thinking," Juan said.

"What *are* you doing, then?"

"I was watching the leaves of those two

317

little palm trees weave together behind you. I was listening to the showering of the fountain and seeing the moonshine blow away in sprays on it. I was listening to the singing from the village, too."

"I cannot hear that."

"Look down to the ground and bow your head a little," he suggested. "Then you will no longer hear the wind itself, but the things which are *in* the wind."

She made the experiment, and then nodded. "That is odd. I *did* hear it! How did you come to learn such a thing?"

"An Indian taught me."

Here a *mozo* came softly up behind her and gave her an envelope, and she, excusing herself, opened it. Juan Oro saw her start a little as she finished reading the note. And then, in haste, she attempted to put it away, but her very haste made her touch unsure. The paper fell, was caught on a current of wind, and floated to his feet. He picked it up and his eye read it all from end to end, for the message was merely this, scrawled in a great, bold hand: **Beware of Maldonado. He is not what he seems.**

What he read did not keep him from returning the paper to her with a bow. After all, the damage had been done already, but he was glad that he had been able to recognize the hand of Alonso. Surely that scoundrel would have to pay for this!

She said suddenly, with the note still in her hand: "You read it?"

"I could not help it," he admitted.

"Why do you not flee, then," said the girl, "while there is time, perhaps, to get away?"

"Why should I flee, *Señorita* Dorotea?"

"Because I guessed long ago what the note says. It merely confirms me. If I give the word . . . what would become of you?"

"They would hang me, of course."

"Have you no fear, then?"

"None, of course."

"Why do you say that?"

"You will not have me hanged, *señorita,* until you know more about me. There is as much curiosity as that in you, surely."

The girl drew a breath — whether of horror or surprise or indignation he could not tell. But then she sat down on the broad, stone bench beneath the palms and pointed to the place beside her.

"Sit down with me," Dorotea requested. "I *am* curious. I shall never meet another like you, I think."

He took the place beside her.

"First, who are you?"

"My name is Juan Oro."

"Ah? Ah? You are Matiás Bordi's lieutenant! You are that terrible young man! Let me look at you again."

He faced into the moon a little so that the light would fall more strongly on his face.

"Juan Oro, Juan Oro," she murmured to herself. "But he is a robber and. . . ."

"Murderer?" suggested Juan.

"They tell frightful stories about you."

"I have taken lives. But man to man in fight, *señorita*. That is not such a great crime. Besides, the odds were against me. They fought for their lives. I fought for their purses."

She gasped. "Do you admit it? Have you absolutely no conscience, Juan Oro?"

"Have you, *señorita*?"

"I?"

"I," he said pointedly, "take only the purses from men."

"I do not understand," she said, but she began to blush in a way which told him that she understood well enough.

She broke in: "First, what has happened to poor Pedro Maldonado, and to his men? Ah, you have not murdered them!"

"They are sitting in the mountains with their hands tied together . . . their right hands, which leaves their left hands free to smoke and to eat. They are not uncomfortable."

"If word comes to them that you, Juan Oro, are hanged by the law?"

"My friends, of course, will hang up Maldonado and the rest. No, they might burn them . . . as a protest, *señorita!*"

"Merciful heaven! Ah, poor Pedro Maldonado!"

"Is he worthy of pity?"

"Being in danger of such a frightful death?"

"Consider, dear *señorita,* that, if I had been he, no robbers could ever have stopped me on my way to you. Unless they killed me first, do you see? But Maldonado and all his men were taken without a scratch. There was not a gun fired, not a knife raised."

"Why did you do it?"

"For the sake of plunder, of course. He is worth a lot of money, that Maldonado."

"And then, like a madman, you came here?"

"For I said to myself . . . 'What a sad thing that the lovely Lady Dorotea should sit in the *Hacienda* Fontana, waiting for a lover, and have this foolish thing . . . this Maldonado . . . come to her? But I, Juan Oro, who am a man, will go to her.' And here, *señorita,* I am."

"My brain whirls," murmured the girl. "You have ridden here with your men and put your necks inside the noose for the sake. . . ."

"For your sake, Dorotea."

"This is a thing out of a book," breathed the girl. "It is impossible."

"But it is done."

"And why?"

"I came, *señorita,* to see if you were not worth saving from such a man, and I have seen enough. You cannot have him, *señorita.*"

"Tell me, then, how you would stop it."

"I shall ride back to Maldonado and free his hands and put him thirty yards from me with a gun in his holster. Then we will decide the question of whether he is to live and have you or die and be buried in the mountains."

"Have we not heard that even Matiás Bordi fears you? It would be murder and no fight, if you stood against Maldonado."

"That, of course, is in your hands."

"Then what am I to do?"

"Look around you, *señorita.* And, if you can find a real man, take him and thank God for him . . . but I shall have your oath, before I go, that you will not choose Maldonado."

"This is a very foolish thing," said the girl gravely. "Do you dictate your terms to me, when I can destroy you with only a word, *señor?*"

"It would be a frightful matter," Juan said, "if that word were given. Yonder in the trees . . . no, perhaps, he is already in the house . . . Matías Bordi and his men are waiting. If that word is given, they will try to cut their way to me. Men will fall by tens and twenties before I am taken. And, even then, they cannot be sure that the noose will have my neck in the end. But, besides that, I know that you will never betray me."

"How can you be sure of that?"

"Because you are brave, and you are generous, *señorita*. Oh, I feel that I am quite safe in your hands. And now the promise?"

"This is a thing not to be believed," said the girl. "But you are right, Juan. And when I see that you have done this thing for me, it makes me see myself with new eyes. What right have I to throw myself away to an unknown man who may be, as you say, not worthy of the name of a man? Juan Oro, I shall give you that promise. I shall not marry *Señor* Maldonado. Not if Don José should cut me off without a penny and give his estate to charity. Not even then! When I marry, it shall be to a man. And now, unless you are a madman, indeed, be up and away. They suspect you already. This warning has been given to me I know not from whom. Do not stay and tempt danger, Juan."

"*Adiós,* then, *señorita.*"

"Farewell, Juan Oro."

He found Steven Marshal at once.

"Well, my fine madman," said Marshal, "what has been done now? I have not seen the lady made ridiculous as yet."

"She never will be," Juan stated. "I came here thinking that I should see a foolish girl, but she is a woman, Don Steven, and she is worthy of you. And now, my dear friend, I have wiped the Maldonado out of her life."

"The devil! Juan, if she breaks off this match that Don José has made for her, he will disinherit her!"

"You, Don Steven, would you care less for her on that account?"

"I wish," said the American heartily, "that Don José's millions were at the bottom of the sea!"

"Then go to her, now. Quickly, Don Steven. For she is full of romance. Go to her and take her in your arms. She will tell you that she will be your wife. And her word is sacred to her. That I know. *¡Adiós!*"

"You are leaving now, Juan?"

"At once."

"Listen to me, lad," said the big man with emotion, "Sombra is in the little paddock at the eastern end of the stables. Take him, saddle him, and be off with him. He is yours, if you have done this miracle with the girl. Are you paid, Juan?"

"Paid?" cried Juan, lifting his head and laughing. "Once on Sombra, they may as well chase a thunderbolt. *Adiós* again, *amigo!*"

Chapter Thirty-Five

Alonso — Traitor

Lurking behind the shrubbery of the garden while the *mozo* delivered his note to the girl, Alonso had seen it fall at the feet of Juan Oro, seen him lift it, heard him admit that he had read it. Like a sensible man, what Alonso did first was to reach for his revolver where it dangled under his armpit. But, afterward, he changed his mind. The moon was too bright on this night, and the horses of the *Hacienda* Fontana were too fast. If he were suspected and pursued, his chances of escape would be very small, indeed.

Yet he knew that the problem before him was the very height of simplicity. Either he must kill Juan Oro, or Juan Oro would kill him. The foolish jealousy concerning Dorotea passed out of his mind at once. Still, there remained the real fear of what would happen, if he were called upon, eventually, to stand face to face with Juan Oro. He knew well enough that in this case his chance would be one in ten. He must tie the

326

hands of Juan. He saw before him a sure means of accomplishing that end, even though there was danger in it to himself.

If it were a selfish and a cruel means, it should not be taken for granted that Alonso was a cruel and a selfish man more than others. Rather, he was an eminently logical fellow, except where women were concerned. And now that fear of Juan had driven the very thought of women from his mind, he was prepared to be as logical as ever in his life. As to what his own future was to be, if he succeeded in this affair, he paid no heed. What was important was that he must brush Juan Oro out of existence, and to that end he started moving at once.

Don José had been losing enthusiasm for these rough guests of his and had withdrawn from the merriment, leaving the poor secretary, Francisco Moreño, to take the brunt of the affair. At the moment of the don's withdrawal, the clever Alonso drew him to the side. They stepped into as secret a place as even Alonso could have wished. That is to say, they stood in an alcove of the garden close to the wall of the house, and through the branches of the shrubbery they could look forth through two small loopholes, as it were, upon the separate groups of Cristóbal, Juan Oro, and the rest, on the one hand, and

Steven Marshal and Dorotea on the other hand. But what they saw mattered nothing to him. What he wanted was to have covert while he confessed to the don.

"There is something you wish, *señor?*" murmured the don wearily.

"There is a thing on my conscience," Alonso said instantly.

"A man's conscience," said Don José, "is about the only really private property that he possesses. I hope you will keep yours well guarded, *Señor* Gonzales."

"That is good advice," said Alonso, "but it happens that this affair of my conscience has to do with throat-cutting."

"In the name of heaven, man!" exclaimed the other. "Do you wish me to know what throats you intend cutting?"

"It is not I, but others."

"If they have opened their hearts to you, the greater fools they. And there is an answer, *señor.*"

"A satisfactory answer . . . except that it will cost certain lives."

"And what have I to do with those lives?"

"I could not tell, Don José, that you are so ready for death."

At this touch of the spur the don started and came a little closer to the other.

"Have you arranged some manner of

jest?" he asked sharply. "Or are you serious?"

"Serious enough, *señor,* to put myself in danger from the two most formidable men in Mexico for the sake of warning you."

"So? So?" murmured the don. "Is it possible? However, I have enough means to requite good services, as you know. But who are the two men?"

"Matiás Bordi. . . ."

"Name of heaven, there is an old thorn in my side. Matiás Bordi, and who is the other?"

"Juan Oro."

"That man I have never seen, but I understand that he is more dreadful then Bordi himself, if that is possible. It is said that it was he who arranged that foolish and wonderful escape of his chief through the herd of cattle. Is it true?"

"It is true."

"And I am in danger from both these devils?"

"You are, *señor.*"

Don José grew pale and trembled. "*Señor* Gonzales," he said, "I begin to foresee that I shall be under a great debt to you. Tell me what you know, and very quickly. First, how you came to know this thing and only reveal it now?"

"Because, *señor,* Gonzales is not my name."

"Well?"

"I myself have been one of Bordi's men."

The don stared helplessly, as though this were a puzzle beyond his power to solve. But he said at last: "You are one of Bordi's men? And you know Bordi, then, and Juan Oro, also?"

"You know them, too, *señor.*"

"I have never seen the second man. Never!"

"Look again. There he stands." And he pointed to Juan Oro, standing by a garden table, waving his hand with the moon turning the smoke of his cigarette to a silver wreath.

"Ten thousand devils," breathed Don José, shrinking away. "I have been fairly touching elbows with death all evening. *Señor,* what is the plan? Quickly!"

"To loot the house and cut every throat in it at midnight," improvised Alonso freely.

"Ah, the demons!"

"They are, *señor.* I was one among them. But when I saw you, tasted your food, drank your wine, and found such kindness in you, my heart relented."

"This is a golden night for you, my friend. This moment you are rich."

"And a dead man, *señor!*"

"Do you say so? No, I shall find means to send you safely out of the country and you shall enjoy your income in Spain . . . in France . . . wherever you choose."

"Don José, you overwhelm me."

"But if this is Juan Oro, what has become of Maldonado? Is he in the plot?"

"He is tied hand and foot in the mountains."

"I see it. I see it. Ah, a very cunning trick. Juan Oro is inside my house . . . Matiás Bordi waits on the outside for a midnight signal?"

"That is the plan, as I understand it."

Don José began to breathe more freely. He even rubbed his hands together in a pleasant expectation. "I have been too kind to this Bordi," he said. "I have pensioned him and given him a house on my lands. I have treated him like a son. But nothing would serve him, except to steal into my house and cut my throat and plunder me by night. Well, friend, perhaps we have time to turn about. What if I sent out a careful warning to my men . . . what if I gather them secretly, and have them set about the house . . . ?"

"It should be done at once, *señor!* At this moment, perhaps, they may be planning some devilishness. Only, *Señor* Fontana, I beg you to put me in some safe place until the danger is over. I am not yet known as a friend or a foe to either side. The guns of both are apt to be aimed at me."

"You shall be as safe as I. Have no fear of that. Ah, the devils! If only I may take Bordi alive, and Juan Oro alive. That would be a thing. They would have reason to remember me before they were turned over to the officers of the law. But all things are possible, if we are swift and secret. Come with me, through this door . . . quickly . . . ah, damnation!"

In the very act of turning, Don José hissed out the last word and pointed with a stiffened arm. The discreet Alonso, staring in the indicated direction, saw through the narrow cleft in the foliage a pleasant picture of the Lady Dorotea dissolved in the big arms of Steven Marshal, and looking up with a smile of dreamy happiness into the face of the *gringo*.

As for Don José, he seemed in such a frightful passion that at first Alonso feared that the rich man would rush out upon the pair. He even went so far as to put a restraining hand upon the shoulder of the don and whisper at his ear: "A single hand and a knife will cure that evil, *señor*."

"He, too, is a thief in my house," breathed

the don. "But she, the fool . . . she shall be disinherited. This moment she is a beggar on the face of the earth. She is stripped of millions at this instant. Yes, I swear to the blessed saints, she is beggared."

"Hush, *señor*, for your voice is raised, and they may hear."

Don José leaned a hand against the wall of the house and passed the other swiftly over his face.

"There is the other work first," said Alonso. "As for the second task, if the *señor* will trust to my hand, then I think that. . . ."

"You, my friend, have been sent to me by the Almighty. Yes, there will be work for you. If you have been trained by Bordi, you are capable of certain work that I shall need. The *gringo* must die! But now come with me."

He led the other hastily in from his garden. They were closeted in a small chamber off the library, and there the don caught up paper and ink and dashed off a few lines on a sheet of paper, signing his name at the end.

"Take this to the village . . . swiftly, swiftly. Take it to the largest house. Take it to the house at the northern end of the street . . . do you understand? Ask for Fernando Guadal. . . ."

"I know his face."

"That is excellent. I have given him his orders in brief. Repeat them to him by word of mouth and more at large. Tell him to come at once. He has forty men constantly with him, day and night. Tell him to gather twenty more. Divide them in four parts. Approach the *Hacienda* Fontana from four sides." He started up and cast open a door at one side of the cabinet. Blackness yawned through it, with a flight of steps dipping down into the dark. "Let Guadal himself come into the house through the cellar. He knows that way. He will find me here. Tell him that. Let him bring four or five of his best men. They shall stay here with me, armed to the teeth, do you hear me? They shall be my bodyguards. . . ."

"Consider, *señor*, that without me, they are only three. . . ."

"Only three! Only three fiends from hell. And any one of them all is capable of sending a bullet through my body . . . and ending me . . . Don José. Think of it, my friend. All the evening I have been in danger of my life. How frightful! Ah, you should have spoken sooner. Not five men, but ten, must enter this room to act as my guard, while Guadal captures the rest of the rascals. Do you hear me?"

"Yes, *señor*."

"Then away with you, and remember that, if all goes well, as I hope, tonight you are a rich man. Away with you at once."

"*Señor,* God bless you!"

"Bless me with the speed of your heels."

"I am gone."

"This way . . . down the cellar stairs . . . you will find a passage that leads straight ahead . . . it rises through a trap door beyond the garden wall . . . then down the hill road to the village. Quickly! Be swift, in the name of heaven. The life of Don José Fontana may hang upon a thread."

Alonso darted through the door and disappeared down the steps into the thick of the darkness beneath. The don listened to the sound of his disappearing steps. Then, with a shudder, he closed and locked the door. He turned to the two other heavy doors that enclosed the chamber. The locks of these he turned. They were secured, moreover, with heavy bolts, and these he thrust into place. And, finally, he sat down at the table and drew from the drawers of it two heavy revolvers. Thus equipped, he began his vigil.

Chapter Thirty-Six

A Mad Dash for Freedom

In the garden, the wine-delighted Cristóbal kept his companions amused with his antics and his ceaseless chatter, until Gregorio suddenly wondered where their comrade, the worthy Alonso, had disappeared. They looked. He did not appear. They searched, but they found only Steven Marshal, sitting most intimately close to the side of the *señorita* in the next little enclosure of the garden.

"The don, too, is not here," said Juan Oro. "And that, friends, I do not like at all."

"He is showing Alonso those wine vaults where he promised to let me browse," groaned Cristóbal, tortured with a deathless thirst. "Is it not so, Juan? The fool, Alonso, with no more nerves of taste in his palate than there are nerves in a sun-baked stone . . . he is pouring delicious old Médoc down his throat. He is gorging himself with ancient Burgundies . . . Pommard, thick as cream."

Cristóbal could go no further. The torment of this picture that he had summoned made him sink into a chair, where he supported his head in both hands and swayed from side to side, perfectly miserable.

Juan Oro appraised the usefulness of poor Cristóbal with one sharp glance, then he called a *mozo* to him and bade him hurry to the stables.

"You will find there my servant," Juan said. "Ask for Miguel. He is a big man with an ugly look. Tell him to come to me at once."

The *mozo* left, a great silver *peso* weighing down his pocket, making him fairly fly upon this mission, and presently Miguel appeared, his hat gripped nervously in his hand, his fierce eyes half cowed and half sullenly defiant because of the great splendor through which he had been led.

"And what do you think of it?" asked Juan Oro.

"It is more magnificent than a church," breathed Miguel.

"It may be more magnificent than a prison, too. Go at once, Miguel. At the end of the stable . . . the big building . . . you will find a small paddock and in it a great black stallion."

"Sombra!"

"Ah, you have heard about him?"

"Of course. They talk of nothing else in the stables. When they are not dicing and drinking pulque . . . it runs like water out of a pipe on this man's land . . . they are talking of Sombra and the *gringo* who rode him."

"Very well. Go back to the stable and take a saddle into the paddock of Sombra."

"*Señor, señor!* There is a constant guard kept over Sombra."

"That may be. All the better. Tell the man that there is a wager between Don Steven and me, and that I intend to ride the stallion tonight by moonlight. Do you understand?"

"*Sí, señor.*"

"Quickly, Miguel."

Miguel whirled.

"One thing more. When you have finished with the black stallion, the other horses must be prepared, and, if you can manage to slip a pair of saddles on a span of the finest horses on the place. . . ."

"Ah?"

"The horse you ride away upon is yours."

"Ah, *diablo*," murmured Miguel. "There is a gray mare that is five years old today. I have looked at her. I have handled her. She is sound as oak. Her mother was the north wind . . . her father was a thunderbolt.

Sombra will stretch his legs, if he keeps at my side tonight."

"Away, Miguel!"

Miguel vanished.

He was no sooner gone than Gregorio said soberly: "It has been several minutes. This is strange, Juan. We are the guests of Don José. You are the betrothed of his heiress . . . and yet he has left us?"

He turned to Cristóbal.

"Cristóbal, there is danger."

Cristóbal started up and, looking wildly about him, caught out from his clothes a pair of heavy revolvers. Juan Oro snatched them from him instantly.

"Fool! Fool!" he hissed. "Do you forget where you are?"

Cristóbal stared stupidly at him for a moment. Then he cast an eye upon the fountain near him, for in every alcove of the garden a small shaft of water showered into the air. Instantly his head was under the wet patter of the water. He stood back, shook his head like a dog emerging from a stream, and then mopped away the trickling water with a big handkerchief. When he turned to the others, his eyes were already cleared.

"So," sighed Cristóbal, "that happy dream is ended now. What comes next to us?"

"I shall speak to *Señor* Marshal," said Juan. "He may have noticed something."

But when he hurried to the place where he had last seen Marshal and the girl, they were gone. He returned, more worried than ever.

"I am going up to my room," Juan said. "After I have left, follow me, one by one, without haste. The people of the house must not think that we suspect . . . in case there is anything wrong. Smile in the face of that rat, Moreño. In your rooms, throw off these clothes. They are too tight for riding or fighting, and I think that we may have to do both before the night is ended. Dress for the saddle and come back into my room. I shall be ready before you."

He left on that word, and in his own chamber undressed and dressed again, hastily. He had hardly ended when the other two were with him. Cristóbal came with a rush, a silk handkerchief knotted about his bull throat and flying over his shoulders.

"Quick!" Cristóbal said. "From my window!"

He led them back to his room and pointed from his casement among the trees that rose shadowy in the moonshine near the house with a stretch of silvery lawn before them.

"I saw them there," Cristóbal explained. "Four men, stealing up through the trees, with rifles in their hands and revolvers at their belts . . . ah, two more!"

Even as he spoke, two men slipped out of a more distant covert and ran with a slinking pace of secrecy across the open, disappearing again under shadows nearer to the big *Hacienda* Fontana.

"Let us go over the edge of the roof," suggested Cristóbal. "It is not a great drop to the ground. And then we can break for the stables."

"Those men among the trees," Juan answered, "have covered our rooms. If we stir outside, there will be bullets in us. We must go back through the house . . . hush."

He held up a hand for silence, and in that silence they heard footsteps, moving through the hall with a cat-like stealth. Juan Oro threw open the door — and they looked forth upon a round dozen of heavily armed men, posted before their doors and jamming the corridors. At their head stood a man with a familiar, rugged face — Fernando Guadal, a revolver in his hand.

"Juan Oro!" Guadal cried, "I arrest you. . . ."

But Juan Oro leaped back and slammed the door behind him. He turned the lock just as a dozen hands strove to tear the door open.

"Put a bullet through the lock . . . then smash in the door with the butts of your rifles!" they heard Guadal shouting. "We shall all be rich for tonight's work!"

The entire house had come to life and noise at the same instant. Voices were shouting from every corner of it. Footfalls were scurrying here and there. Heavy heels thronged, pounding up and down the great stairways. Beyond the house the same tumult was spreading. A man shouted here and again there. A horn was shrilling the alarm. A gun exploded, and another and another, carrying the signal to the village.

"They will be out after us thicker than rabbits in a green field," said Juan Oro. "Cristóbal, you are right. There is only one way left for us, and that is over the edge of the roof. Quickly, then, before they send their men out onto the garden on the roof!"

They were lurching forward even as he spoke. Through the garden door they burst into the white flood of the moonlight and into the most mortal danger. A sharp voice barked an order from the side, and yonder, hurrying down the roof garden, they saw half a dozen armed servants pouring, who halted and pitched their guns to their shoulders. There was no need for Juan to give commands. For each man with him had the wit and ferocity of a weasel. They were on their bellies instantly and sending a storm of bullets toward the foe, while high above their prone bodies the answering rifle fire sang, but only for an instant. Two or three of their revolver bullets had knifed through the flesh of the *mozos* and given them quite enough of battle for the moment. They broke for cover, yelling with pain and with terror.

In that moment Juan was on his feet again. Those feet were naked, and his brown body was naked to the waist, also. Juan Oro, Mexican or *gringo,* was left behind him with civilized clothes. Now, in time of need, he was the Yaqui once more. He went over the edge of the roof like one who expected to find water rather than dry land beneath him. And, indeed, his feet sank deeply into the soft garden mold, breaking the shock of the descent. He tumbled forward, head over heels, but rolled to his feet, running.

Straight ahead lay ruin. Small jets of fire were darting from the shrubbery, and bullets were whining around his head. Something pressed against his cheek like the sharp edges of a red-hot iron, searing the flesh — a bullet had clipped him, he knew.

He dodged to the right and dropped to his belly behind a little hedge. Gregorio and

Cristóbal had made for the same haven of refuge, but a rifle bullet met poor Gregorio. He bounded into the air with a scream, and fell in a twisted heap into which the men of Don José still fired. But here beside Juan lay Cristóbal, gasping for breath.

"We are lost, Juan," he panted. "We can never reach the stables."

"Aye," murmured Juan. "You are right. We can never reach them, and we are lost."

Chapter Thirty-Seven

Bordi to the Rescue

For they were perfectly encompassed round-about by dangers. Not only were the trees lined with marksmen who, momentarily, became more numerous as the entire army of *mozos* rushed toward this side of the house, but, from the roof of the *Hacienda* Fontana itself, a score or more were raining a confused fire toward the spot where the pair had disappeared in the low-lying hedge.

Guadal directed the movements from the house, and from the trees the wretched pair heard the ringing voice of none other than Alonso, issuing commands.

"Ah, Lord," groaned Cristóbal, wincing closer to the face of the soft earth as a brace of bullets whirred just above his head. "If only I might put my hands upon Alonso . . . it is he, Juan. Ah, may the devil burn ten million ages in hellfire."

"Work forward," Juan told him.

"To what purpose?"

"We cannot stay here. They will set the

brush on fire, presently, and burn us out like rats."

"We can never rush them."

"Better to die rushing them, or trying it, than to lie here. Crawl forward, Cristóbal. . . ."

Here a loud voice shouted from the trees, and the firing instantly died off. Then they heard Alonso calling: "Juan and Cristóbal, it is I, Alonso!"

"Oh, devil!" snarled Cristóbal in answer. "Step out to meet me, Alonso, and I shall step out to meet you, man to man."

"You talk like a fool, Cristóbal."

"Do I talk like a fool? And you, Alonso, talk like a traitor and a coward."

"Use better words on me, or you may sweat for it!" said Alonso angrily. "Let me tell you that I, Alonso, still have enough friendship for you to get good terms from the *señor.* If you will surrender yourselves, I shall arrange excellent terms, Juan Oro. Do you hear me?"

"You will arrange to have us hung with a soft rope rather than a hard one . . . you will arrange to have us fed meat while we are in prison waiting for the hanging. Oh, Alonso, you are a very kind fellow. I wish that I were closer to you, or could see you, so that I could make you understand how I appreciate your kindness."

"Juan, unless you are a madman, you will. . . ."

"Thank you thus!"

And, having spent the last moment locating as carefully as he could the exact spot where Alonso was standing as he talked, Juan Oro touched the trigger and sent a bullet combing through the brush. Whether it badly hurt the traitor or not, at least it stung him and made him yell with pain and with surprise. At once the trees blazed with quickly working rifles. And next the wind rolled to the nostrils of Juan and his companion a smell of smoke unlike the pungent smoke of burned gunpowder.

"They have lighted the brush," Juan said to Cristóbal. "The flames will be at us at once. Let us stay until the last moment, however. Cristóbal, we are both no better than dead. But if one of us lives, what can he do for the other?"

"Speak first, Juan, my friend."

"If I die, and you live to escape from these devils, ride north, Cristóbal, and in the village under Mount San Vicente . . . do you know it?"

"Yes, I have eaten there three times and slept there once."

"There is an old priest in that town that. . . ."

"Ha?" murmured Cristóbal. "Have you grown superstitious, Juan? Will you become a religious man before you die?"

"I scorn it, and I scorn you. No, but once, for lack of something better to do, I robbed the poor priest of three *pesos*. And, afterward, I learned that he is a good man, who keeps money only that he may pass it on to his poor. He is a saint, and not a man. Now, Cristóbal, if you live, and I die, swear to me that you will ride north and find Father Sebastian . . . that is his name . . . and pay him three hundred dollars for the three. Do you understand?"

"I swear to you, Juan, that I shall do what you ask of me. But if I die, and you, Juan, lose only eight of your lives and run away with the ninth. . . ."

"Ah?"

"If you should do that, Juan, swear to me that you will ride to Mexico City and go to a vineyard north of the city in the hills. There is a white house with a red roof, and there are three windmills behind it. You cannot fail to know it. Besides, you may learn by asking where it is that the Mantegna wine is made. Well, *amigo mío,* my father once described that wine, and I heard him talk of it.

Since that day I have sworn that I would visit Mantegna and drink. But I have never done it. When I have had the leisure to go to it, the law has had too much leisure at the same time to chase me. Do you understand? But at the roots of my tongue there is still a mighty longing for the taste of that musty wine. Do you understand me, Juan?"

"I understand you, Cristóbal."

"If you live, then, ride south to the place. There is a cool pergola near the house, all wrapped in vines. Sit there, where my father sat. And for every bottle that you drink, pour one out upon the sand. For I tell you, Juan, that the wine will seep down to my thirsty soul where it is roasting in hellfire, and I shall stop groaning and screaming and sweating in order to bless you, my friend."

"I swear to you, Cristóbal, that I shall do as you wish. Is there no other message to no other human being?"

"None. And from you?"

"None that is worth sending. I am content to die now, without more talk. Bah! The smoke is choking me, Cristóbal. Who starts up first and draws the fire?"

"I have a coin here."

"Throw it in the air, then."

"I shall have an advantage. *You* throw up the coin, Juan. For I know a trick with it that will make it come down as I wish it nine times out of ten."

"Very well, Cristóbal. I know no tricks with money except how to spend it. Call." And he quickly spun the coin high into the air.

"Heads!" exclaimed Cristóbal as the coin rose and seemed to hang in the moonlight for an instant in the top of its twinkling rise. It shot down, a silver streak, and spatted upon the ground between them.

"And heads it is!" Cristóbal announced triumphantly.

Juan Oro looked down upon the face of the coin that finally sealed his destiny. For although the first man to rise from the brush had all the fortune in the world, nothing could keep him from being riddled with bullets, for the night was brilliant with moonshine, and there were many calm marksmen among the men of the don.

"Very well," said Juan, "I shall keep this *peso* for a souvenir."

He reached his hand for it, but at that moment a driving rifle bullet split the silver dollar in twain and drove the halves of it flying far away.

"*Adiós*, Cristóbal."

"*Adiós*, Juan. Ah, what a cruel thing luck is, Juan, that it will throw away a handsome youngster like you to save an old, tough drunkard like me."

Juan Oro turned on his stomach, gathering legs and arms under him, prepared for his leap, for he intended to spring like a panther from that scant covert and race straight at the muzzles of the nearest rifles. He said softly: "Whatever God there be of the Yaqui or the *gringo,* give me strength enough to find one enemy and to kill him with my hands before I die. For the sake of the many great fights I have fought, grant me this."

So, as he spoke, he gathered himself tensely and swayed up a little for his leap from the hedge, but that leap was never made. Behind the trees there broke out a sudden babble of conflicting voices and then an overwhelming shout which was the divinest music to the pair.

"Bordi! Bordi! Bordi!"

Then a rush of voices storming along at full speed. Guns rattled; a dozen men were shouting that name in a wild unison, and the very weight of the sound of it seemed to split asunder the fighting men of the don. They ran yelling to the right and to the left, and, breaking from the trees and the shrubbery, Juan and Cristóbal saw some twelve or fifteen men on magnificent horses storm toward them.

They leaped to their feet with a yell. There was Bordi himself in the van. Beside him rode none other than the muleteer, Miguel, winning his spurs gloriously this night with the men of the outlaw, and by the reins he led the great black stallion, Sombra.

They hardly paused, that charging troop, for the rescued men to mount. Here and there a man threw up his arms and dropped with a yell from the shadow. There was no stay to lift them again. But Cristóbal caught one horse and leaped into the saddle. Juan, like a great cat, was instantly on the back of the stallion, and on they swept with their revolvers spouting.

They did not bear straight away, where they would have passed for some distance under the fire of the men in the *Hacienda* Fontana, but Bordi led his troop straight back at those disorganized fellows through whom he had just charged. The trees closed behind them. Voices were screaming orders to take to horse, and from before them frightened *mozos* were dropping their rifles and fleeing into the brush. Among the rest, Juan Oro saw the moon fall white on a familiar face — Alonso.

As the man reached the brush, the bullet from Juan's gun struck him. He seemed to hang in mid-air for a moment, clawing before him with desperate hands as though he were striving to swim upward through stifling water. Then he fell on his back and lay still with his arms thrown out crosswise on the ground.

Chapter Thirty-Eight

The Fleeing *Gringo*

There was no difficulty in breaking through the remainder of the guards. Not a man fell from the saddle among the little troop of Bordi after they had turned the second time through the line, but already they had paid heavily for their work, and out of a dozen riders only seven were left. Such was the tax upon them. Yet they bore it without a murmur. The dead and the abandoned were completely forgotten. And if they had paid the price of five men in order to bring off two, they could balance against that the sheer loss that they had inflicted upon the foe — loss in men and in money, also, since these magnificent stolen horses came from Don José Fontana.

From Matías Bordi, Juan Oro could learn none of the things that had led up to this rescue, at first. The leader was too busy rejoicing to give any explanations, and not a word would he speak until Juan Oro had assured him that he was not hurt.

"It is false," said Matías. "For I see the blood on your head."

"It is only a little scratch . . . Matías."

This as they flew a ditch side by side, the black coming up powerfully upon the curb.

"Now, that is well!" Matías Bordi cried. "For if that has really wounded you, I should have burned the town of Fontana by night and shot them down as they ran from the flames. But you are free . . . more than my greatest hope, Juan! There was a time when I said to myself that all was lost, lost! And the most that I expected was to bargain with the don for your dead body, so that I might give it a decent burial . . . not in some churchyard, but in the free mountains, Juan, where you and I have been happy together."

And he began to laugh and shout and whirl his quirt like a foolish child on an outing. Juan Oro watched and listened in amazement, for, although he had had proofs before that the man loved him, he had never dreamed to what degree.

From Miguel, the muleteer now turned into bandit extraordinary, he heard some of the details — how José and Gabriel Donato had saddled the horses, beginning with the great Sombra, according to instructions. How the other servants had wondered when they heard that the Maldonado really intended to attempt to back the great stallion by night — how they had gathered to watch and to stare, making both Miguel and Donato certain that they could never get away from such an audience to help their companions. Then there came a burst of firing and of many shouts from the *Hacienda* Fontana itself. The stable grooms paid no more heed to the two, but caught up weapons and rushed for the great house to serve where they could in the time of trouble.

After that, Miguel and Gabriel had gathered together quickly the horses that they had saddled, and had struck off through the place in the moonlight, feeling that their friends were surely hemmed in and destroyed by numbers, and that they would at least save these glorious horses from the wreck. So, as they drove across the night, they had come fairly upon Matiás Bordi, swinging at a round gallop toward the sound of the guns — a furiously incensed Bordi, pouring forth oaths and swearing to destroy them all with his own hands, if they did not save Juan Oro from the danger. They had turned back, therefore, with Bordi and his nine men, and the rest of the charge. Its result Juan already knew.

While he heard this story, shouted at his

ear above the noise of the pounding hoofs, they were whirling through the gardens and the open lawns of the *Hacienda* Fontana and finally dipping down toward the valley where the town lay. Twice they passed dense bodies of armed men, hurrying up the slope from the town toward the big house, and twice they shouted that they were friends, riding to bring more aid — for the *Hacienda* Fontana was beset by hundreds.

Hundreds of madmen, indeed, and that was the truth. For the don had endured a double loss on this night, and, when he learned about it, his reason staggered. While his men swarmed into saddles, while his great stable gave forth their horses by the score, and while the saddle animals were roped and made ready in the great fields and the corrals near the house, the don was seen running about bareheaded, cursing one man for a sluggard, begging another with outstretched hands, and then screaming out the sums of his rewards — "To him who captures or kills Bordi, fifty thousand *pesos* . . . in gold. For Juan Oro, the same amount. For the thief of a *gringo* dog, another fifty thousand. For the foolish girl, snatched away to ruin as the bride of a dog of an American . . . a hundred thousand *pesos* for her alive . . . or dead!"

Such was the language which was repeated through the crowd of pursuers as they started off, singly, spurring away hard through the night. There, as they rode, they instinctively spurred the harder or else drew rein to wait for companions from the rear, for who but a madman would dare to pursue the Bordi and Juan Oro single-handedly?

In the meantime, the fugitives reached the head of the village street. Half a dozen stragglers, even now hurrying out of their houses to trail toward the *Hacienda* Fontana, saw and recognized the terrible squad of horsemen that was flying toward them. They turned and fled back as fast as they could go. And Bordi and his men went crashing down the street, then whirled in thunder across the bridge beyond the Río Fontana, then up the slope beyond.

They were formed into two sections as soon as they gained the tops of the hills beyond the river, with the darkness of the pines closing about them. Juan Oro and the chief himself made one section — they were to ride straight on and draw the pursuit after them, probably, by the straightness of their flight. The others were to fall off to the side, one by one, and so eventually join each other at a designated spot on the shoulder of a distant mountain.

As they talked, Juan, from the edge of the woods, reining the dancing, impatient black beneath him, could see the men of Fontana rushing through the village, and then in black clusters across the bridge — yes, the dull thunder of the horses with their armed hoofs on the hollow bridge came, vague and muffled, up to him. They rode fast, and they rode hard, and with such determination that any mishap to the fugitives would cause a disaster.

By the eagerness of their riding, Juan Oro guessed shrewdly enough what quantities of gold were promised. He came back to the band just as Bordi finished giving his directions, and then the entire group pushed off through the trees. But, as they galloped, one by one the others fell away to the left, and, when they had pushed through the thick belt of the forest that lay before them, they were alone. All the band had drawn away.

"Now, Matías, I owe you my life again."

"You see, Juan, that I dare not let you get out of that debt . . . for fear that my throat will be cut for me. Listen, Juan. Those fat dogs of the don's are already tired of running. And I, Juan, am tired of leading this spare horse."

"Do not turn it loose. It is a fine beast . . . it is one of the best from the stable of the don."

"What is horseflesh to me?" He drew his knife to sever the rope.

But Juan reined the black close and caught at his arm.

"I myself shall lead the gray mare," he said. "Poor Miguel would have a broken heart, if he lost that horse. I heard him describe her with a trembling voice. Besides, look at her action. Is she not a queen? Ha!"

The last exclamation came as Sombra, quite unexpectedly, hurled himself into the air and almost from under Juan Oro as he veered from a dead thing, lying in the trail.

A fallen body of a horse, with a saddle strapped on its back, a woman's side saddle, heavily decorated with gold.

"It has not been dead for more than a few minutes!" Juan shouted. "And do you know to whom it belongs?"

"How should I guess the name of every dead horse I find in the mountains?"

"Oh, Matiás, I dare not guess . . . but I think, unless I am very wrong, that Don Steven, the *gringo,* has done a wild thing on this night. Heaven help him, if it is as I think. Look, Matiás, for one horse, carrying two riders. . . ."

They shot over the shoulder of the next hill as he spoke, and there was the sight which he wanted — a single strong horse, shining with sweat in the moonlight, and carrying a man in the saddle and a woman before the saddle, clinging to her companion and pointing a frightened arm back at them — yes, that was her scream that tingled through the air.

But now Juan Oro floated away into the lead with the black stallion — drifted away before even Bordi on his fast horse, and shouted as he came in a ringing voice: "Don Steven! It is I! You are safe!"

The laboring of the horse before them stopped at once. They swept up to Marshal and, now, slipping to the ground beside the horse of her lover, the proud Lady Dorotea herself. Oh, strange, indeed — fleeing through the night away from all the millions of the don, and with a *gringo!*

"Halt, by the heavens!" cried Juan Oro, as he drew rein. "I thank God that she has sense enough to choose a man. But where will you go, Don Steven? Where will you go? Do you know the trails north to the Río? Do you know that every trail will be watched for you? Do you know that there will be a price for both of you, alive or dead?"

"We thought of it all," Steven Marshal responded quietly. "And I suppose that was the reason we decided we must ride away and ride at once."

He was interrupted by the angry cry of Matiás Bordi: "It is the *gringo!* It is Steven Marshal! *Señor,* defend yourself. . . ."

Juan Oro barely threw himself between them in time.

"But, consider, Juan," cried the bandit, "that this is the man who shot me down . . . put me in the hands of the law . . . made me laughed at and scorned . . . made every boy, learning to ride a horse and shoot a gun, swear that he, too, would take Matiás Bordi, because a *gringo* dog had been able to do it!"

"Hush, Matiás. This man is my friend."

"Juan, Juan, are you to choose between me and the *gringo,* and leave me for him?"

Chapter Thirty-Nine

The Cavalcade

That was the beginning of a strange contract. Matiás Bordi, who could not in honor and in pride allow himself to ride at the side of the man who had brought him down, until they were ready to do battle for a second time, now rode ahead, acting as an advance guard of the pair. And at a distance behind came Steven Marshal and the girl herself. Far to the rear again was Juan Oro, and between these two guards they worked every day through long, long marches.

There were a thousand miles to cover to the border and safety for Marshal under the flag of his country. They kept up a pace of forty miles a day, driving forward relentlessly. Yet, hard as they rode, Juan Oro came up with the fleeing pair close enough for conversation only thrice. Matiás Bordi came up only once.

That was for the marriage. They came on the second night of the northward journey to a little village tucked under the elbow of a forested mountain — a tiny little village, announced from afar by a straggling row of lights. Toward it they made, and there they found the priest, and there the priest took them into the strange old church, with shadows plying above the reach of the candlelight among the ancient, naked rafters of the ceiling. There stood Steven Marshal with the girl beside him. Behind them were two witnesses — and, oh, how the knees of the priest shook when he heard those names, one by one: Steven Marshal, Dorotea Calderon, Matiás Bordi, Juan Oro.

And how the good old man wept and blessed them when they filled his hands with gold for his poor. And how he followed them to the door of the church, and how they saw him fall upon his knees in prayer for the fugitives.

"We shall have luck," declared Matiás Bordi. "There shall be no trouble between this place and the border. You will see."

"That is a cheerful thing," Steven Marshal said. "What makes you think that?"

"Hush," said Juan. "Don't ask him questions. That is the way of Matiás, when he has a revelation from Providence, as he calls it. Let him ride ahead . . . now follow . . . I fall behind once more . . . do you know the trail?"

"You have explained it to me clearly enough. But, Juan, while I do not scruple to use you as much as I can, how can I let Bordi, who hates me and wants my blood, continue to serve me?"

"So long as he does not see you, he is happy enough. He will do for me what I am glad to do for you."

"But when you part from him at the frontier, Juan. . . ."

"Part from him . . . I?"

"You will ride on with us, into your own country, Juan?"

"The devil!" said Juan. "Do you still make me out an American?"

"By the color of your skin and by the. . . ."

"I do not care to think about it, or to argue," Juan stated gloomily, and fell back to the rear once more.

It was not an unharassed journey, in spite of the prophecy of Bordi. Twice he himself found danger ahead and turned them into new trails. And once a flying body of horses, sweeping up from the rear, plunged into the gunfire of Juan and scattered for safety among the rocks. After that, they journeyed on without further trouble. They had veered far to the east, planning to reach the border near Juárez, but still keeping from the main roads at the guidance of Matiás. By night,

Marshal and the girl made their own small campfire, and Matías and Juan sat over another.

"Matías, will you not bury the knife?" Juan would ask him, and he would always answer: "He is marked down . . . either he or I must destroy the other. Look, Juan, do you choose him above me?"

And Juan would deny. But every night the denial was fainter, for, as they swung north and east, league after league, there arose in him a great hunger to know the lands beyond the famous Río Grande and see the people there. For perhaps he would find others like Steven Marshal among them.

Matías himself understood. "It is the call of the blood to blood, Juan," he said, "and I shall ride back alone."

"No, no!" Juan would cry. But, nevertheless, he knew in his heart that this was true prophecy, indeed.

So, on the last night, when the narrow little, muddy river lay in view before them, speckled with the stars, he went to the two to say farewell.

Steven Marshal did not attempt to argue. "We are going to wait until the morning," he said, "on that hill beyond the river. We will wait until the sun is well up in the east.

For, by that time, I think that you will be with us, Juan."

Then he and Dorotea mounted and rode down the long slope toward the river. But Juan rode back to Matiás, where he knew the bandit waited. He found Matiás with his horse unsaddled and hobbled to graze on the sun-cured grass of the desert.

"Saddle, Matiás!" he called. "They are gone, and you and I have a long march ahead of us tonight."

"A long march?" echoed Matiás. "And why, Juan?"

"It is best for me to put many miles between me and that river."

"I understand. It is because you feel the hunger to cross it, and you wish to turn your back on the sight of it. But listen to me, Juan. A man cannot turn his back on his fate. That thing to which you close your eyes looks into the dark of your mind brighter than ever, and the farther you ride from it, the more you will hunger to turn and come back. No, we will camp here tonight. If I am to lose you, Juan, and there is a voice in me that tells me that I will, my son, let it be here and now. Not after we have turned back and I have made sure of you."

"Very well," Juan said gloomily. "We stay here for tonight. But hear me swear to you,

Matiás, that I shall never. . . ."

"Peace!" broke in Matiás. "An oath is the staff of a weak man or a woman. Do not tie yourself to it. For if the oath is broken, we will both despise you."

"Well, you will see."

And Juan Oro rolled himself in his blanket and lay down. In another moment he was asleep, as though all the problems in the world did not have the strength to rouse him.

It was Matiás who did not close his eyes that night. For a long time he sat with his back to a rock, smoking one cigarette after another and watching the smoke drift up and put out the faint stars. Finally he, in turn, stretched himself in his blanket. But it was not until the coolness that comes just before dawn that he drowsed a little.

Out of that drowsing he was awakened by the leaning of a shadow over him and a voice that whispered softly: "Matiás." But he closed his eyes again and did not answer. But there was a great weakness in his heart, and he knew the thing that was about to come.

"It is fate," he heard Juan whisper to himself, "and he will not waken."

After that, staring blankly up at the stars, Matiás Bordi heard the soft preparations, as

Juan, carrying his pack and saddle to a distance, made Sombra ready for the ride of that day. Then a sharp squeaking of the stirrup leathers announced that Juan was in the saddle. Afterward there was the soft, soft crunching of the sand under hoof, lighter than a whisper. It trailed away toward the river.

Then Matías Bordi sat up, and saw the phantom horseman, disappearing toward the river. The dawn sent a little ring of gray light around the horizon, and under that quickening light the rider was clearly seen as he forded the river, and then as the horse went up the farther hill.

And Bordi stretched out his hands to the heavens. "What have I done," he said, "that I should be left alone now?"

But Juan Oro, once he had crossed the river, was immune to regrets. When the water rose to his knees and then ebbed away as Sombra climbed into the shallows and then to the dry bank beyond, it seemed to Juan that the beginning of this new day was the beginning of a new life, and a happier and greater life.

And now, leaving all the years dead behind him, and the thought of Matías Bordi dead with all the rest — for nothing is so cruelly easy to the young as forgetfulness —

he rode up the hill with the rose of the morning all about him. And he heard the joyful shout of Steven Marshal from the hill crest, and then he saw Steven and his wife coming, running down to him.

He knew, by that, that all of his life lay face forward before him, and he knew that what he had been must be wrapped in night behind him. Down the hillside, flaming like a sword in the morning light, ran a new barbed-wire fence. It was the sign of the law. In the old life the law had been a jest and a joke to him. In the new life it was sure to be a wall over which he must not jump.

And a little shiver ran through Juan Oro. So apprehension was mixed with even this first joy. But when he took the big, strong hand of Steven Marshal, he knew, indeed, that he had come back at last to his own kind.

About the Author

Max Brand is the best-known pen name of Frederick Faust, creator of Dr. Kildare, Destry, and many other fictional characters popular with readers and viewers worldwide. Faust wrote for a variety of audiences in many genres. His enormous output, totaling approximately thirty million words or the equivalent of 530 ordinary books, covered nearly every field: crime, fantasy, historical romance, espionage, Westerns, science fiction, adventure, animal stories, love, war, and fashionable society, big business and big medicine. Eighty motion pictures have been based on his work along with many radio and television programs. For good measure he also published four volumes of poetry. Perhaps no other author has reached more people in more different ways.

Born in Seattle in 1892, orphaned early, Faust grew up in the rural San Joaquin Valley of California. At Berkeley he became a student rebel and one-man literary movement, contributing prodigiously to all campus publications. Denied a degree because of unconventional conduct, he embarked on a series of adventures culminating in New York City where, after a period of near starvation, he received simultaneous recognition as a serious poet and successful author of fiction. Later, he traveled widely, making his home in New York, then in Florence, and finally in Los Angeles.

Once the United States entered the Second World War, Faust abandoned his lucrative writing career and his work as a screenwriter to serve as a war correspondent with the infantry in Italy, despite his fifty-one years and a bad heart. He was killed during a night attack on a hilltop village held by the German army. New books based on magazine serials or unpublished manuscripts or restored versions continue to appear so that, alive or dead, he has averaged a new book every four months for seventy-five years. Beyond this, some work by him is newly reprinted every week of every year in one or another format somewhere in the world. A great deal more about this author and his work can be found in THE MAX BRAND COMPANION (Greenwood Press, 1997) edited by Jon Tuska and Vicki Piekarski.